Praise for Tamar Myers's
Pennsylvania Dutch Mysteries

"A pinch of acerbity, a scoop of fun, and a pound of originality . . . a delicious treat."   —Carolyn Hart

"A piquant brew, bubbling over with mystery and mirth. I loved every page of it."   —Dorothy Cannell

"Rollicking suspense."   —*The Washington Post*

"Feisty Mennonite innkeeper and talented sleuth Magdalena Yoder offers a mix of murder and mouthwatering recipes."   —*Publishers Weekly*

"Snappy descriptions . . . humorous shenanigans."
     —*Pittsburgh Tribune-Review*

"A hoot. Guaranteed you'll be laughing by the third paragraph."   —*The Charleston Post and Courier* (SC)

"Think *Mayberry R.F.D.* with Mennonites. Think *Murder, She Wrote* with a Pennsylvania Dutch accent. Instead of Jessica Fletcher, think Magdalena Yoder, a plain-dressing, blunt-speaking, middle-aged innkeeper who frequently rescues the incompetent chief of police by solving his cases."   —*The Morning Call* (Allentown, PA)

HELL HATH
NO CURRY

A PENNSYLVANIA DUTCH MYSTERY
WITH RECIPES

Tamar Myers

AN OBSIDIAN MYSTERY

OBSIDIAN
Published by New American Library, a division of
Penguin Group (USA) Inc., 375 Hudson Street,
New York, New York 10014, USA
Penguin Group (Canada), 90 Eglinton Avenue East, Suite 700, Toronto,
Ontario M4P 2Y3, Canada (a division of Pearson Penguin Canada Inc.)
Penguin Books Ltd., 80 Strand, London WC2R 0RL, England
Penguin Ireland, 25 St. Stephen's Green, Dublin 2,
Ireland (a division of Penguin Books Ltd.)
Penguin Group (Australia), 250 Camberwell Road, Camberwell, Victoria 3124,
Australia (a division of Pearson Australia Group Pty. Ltd.)
Penguin Books India Pvt. Ltd., 11 Community Centre, Panchsheel Park,
New Delhi - 110 017, India
Penguin Group (NZ), 67 Apollo Drive, Rosedale, North Shore 0632,
New Zealand (a division of Pearson New Zealand Ltd.)
Penguin Books (South Africa) (Pty.) Ltd., 24 Sturdee Avenue,
Rosebank, Johannesburg 2196, South Africa

Penguin Books Ltd., Registered Offices:
80 Strand, London WC2R 0RL, England

Published by Obsidian, an imprint of New American Library, a division of
Penguin Group (USA) Inc. Previously published in a New American Library
hardcover edition.

First Obsidian Printing, January 2008
10 9 8 7 6 5 4 3 2 1

Copyright © Tamar Myers, 2007
Excerpt from *As the World Churns* copyright © Tamar Myers, 2008
All rights reserved

OBSIDIAN and logo are trademarks of Penguin Group (USA) Inc.

Printed in the United States of America

This book is dedicated to
Shabnam Mahmood and her family.

Acknowledgments

All the recipes in this book are authentic and were supplied by my dear friend Shabnam Mahmood.

1

It was the best of crimes; it was the worst of crimes. Cornelius Weaver had everything going for him—except a pulse. He was tall, handsome, and exceedingly rich. It is said that he flossed on alternate Tuesdays. Even now, as he reposed in his extra-long, sinfully expensive, antibacterial casket, I had no doubt that there was at least one woman in Hernia, Pennsylvania, who wouldn't mind taking him home with her. That someone, by the way, was not me; dead or alive, Cornelius was not my type. But I seem to have gotten ahead of myself.

I was sitting at the kitchen table of the PennDutch Inn, which is both my business and my home, when Sergeant Chris Ackerman tapped gingerly at the door. On second thought, maybe the only ginger present was the powder my cook, Freni, was adding to her stew, but nonetheless it was a very weak sort of knock; one that I found irritating. My knuckles are the envy of woodpeckers, you see, and I firmly believe that if one must knock, then one must do it with panache.

"I can't hear you," I shouted pleasantly through cupped hands.

Sergeant Ackerman knocked a wee bit louder.

"Hark, who goes there? Art thou a man or a mouse?"

"Miss Yoder, it's me, Chris!"

"Chris who? If it's Kris Kringle, then you're either six

months early or six months late. No matter which way you slice it, an apology is in order."

"Miss Yoder, this is very important."

"Ach, enough," Freni said and, wiping her hands on her apron, went to open the door. Freni serves triple duty; not only is she my cook, but she's my cousin and my friend. Occasionally she acts as my conscience.

The second Chris tumbled into the room, I knew she'd been right to put an end to my shenanigans. The young man was as pale as uncooked bratwurst, and only slightly more coherent.

"It's the chief," he said. "It's awful. He's dead."

For the record, Police Chief Olivia Hornsby-Anderson is all woman, not that I've ever checked, mind you. Surely he was referring to someone else.

"Are you sure it's the chief?"

He nodded vigorously. "She said to come get you. That you'd know what to do."

Dead women rarely talk in my experience, but if indeed our deceased chief had recommended my services, she'd been right to do so. Sergeant Ackerman had only recently moved to Hernia from California, and was still quite unfamiliar with our ways. Besides, there was the issue of his youth; although no fault of his own, the man was younger than most of my sturdy Christian underwear. The chief also hailed from the land of fruit and nuts, but at least she had the benefit of wisdom, which, if you ask me, can come only with age.

"How did she die?" I asked as I reached for my purse, which hung from a hook by the door.

"She isn't dead, Miss Yoder."

"But I thought you said—"

"It's Mr. Weaver who's dead."

Ours is an Amish and Mennonite community. We have more Weavers in the phone book than we do Smiths and Joneses combined. Off the top of my head I could think of at least three Weavers who had one foot inside the grave and the other on a banana peel.

"Which Weaver, dear? Augustus?"

"The rich one."

"Both Seth and Elias have money—"

"The hottie, if you'll excuse the expression."

"Cornelius! Why didn't you say so? But wait, there's nothing wrong with Cornelius that a stern lecture and a fused zipper couldn't fix."

"Apparently it was a heart attack. Miss Yoder, what do I do?"

"Well, I assume you called 911. You did, didn't you?"

"But I *am* the police—well, one of them."

"Touché. Did you call the paramedics?"

"Yes, of course."

"Then write up your report and turn it in to the chief, who will read it and give it back to you to file. It's really very simple. Even Freni here could do it."

"Ach!" Freni glared at me from behind thick lenses that were perpetually smeared with shortening and flour.

"I didn't mean anything by that, except that you don't have any police or office experience. My point is that this is a fairly run-of-the-mill case and that anyone could do the job. Oops, perhaps I best quit speaking now."

"But you see, Miss Yoder," Chris said, not sounding at all insulted, "this is an unusual situation in that Chief Hornsby-Anderson was actually there when Mr. Weaver died."

"Well, heavens, then, let her write it up."

"Yes, but you see, uh—how can I put this?"

"Put it quickly, dear. The sands of time are slipping quickly through this hourglass figure of mine." I meant that as a joke, of course.

"Miss Yoder, I guess I'm going to have to come right out and say this; it's possible the chief contributed to Mr. Weaver's demise."

One must give a certain amount of begrudging respect to any twenty-some-year-old who can use the word *demise* in a sentence, even if he appeared to have been smoking marijuana and had porridge for brains. I prayed in vain for patience.

"Just because the chief was there," I said, "does not make her responsible. I'm sure she did her part."

"That's what I'm trying to tell you."

I sighed. "So now you tell her that since she did her best, she needs to stop feeling guilty. And believe me, I'm an expert on guilt."

Sergeant Ackerman is a good-looking young man with a pleasant disposition. I was quite shocked to see his demeanor change.

"Miss Yoder, I always thought you were a very intelligent woman."

"But I am!"

"Then why is it that you don't grasp the situation?"

Freni, who had been standing silently at my elbow, gasped and covered her mouth with her hands. "Ach, the English," she said behind her protective shield of stubby digits. "Always the sex, yah?"

"Sex?"

Chris nodded again. "The chief and Mr. Weaver were doing the mattress tango, as I believe I've heard you refer to it."

"That's mattress *mambo,* dear. It's the two-sheet tango—oh, never mind. You don't say! Are you sure of this?"

"She told me herself. That's why she sent me to you. I'm quite capable of writing up the report," he said, no doubt emboldened by my state of shock. "I don't need help with that. It's damage control that the chief and I are worried about."

"Damage control? Why me?"

"Because you're the mayor, Miss Yoder."

"And very bossy, yah?"

"Freni!"

The young man had the temerity to smile. "And not just that. These are your people, Miss Yoder. You know their ways. You know how to reach them, how to prevent this from becoming a huge scandal. Besides, like the chief says, you have a vested interest in keeping this incident under wraps."

"I do?"

"The chief says because you appointed her to the job, if word of this gets out, the people will start to question your judgment. She said that if you don't help us—I mean, her—you could be voted out of office."

"Is that a threat? It sounds like one to me."

Freni lacks a neck, or she would have nodded her head in agreement. "Yah, a threat."

"Ladies, it isn't a threat, but a fact. You appoint the chief; the chief does the hokeypokey with one of Hernia's most upstanding citizens; said citizen croaks. Who's ultimately to blame?"

I sighed so hard a layer of grime was blown from my kinswoman's glasses. "All right. I'll call the town's biggest gossip and see what she already knows. I'll take it from there."

"But, Miss Yoder, she couldn't possibly know anything. I came straight over here from Mr. Weaver's house. The paramedics hadn't even arrived yet."

I chuckled while Freni snorted. "My dear boy," I said. "Welcome to Hernia."

2

Agnes Mishler's landline was busy, but I got her on her cell. She said she was happy to be of service and promised to be right over. I relayed this to Chris, who, it was obvious, didn't put much stock in Agnes's ability to help. It was also clear that he didn't believe her promise to be right over. No sooner did he pull out of my driveway, on his way back to the Weaver residence, than Agnes squealed up to the kitchen door. Her car made some funny noises as well.

"Ach," Freni mumbled, "the nosybody."

The dear woman, it must be noted, is Amish, whereas I am Mennonite. I have a high school diploma *and* an associate's degree in English. Freni has only an eighth-grade education, not to mention that English is her second language. The fact that some of her phrases are colorful is to be expected, sometimes even enjoyed.

"Just plain nosy would work, dear," I said, and jerked the door open to admit Agnes. The latter is on the fleshy side, to put it kindly, so she almost lost her balance. It was not, however, my intention for her to do so. To make amends, while I shoved a chair under her, I offered her something to drink.

"No thanks, Magdalena. This may come as a surprise to you, but I'm trying to lose weight."

"I've got diet soda. My guests insist on it, but why I

should pay good money for what is essentially colored water is beyond me."

"From what I hear, you charge your guests so much that you could fly that water in from a mountain spring in Switzerland and still make a profit."

"Quite true. So I guess that makes me a profit-ess. Agnes, are you aware that Hernia's most eligible bachelor just went to his final reward?"

Concern flooded her eyes. "Oh, Magdalena, I'm so sorry. How did it happen? Gabriel Rosen was such a healthy-looking man."

"Gabriel Rosen is my fiancé, for crying out loud! He's *not* an eligible bachelor. And he's perfectly fine."

The concern drained from her eyes. "Cornelius Weaver?"

"I'm afraid so. It appears to have been a heart attack."

"Oh, dear. Poor Priscilla Livingood. They were supposed to be married in three days. Now this, on top of everything."

"Exactly."

She recoiled with interest. "You know about that?"

"There are those who say I know something about everything." You can bet I'm not the only one to say this. "So spill it, Agnes. What do *you* know about Cornelius Weaver doing the horizontal hootchy-kootchy with a woman other than his intended?"

"Well, you're not going to believe this. Just yesterday Imogene Cornswaller was saying she couldn't understand why Priscilla Livingood put up with it. And I don't mean to be cruel, Magdalena, merely observational, but you and I are both better looking than she."

It took a second or two for my brain to sort out the possible interpretations of that last sentence. Was I to feel insulted having been lumped with Agnes, who is no bathing beauty, or flattered, given that Chief Hornsby-Anderson was generally considered quite comely?

In the end I decided that pride took less energy than anger.

"Thank you. But to be honest, I don't deserve to be included in your comparison. She may not be perfect, but she comes pretty close. In fact, she once confided to me that she'd been approached by a TV producer about possibly starring in a series of some sort."

"Now *that* is interesting. I hadn't heard that. Lots of stand-up comediennes are getting their own shows these days, but I surely wouldn't put her in the same class as Ellen DeGeneres. Now *there* is a genius."

I've known Agnes for years but have only recently become friends with her. Apparently our newfound bond was not built on communication.

"Agnes, dear, we couldn't possibly be talking about the same person."

She frowned. "Short, squat, with a nose like a radish? A sex addict, if there ever was one."

"Ach," Freni squawked and made a beeline to a side table where she had a bowl of bread dough rising. Without further comment she raised the dish towel covering the bowl, pinched off two wads of the sticky stuff, and crammed them into her ears.

"What is that all about?" Agnes asked.

"She must have thought you were describing her. Who were you describing, by the way? It certainly wasn't the chief."

"The chief?" Agnes managed to stretch one syllable over the span of a full octave.

"Uh—ah—just a minute, there is something in my throat." That wasn't a lie; that something was my heart. It was suddenly clear to me that the queen of gossip hadn't a clue about the chief's indiscretion. And to think I'd nearly blown it! On the other hand, it was obvious that Agnes was still in possession of a juicy morsel of hearsay. Although it had nothing to do with Cornelius's death, it was important that I be privy to this bit of information. Important to me.

"There's nothing wrong with your throat, Magdalena. You're stalling, aren't you?"

"*Moi?* Why on the earth would I do that? No, I was just thinking how the woman Cornelius was cheating with was doomed from the start, having been given that horrible name by her parents."

"Alice is a horrible name? Really, Magdalena, people who live in glass houses shouldn't throw stones."

Ding, dang, dong, I swore to myself. Normally I don't allow myself to think such foul language, but *Alice* wasn't much of a clue. In Hernia it was practically a throwaway.

"Yes," I said, "Alice is a horrible name when you combine it with her last name. What were her parents thinking?"

Agnes pushed herself clear from the table. "I'll be sure to tell Ned and Frieda that next time I see them."

"Troyer?" Of course, the radish nose was as good a clue as the Yoder nose on my face. My probing proboscis is also shaped like a root vegetable: a carrot. Only not quite as orange.

"Tsk, tsk, Magdalena, you were toying with me like a cat with a mouse. Cornelius was multitasking, wasn't he?"

"Excuse me?"

"Sowing his seed in more rows than one. You know what I mean. Now it's your turn to spill the beans."

"All this talk of comestibles is making me hungry. Are you sure you wouldn't like a bite of something? There's some shoofly pie left over from supper last night—my guests found it too sweet—and the cookie jar is almost full of fresh gingersnaps."

"You're stalling."

"I am not."

"You are so. Magdalena, I thought you wanted to be friends."

"I do. But my hands are tied. With the chief having to distance herself from this case—"

"Oh, my aching liver spots! Cornelius was sleeping

with Chief Hornsby-Anderson, am I right? I am! And then she killed him!"

"She most certainly did not!"

"Then why did you call it a case?"

"I did?"

"Magdalena, I can see by your face that I've struck gold. Oh, thank you, thank you, thank you. You are such a good friend." She heaved herself into a standing position, planted a kiss on my cheek, and then barreled for the door. A team of draft horses wouldn't have been able to stop her.

The rumor spread like head lice in an overcrowded schoolroom. The chief, bless her cheating heart, holed up in her house behind locked doors, while the paparazzi camped on her front lawn. And although he was furious with me, young Sergeant Ackerman relied on me more than ever. Thus it was that I was able to convince him to order an autopsy on Cornelius. *"Tout de suite,"* I said, almost exhausting my French vocabulary. I called in a few favors, canceled a few loan obligations, and within twenty-four hours I received the news that Hernia's most eligible bachelor had died of a heart attack. Given that it was common knowledge that Cornelius suffered from a temperamental heart, this was no surprise.

But the report went on to say that a major contributor to the heart attack had been the ingestion of an unusually large amount of amitriptyline. This is a drug, sold under the brand name Elavil, that is often prescribed for depression and can be used as a pain reliever. At my direction the young sergeant had Cornelius's medical records subpoenaed, and they, in turn, revealed that at no time had he been prescribed amitriptyline. Since this is not a drug that delivers a "buzz," we deduced that Cornelius either had accidentally consumed it or, more likely, had been tricked into taking it. And because the odds of a competent adult accidentally ingesting a prescription drug like Elavil were slim to none, it was evident that someone, knowing Cornelius's history of heart disease, had taken the fate of his faltering ticker into her own tiny hands. In other words, Hernia's version of a playboy had been murdered.

Could it have been Chief Olivia Hornsby-Anderson who committed the dastardly deed? When it comes to human behavior, anything is possible. But if the chief had, for some reason, administered a prescription drug to her lover, she wouldn't have been so stupid as to report his death to *anyone,* especially Sergeant Ackerman. I am not a betting woman, but had I been, I would have put my money on one of Cornelius's lovers, starting with Priscilla Livingood, his fiancée.

Priscilla has been obsessed with her appearance ever since I've known her, which has been virtually our entire lives. The woman is my contemporary, and therefore a good ten years older than her deceased fiancé. Upon occasion folks have remarked that I am well preserved for my age, but Priscilla is way out of my league. I can remember back in high school when she played the trumpet for the sole reason that it gave her pouty lips. Those lips, I hate to recall, got her dates with anyone she pleased, including the one boy I ever truly desired in that shameful, carnal way—Jimmy Skinner.

Not many people would argue that Priscilla was, and will probably always be, a beautiful woman by Hollywood standards. But upon meeting the well-endowed receptionist, who works in nearby Bedford, savvy folks will immediately recognize the telltale signs of excessive plastic surgery: her endowments are unnaturally large for her petite frame, and project abruptly from her chest, like two halves of a cantaloupe, her nose is pinched at the tip, her cheekbones too sculpted, and her chin a mite too pert. In other words, Miss Livingood has more store-bought parts than a John Deere tractor. It has been said—if only by yours truly—that over the years her nips and tucks, and implants, have produced a face so tight that when Priscilla opens her mouth, her eyes snap

shut, and vice versa. Alas, somewhere along the way her
eyebrows migrated to the middle of her forehead, where
they hover like the disjointed wings of a bat. Despite all
this, men still find the woman attractive. Go figure.

I received the coroner's report early on a Tuesday
morning, and rather than wait until she got off work, I
decided to visit Miss Livingood at her place of employment. I might be a fool, but I am not a masochist. You
can be sure I primped as much as possible without slipping into the valley of the vain. I wound my bun extra
tight, and used twice as many hairpins to secure it as I
normally do. The prayer cap was new, crisp, and white.
Over my sturdy Christian underwear I donned a freshly
ironed navy blue broadcloth dress that had a shock-
ingly short hem, one that barely fell below the knees.
Practically daring the Devil to embrace me, I slipped
my stocking-clad size elevens into sandals, instead of
my usual brown brogans. Apropos of nothing, just about
every article of clothing I owned had recently shrunk,
except for my shoes.

Then, throwing caution to the wind, I rummaged
through my foster daughter's things until I found a tube
of peppermint-flavored lip balm that promised to de-
liver a translucent pink. After having applied the gunk,
I discovered, to my dismay, that the manufacturer and I
had decidedly different views on what defined *translucent,* because quite frankly, even the Whore of Babylon
would have been embarrassed to go out with lips the
color of mine. I scrubbed the balm off with soap and
warm water but was unable to remove it completely.
To be completely honest, this pleased me. A faint tinge
of palest pink was admittedly more alluring than my
natural color, which approaches that of boiled liver.
Needless to say, I felt quite racy as I stepped out to face
the world of Priscilla Livingood.

3

I knew that Priscilla worked for a Dr. J. P. Skinner, but I had no idea that her boss was a plastic surgeon. The riddle of how this medical receptionist was able to afford so many procedures was finally solved. But, silly me, I had neglected to call first and so discovered, to my irritation, that the office was not officially open to business until ten o'clock. It was just now only a quarter till the hour. The woman who informed me of this, through a cubbyhole too small to admit a cat, sounded just as put out as I did.

"Miss Livingood isn't here yet, so you're just going to have to wait like everyone else."

I glanced around at a room full of swollen and bandaged faces. Priscilla, the trumpet-playing strumpet, must have gone through a lot of pain to get where she is. For a second she had my admiration. Then the door to the examining wing opened and in strode a man in a white lab coat. By the arrogant way he moved, I knew without being told that he was a doctor. He walked right past me and disappeared through a door that led to a room, or rooms, behind the receptionist station.

With nothing else to do but fume, I plunked my patooty down on a chair with stained upholstery and grabbed a dog-eared magazine off a side table: *Lift Magazine: True Stories of People Who Have Improved Their Lives by Going Under the Knife.* I thumbed through the pages until I saw a headline that was so salacious, it nearly stopped my heart. I looked again at the cover. Then back at the article. I couldn't believe the smut before my eyes. If I were to describe this moment in a novel, I would warn my gentle readers to skip to the next paragraph so as to protect their souls from unnecessary sin. It was about a woman's quest for the perfect breast size, and her final realization that there was no such thing—although Dr. J. P. Skinner's work had certainly added to the quality of her life. Yes, the story had some merit, but the title, "A Tale of Two Titties," was uncalled for.

What if I'd brought a child with me? What if I'd been someone with less life experience? Both the child and I would have been damaged irreparably by the T word. There is nothing so energizing as righteous indignation. I leaped to my feet just as the aforementioned doctor strode back into the packed waiting room.

"Hold it right there, buster," I bellowed.

He stopped and turned. "Are you talking to me?"

"None other." I advanced until I was well within speaking distance. "This"—I tapped the offending page—"has no business being in a public waiting room."

"It's my waiting room; it isn't public. And I haven't the slightest idea what you're talking about."

"This titillating language—well, you get my drift."

"Actually, I don't."

There was something vaguely familiar about the man. Perhaps I'd seen him over at Pat's IGA, or had gotten a glimpse of him on the golf course as I drove along it in and out of the city of Bedford. The way he was looking intently at me made me think we'd met formally at a fund-raiser of some sort, but I couldn't for the life of me figure out what that would have been. To be sure, Dr. Skinner and I did not move in the same circles.

A smile played at the edges of his mouth. "Magdalena, could that possibly be you?"

"Possibly," I said. "That all depends on where, and how, we met."

"Try just about every day in sixth grade. My parents decided to try life in Hernia for a year, but gave it up when they realized they were about to drop dead from boredom."

"*Jimmy?* Is that you?"

"Skinny Jimmy Skinner," he said, and then, much to my surprise, threw his arms around me in an unscripted hug.

My people are Swiss-German. We don't hug. At best we place our arms gingerly around blood relatives and pat them on the back. We slap hard if we really like a person, although in almost any situation, a handshake will suffice. But I'd been dating a Jewish man from New York for the past year, and had learned that it is possible to survive a full, gentle embrace—at least from someone you know. And Skinny Jimmy was no stranger.

I shot up like a weed the summer between fifth and sixth grades. When school started that fall I was five foot eight and towered over everyone in the classroom including our teacher, Miss Thumbernickel. Puberty brought with it a whiff of maturity, so to speak, but Mama would not hear of an eleven-year-old wearing deodorant. In no time at all I was dubbed Yoder with the Odor, then just Odor, which edged out Stretch and Pole only because of the rhyme. It would have been an even more horrible year, had not the skinniest boy on the planet moved to Hernia.

At first our friendship was based solely on the fact that we were the oddballs, the butts of most of the juvenile jokes thought up by our insensitive classmates. Eventually, however, I grew rather fond of Skinny, and was practically heartbroken when he moved back to Bedford a year later. We vowed to stay in touch forever, which lasted for almost two whole months. To be frank, I'd rarely thought of him over the years, and when I did, it was never even with enough curiosity to look for him in the phone book.

"Jimmy," I said, giving him the once-, twice-, and thrice-over, "you aren't skinny anymore." I spoke the truth. He was wearing an expensive sports jacket, but it couldn't hide a weightlifter's physique.

He pretended to sniff the air. "And you no longer smell. How about that?"

"Yes, how about that. Say, Jimmy, back to the smut in this magazine—"

"You ever think about modeling, Magdalena?"

"Excuse me?"

"Not only are you tall, but you have the perfect face and figure for the job. Of course, you'd have to do catalog modeling, as opposed to runway modeling, now that you've reached a certain age."

"How is life on Mars, Jimmy?"

"You think I'm joking, don't you? Magdalena, I know that you've been occupied building up a thriving, successful business, but it's time to smell the roses—no odor reference intended. I know some catalog people in the modeling division. I could help you get started."

"Enough is enough! How can you be so cruel?"

Jimmy must have known someone in the acting profession as well, because he appeared genuinely surprised. "I beg your pardon?"

"And what gall you have! Your patients are staring at us, for crying out loud. Does that give you the jollies? Stick-thin Magdalena with a nose deserving of its own zip code—who are you to make fun of skinny people, by the way?"

Jimmy grabbed my hand, and even though I protested, he succeeded in dragging me into one of his consulting rooms. Although I was seething, he gripped my wrists tightly and forced me to look into a mirror.

"What do you see?"

"Steam coming out of my ears."

"What else?"

"A beaked scarecrow in a clean broadcloth dress and surprisingly sturdy sandals."

"Take a better look," he growled.

"Well, I see you, someone who has somehow managed to grow into a hunk—I mean a hunky-dory-sort-of-looking person."

"I'll tell you what I see. I see a woman who has a body most of my patients would kill for. I also see a woman whose striking good looks should be the envy of every woman in the Commonwealth of Pennsylvania."

"Since you're not wearing glasses, I'd have to say it's your contacts that need changing."

"So, what are you, Magdalena? A full B cup? Almost C?"

"*Excuse* me?"

"Your bra size. I'm a doctor; I think I can handle it."

"For your information, although I wear a B cup, it's only so that when I stuff it with tissues, my bosom looks almost normal. Once I even had room for a pussycat in there."

He smiled. "And now?"

"Now the darn thing—oops, pardon my swearing—has shrunk."

"Has your dress shrunk as well? It seems to be hugging your hips a bit snugly."

"It's the funniest thing; everything I own has shrunk. I don't do anything different with the laundry, except that I got rid of the washer with the wobbly leg. The loads always ended up being unbalanced, so I had to sit on it, which led down a path of sin—uh, never mind."

"Magdalena, have you ever heard of body dysmorphic disorder?"

"I don't listen to rock and roll."

He grinned. "It's when one's body image doesn't match up to reality. It can go both ways, but usually it involves a man or a woman thinking that they're ugly, or have some very unattractive feature, when virtually everyone else sees them quite differently. Some very beautiful women, as well as handsome men, think they're ugly."

"Like in the *Ugly Duckling*?"

"Exactly."

"Why, that's just silly. If I was a beautiful woman, you can bet I'd have no trouble seeing that."

"Oh, but you do."

"What?"

"When is the last time you looked in a mirror—I mean *really* looked in the mirror. With an open mind."

"This morning."

"And what did you see?"

"An extremely tall, skinny woman with a horsey face. Neighhhhhh! When the Good Lord made me, he put a saddle on my back and hollered giddyap."

"That isn't funny. You're a damn—now it's your turn to pardon my swearing—good-looking woman, Magdalena. Honestly, you have a classical face and a killer bod."

"But my nose—"

"You've grown into your nose, Magdalena. It is in perfect proportion to your face. Everything about you is in perfect proportion. Trust me, I'm a plastic surgeon. I try to make people look like you for a living. A mighty good living at that. I redo what God has done, but only when I honestly think the patient could use some improvement. If you came to me requesting any procedure—more extensive than removing a bunion—I'd throw you out of my office. No, I'd kick you to the nearest psychiatrist, that's what I'd do. Come to think of it, I should do that anyway."

Pride is the worst of sins. That said, I've always been proud of my mental prowess. I may have the face of a mare and the body of a scarecrow, but at least I have a top-notch brain. That brain now asked me to consider what the doctor was saying. Could it possibly be that I wasn't as ugly as I believed myself to be? I mean, Jimmy had been a good buddy in the sixth grade, but I didn't for a second doubt that he would be happy to fix any of my many flaws, and charge me an arm and a leg for the privilege. What was in it for him to make me feel good about myself? Absolutely nothing; zilch; zero.

Again I looked at my image in the mirror, this time with open eyes—well, one open eye. "Oh, my heavens, oh, my stars," I said, feeling faint.

4

Jimmy stood over me, fanning me with his filthy magazine. "You fainted, Magdalena; you'll be all right in a minute."

"Fainted? I think not. I was dreaming, and one doesn't dream whilst fainting—does one?"

As always, Skinny Jimmy was easily amused. "What were you dreaming about?"

I could feel myself blushing. "That is for me to know, and you *not* to find out."

"That you're not ugly, but beautiful?"

I struggled to my feet. "How did you know that?"

Jimmy grabbed my shoulders and turned me to face a full-length mirror this time. "You weren't dreaming; you were in shock. I can't imagine what you're feeling. I worked out forever to beef up, so the change was gradual for me."

If allowed, I think I would have stood there staring at my reflection in the mirror until I turned into a pillar of salt. Fortunately the intercom on Jimmy's desk buzzed.

"Yes?" I heard him say, although he sounded a mile away.

"Dr. Skinner, your first patient is ready in cubicle nine."

"Thanks." He turned to me. "Sorry, Magdalena, but I've got to go. Duty calls."

"Sure thing, Doc." My voice still sounded like it

belonged to a homely woman. Would that change as well?

"Before I go, just one quick question. What brought you here today? You weren't actually thinking of having a procedure, were you?"

I shook my head. "I came to speak to Priscilla Livingood."

"What about? Is this personal?"

"It's police business."

"That's right; I heard you solve their difficult cases—which seem to be just about all of them lately. Then you know, of course, that her fiancé died the day before yesterday."

"Yes. I also know that she came to work yesterday. Don't you think that's odd?"

He shrugged. "We all have a right to grieve in our own way. Priscilla is a hard worker. Coming in yesterday and today is how she copes."

"Is she in now?"

"Yes, that's who I just talked to."

"May I speak with her?"

"You can use my office. I'll send her in." He picked a folder off his desk and started for the door. Halfway there he stopped. "Please go easy on her."

"I will."

"And enjoy your new self. You're a knockout, Magdalena. Remember that."

"Aye, aye, sir. And thanks, Jimmy. From the bottom of my heart."

But it wasn't easy to remember Jimmy's words. When Priscilla walked through the door, doubt was close on her heels. Yes, I knew that the woman owed a lot of who she was to petroleum by-products and Jimmy's skillful fingers, but nonetheless, she was the epitome of what society now regards as female beauty. The cantaloupe bosoms, the batwing eyebrows—I'd seen them a thousand times on covers of the magazines in the checkout line of Pat's IGA. Surely my homegrown assets, if indeed I really had them, seemed bland by comparison.

Priscilla appeared resigned to see me. "Magdalena Yoder, what took you so long?"

"I beg your pardon?"

"I was expecting to see you yesterday. Don't you usually pounce on your victims almost immediately?"

"I'm sorry for your loss," I said, at a loss to say anything else.

"I'll just bet you are. I'm sure you and every other hoochie in Hernia have been crying buckets."

"*Excuse* me?"

"Oh, did I step on a nerve? Magdalena, you have a reputation for being blunt, straight to the point. Are you going to beat around the bush, or are you going to come right out and confess that you too had an affair with my Cornelius?"

"Ew!" I could feel my face take on a life of its own; it was as if I'd just tried to suck a slice of rotten lemon.

"What was that all about?"

"No offense, dear, but Cornelius Weaver never did a thing for me. Not that there was anything wrong with him, but I have my own fiancé."

"So this is strictly police business?"

"Strictly. I just need to ask you a few questions."

There were two chairs in Jimmy's office. A straight-back with a plastic seat, intended for anyone other than him, and the leather swivel behind the desk. Priscilla had the chutzpah to slip into the latter and offer me the plastic chair.

"Shoot," she said.

I consulted my list. "Were you and Cornelius living together?"

"I slept at my own house. Sometimes he did too, but more often not."

"Was yours an exclusive relationship?"

It surprised me that such a beautiful woman, albeit a

man-made one, should have such an unpleasant voice. It was like the sound of toenails scraping on a chalkboard. I've heard enough of that to be a good judge, by the way.

"Exclusive, my eye. Cornelius knew he was the most illegible bachelor in town." Priscilla Livingood is syntaxically challenged, to coin a new word.

"Come again?"

"You know, he has the most to offer, so every woman wants him."

"I most certainly do not!" I shuddered just at the thought. I'd rather eat a plateful of boiled eels.

"That's because a woman with your looks can reach far beyond Hernia to get a man. Bedford too. That handsome doctor of yours is from where? South Carolina?"

"New York. And he came here; I've never been to the Big Apple."

"All the same, he wouldn't have looked twice at a girl like me."

I'm sure Gabe would have looked several times, but I wasn't about to point that out. "Tell me, Priscilla, if Cornelius was a lothario, why did you agree to marry him?"

"Because he was rich, handsome, and single. Sounds shallow, doesn't it? I don't care. I'm forty-three, Magdalena; my eggs are getting old. I want to have babies, lots of them. I only need two more procedures; then I'm through. After that Cornelius would have had eyes only for me."

"I didn't realize Dr. Skinner did brain transplants."

"What? Was that a dig?"

It was. And I should have been ashamed of myself. But what woman in her right mind would put herself under the knife so many times? Why couldn't she just suffer in silence like I did all these years?

I cleared my throat. "What I meant to say is, I wouldn't think Dr. Skinner would agree to do so many surgeries on the same patient. Is there a code of some sort?"

"You mean the Hypocrite's oath. Yeah, well, Dr. Matthews is going to do it, not Dr. Skinner. But I still get my twenty percent discount, because they have this Episcopal thing."

This one took me a minute. "Ah, reciprocal."

"That's what I said. Now, are we done here?"

"Almost. Where were you when you learned that Cornelius had passed?"

"Passed on what? I told him to sell that '67 Mustang convertible of his and buy an SUV like everyone else. I can't have my babies riding around without a roof over their heads."

"Indeed. But I'm speaking of his death. Where were you when you learned that he'd had a heart attack?"

"At my house, sleeping in my own bed. Cornelius said he had a killer multigrain and was just going to lie low for the evening."

"Now, that's what I call a cereal killer."

"Huh?"

"Never mind. Who called you?"

"That cute young police sergeant, what's-his-name."

"Chris Ackerman."

"Yeah. He said Cornelius had suffered a heart attack, and that I should meet him at Bedford County Memorial Hospital. I didn't even take time to get dressed; I just put on a robe. I got to the hospital the same time the ambulance did, but Cornelius was already dead. It doesn't surprise me that Cornelius hadn't called for help when the attack began; he was such a stubborn man. He thought he could tough out anything, but you can't tough out a heart attack."

That was interesting. Priscilla had unwittingly exposed a cover-up. Chief Hornsby-Anderson and her protégé had conspired to make it look as though Cornelius had called 911 himself, and died on the way to the hospital. When I agreed to keep secret the fact that the Grim Reaper had caught Cornelius and the chief in flagrante delicto, I hadn't fully realized the ramifications of such a problem. It was one thing not to mention the chief's presence at the house, but quite another to be party to a story that had Cornelius dying someplace else altogether. What was I thinking?

"Magdalena," Priscilla said, waving her hand in front of my eyes, "you've zoned out on me. Have you been hitting the sauté again?"

"Excuse me?"

"The bottle. You know, drinking."

"I most certainly have not! And for your information, I don't hit the sauce on a regular basis, not unless it's au jus. The three times I *did* partake of the funny juice were all by accident."

"Whatever. So, then we're through here?"

"One last question. Are you on the drug Elavil?"

"Just because you drink, doesn't mean I take drugs."

"Indeed it doesn't. This is a prescription drug."

"For your information, I don't take any drugs, not even an aspirin, unless I've just had a procedure. Then the doctor gives me pain pills, but I get off them as soon as I can."

"Did Cornelius take Elavil?"

"Not that I know of. But I never snooped in his medicine cabinet, if that's what you mean."

"No. You've been very helpful." I headed for the door, but stopped when the most important question of the day occurred to me. "Priscilla, just out of curiosity, what are the two procedures you'll be having?"

"Liposuction on my upper arms, and floating rib removal."

I jiggled pinkies in both ears to make sure they weren't blocked and I could hear right. "I'm sorry, I thought for a second you said 'rib removal.' "

"I did."

"But that's so bizarre. And painful, I would imagine."

"Magdalena, don't you be judging me until you've

walked a mile in my pumps. What does a perfect woman like you know, anyway?"

Apparently not as much as I thought. But until that morning I thought I knew everything there was to know about having a poor self-image. Well, color me wrong! I never could have dreamed that I would meet someone who felt even worse about her body than I did. And I still did. Jimmy's lecture had yet to sink in fully, although I had already begun to pray that he was right.

To have a woman as beautiful, albeit unbalanced, as Priscilla Livingood call me perfect—well, it was an indescribably wonderful experience. The sad part is, there may have been many nice things said about my appearance over my life span; things I'd managed to block out because I couldn't possibly believe they were true. Perhaps my ears were deceiving me now. Perhaps I was nuts, as well as ugly. Perhaps I was dreaming. Whatever the case, I wasn't going to hang around Jimmy's office any longer to find out.

"Toodle-oo," I said, and sailed from the room.

My full name is Magdalena Portulaca Yoder, and I have a life apart from my amateur detecting work and my killer bod. I'm the co-owner, but sole proprietress, of the PennDutch Inn, one of the most desirable full-board establishments east of the Mississippi. I am a sister to Susannah, a well-meaning, but slovenly, slothful, and slutty woman who is married to a jailed murderer. I am also a foster mother to a fourteen-year-old girl, who is the issue of my pseudo-ex-husband's loins. And last, but not least, I am engaged to Dr. Gabriel Rosen, a retired physician, who fancies himself a mystery writer.

When I got back to my car, the first thing I did was consult the rearview mirror. "Mirror, mirror, in the car, who's not pretty, har, har, har?"

The mirror usually doesn't hesitate to scream right back at me, "You're not pretty, you dummkopf."

Now the mirror was mute.

I tapped it with my index finger. "Come on, wake up. This is an important question."

The mirror mocked me with its silence.

"Okay then, mirror, how about this: I have a classical face and a killer bod."

The mirror didn't even snicker. "Congratulations, Magdalena. You've finally seen the light."

I turned on the ignition, squealed out of the parking lot, and careened down the highway to the Sausage Barn, where I was scheduled to meet four people for brunch. I knew for sure that one of these, in particular, would not hesitate to tell me the truth.

5

Curries

All of the following recipes reflect typical curries of either meat or vegetables with a masala or curry sauce, which can be wet or dry. Different regions of India and Pakistan account for the variations in ingredients and preparation methods involved. Northern India and Pakistan see cooler, fragrant ingredients given the climate and spices indigenous to those regions. The farther south you go, the hotter the palate, thus the spicier the cuisine. Why eat hot foods in hot climates? Because the excess heat induced by the cuisine promotes perspiration, in turn cooling the person enjoying the dish. Coastal areas will have more seafood, rugged regions more meat; regional vegetables abound everywhere.

All of these curries came from our kitchen. Curries vary, as do people. There are authentic curries that demand an acquired taste, and very modernized curries that do not resemble anything of the original curry, save for curry powder. These recipes are as homemade as they come. But they also allow one to experiment and make these curries one's own. Also, since these are curries, and like any dish, really, they are reflective of one's capacity to withstand spices. Adjust the spices to your liking, and experiment. There is no one right way to make a curry, but don't let Granny know that!

Garnishes may include finely chopped cilantro (or coriander leaves), julienned ginger, shredded coconut, lime wedges, or fried onions.

Raita is a yogurt salad used to cool the palate while eating spicy foods or to just add a little something to the meal. The basic recipe is as follows.

Ingredients

1–2 green chilies, finely chopped (optional)

1–2 teaspoons cumin seeds, slightly roasted

Salt and black pepper to taste

1 garlic clove, finely chopped

¼ cup coriander leaves, finely sliced

2 cups yogurt, whipped

1–2 cups cucumber, grated

Coriander leaves, crushed cumin, and black pepper for garnish

YIELD: 4 SERVINGS

Preparation

1. In a blender add chilies, cumin seeds, salt and pepper, garlic, and coriander leaves and process.
2. Add this mixture to yogurt.
3. Fold in cucumber.
4. Garnish with some coriander leaves, crushed cumin, and black pepper.

Notes

Variations are limited only by your imagination: Add ¼ cup chopped mint leaves, a tablespoon or two of a favorite chutney, roasted mashed eggplant, shredded lettuce, or a garden confetti mixture of finely diced onions, green bell pepper, and red bell pepper.

Another idea is to use yogurt and any prepared chutney, whether sweet or hot. Mix a cup of yogurt with the desired amount of chutney for a wonderful sandwich condiment or as a salad dressing.

Ginger-garlic paste is mentioned in these recipes, but you can buy ginger paste or garlic paste separately as well. Or make your own by blending enough water with ginger and/or garlic to make a paste. Store in the fridge; it should last two weeks.

Garam masala is a dry ground powder made from a mixture of whole spices such as cloves, cinnamon, and the like. New cooks should use it sparingly.

As you cook, keep tasting the curry, and make adjustments accordingly. If you think a curry is too hot and spicy, add a peeled and diced potato to absorb some of the heat.

Using canned stewed or crushed tomatoes is just as good, and in some cases better than fresh, since canned tomatoes tend to make much smoother gravies. I prefer canned.

6

As is usually the case, I was the first of my party to arrive. It was not quite eleven; too early for the lunch crowd, and past time for breakfast—at least for most working folks. This meant that Wanda Hemphopple, the world's meanest restaurateur, would be free to play the part of hostess. She does not, however, have the mostest.

"Well, well, look what the cat dragged in."

I scanned the sticky linoleum floor around me, looking for bunny heads and bird legs.

"I meant you, Magdalena."

"And a cheery good morning to you too, Wanda."

"I suppose you want your usual booth, and your usual breakfast. How boring, Magdalena."

"Actually, I'll be wanting one of the round tables, instead of a booth. There's going to be five of us."

Wanda quickly considered, and just as quickly rejected, the idea that I might have friends. "It's gotta be some church thing."

No comment from the new, and improved, Magdalena.

"So? Am I right?"

I nodded resignedly. It was better to let her continue to think I was a pariah than to let her know what was really going to take place in her restaurant.

"Ha! That's what I thought."

"Wanda, I know we're not exactly friends—we've

even had our differences—but I'd like to ask you a personal question."

"It's one hundred percent natural. All me. And no, I don't dye it."

I knew immediately that she was referring to her hair. Wanda wears her long brown hair coiled on top of her head, around an opening at the top that goes all the way down to her scalp. Imagine, if you will, a model of a volcano made from clay. This hideous do is held in place with thousands of hairpins and gallons of hairspray. This is only a slight exaggeration.

I am convinced that Wanda has neither washed, nor combed, her hair since we were in high school, lo some thirty years ago. Over the ensuing decades, new species of vermin have developed in this teetering tower of epidermal outgrowth. Should this unsightly mass ever break loose, plagues will be unleashed that could decimate this nation. In my humble opinion, it was foolish for President Bush to search Iraq for weapons of mass destruction, when all along they were hidden in plain sight on Wanda Hemphopple's head.

"No, dear," I said with a pleasant smile, "I'm not talking about your WMD."

"My WMD?"

"Yes. Wanda's marvelous do. What I want to know is, do you think I'm pretty?"

The coil teetered precariously as Wanda recoiled in surprise. "Magdalena, I always knew you were a bit odd, but I never thought you were gay."

"I'm not gay—not that there's anything wrong with it. I just want to know if you think I'm pretty."

"No, I don't think you're pretty."

My hopes were dashed, like a bottle of bubble bath in Mr. Gawronski's backyard fountain on Halloween. Not that I know about such a thing. And it could have been anyone; the geometry teacher was hated by everyone in the tenth grade.

"Oh. Thanks for not being mean about it."

"Don't be so dramatic, Magdalena. Of course you're not pretty; you're beautiful. Everyone knows you're the most beautiful woman in Hernia. But just in case you haven't figured it out, nobody likes a woman with a swollen head."

"You really mean that?"

"Get over yourself. Lord knows I did."

"I beg your pardon?"

"I always thought we could be friends, Magdalena. In fact, I thought we were—until that day you purposely, and maliciously, dropped a hotdog down my hair."

"You *knew* about that?"

"I'm not stupid. And I may not have such a good sense of smell, but even I could smell it after a week. But you see, that was the beauty of it. A little bit of Vicks VapoRub under my nose, and I could no longer tell it was there. But you kids sure could. If I recall correctly, you sat behind me in bookkeeping class."

"You mean you *never* removed it?"

She never got a chance to answer, because my brunch party showed.

I am an Amish-Mennonite, which is to say I am a Christian whose ancestors were at one time Amish, but who eventually became Mennonites, and one even became a Presbyterian. So you see, Mennonites and Amish are not the same thing, although both denominations stress pacifism and the belief that only persons old enough to make a confession of faith can be baptized.

Amish generally marry other Amish, and so that part of my family tree is as tangled as any jungle. Scratch me, and my cousin bleeds. Give me a sandwich, and I *am* a family picnic. Freni, my best friend and cook, is not only my first cousin, but cousins number two, three, and four, as well. But I am almost positive she is not my mother.

Speaking of Mama, she and Papa, who were double second cousins, were squished to death in a traffic accident. The car they were riding in was rear-ended by a truck carrying Adidas tennis shoes, and they were pushed into the back of a milk tanker. It happened in the Allegheny Tunnel, one of America's longest tunnels, so there wasn't any room for them to get out of the way.

Upon their death, my sister, Susannah, and I inherited the family farm, which I soon converted into the PennDutch Inn. My inn, by the way, was immediately discovered by *Condor Nest Travel* magazine, and became an instant hit with the celebrity crowd. Starving models from New York, remodeled Hollywood stars, and fat cats from Washington all vie for my limited space, and for the right to be gently abused by yours truly. In fact, they pay big bucks for the experience, and I have become an exceedingly wealthy woman. I have also discovered that the axiom "Money can't buy happiness" isn't necessarily true. I've been poor, and I've been rich, and I'd rather be rich and unhappy than poor and unhappy.

Susannah is now a wealthy woman. Her portion of the inheritance, as well as her profits from the business, are in a trust, over which I have control. The trust was originally my parents' idea, because, sadly, they knew that their youngest daughter was every bit as responsible as a poodle in heat. I say that lovingly. My parents' lack of faith in their youngest daughter was validated when Susannah's husband, Melvin, turned out to be a murderer. Fortunately for them, they were both dead at the time.

I remained a spinster, and a virgin, until a few years ago when I married a very handsome man who, in addition to being a distant cousin, was still married to another woman. I discovered this horrible fact after having given him the flower of my maidenhood, and have ever since been somewhat of a social pariah to the more devout members of our community. Whilst they refer to me as an adulteress, I prefer to be known as an inadvertent bigamist. Sort of like the *Accidental Tourist*—a very good book, I might add.

Hernia's Holier-Than-Thous, of which I used to be a charter member, were about to get new grist for their gossip mill, new fodder to fuel their righteous indignation. I, a believing Christian, was about to get unevenly yoked to a Jew.

As I stood there wondering whether Wanda had ever disposed of her wiener, my Jewish future mother-in-law barged through the door of the Sausage Barn. Her face was so grim, one would have thought she'd just eaten there.

"You," Ida Rosen said, pointing a stubby finger at me, "are *meshugganeh*."

"Ma!" My beloved, Gabriel Rosen, aka the Babester, was clearly pained by his mother's accusation. He had a firm grip on her other arm and was mouthing words to me over the top of her head—*well* over the top.

I have never been much of a lip-reader, and what little ability I had vanished with the onslaught of collagen-enhanced celebrities. Take two inner tubes, smack them together repeatedly, and then try to decipher language from the experience. Now *that's meshugganeh*. At any rate, I couldn't read Gabe's wonderful, and entirely natural, lips.

"What did you say, dear?" I asked.

His lips moved in an exaggerated fashion, but I was still clueless. It was even less enlightening than watching Pamela Anderson eat corn from a cob while talking.

Gabe tried hand signals just as Ida looked up. "There was a fly on your head, Ma," he said. Thank goodness my intended is a would-be novelist and thus quick with the words.

"There are no flies in my restaurant," Wanda snapped.

"You call this a restaurant?" Ida said, rolling her eyes. "I ordered a toasted bagel last week, and it was cold in the middle. Frozen. In New York you get only fresh."

"Then you should have stayed in New— Welcome!"
Wanda, a serious businesswoman like myself, can turn
on a dime if it means adding coins to the coffer. In this
case, the potential cash cows walking through the door
were the Reverend and Mrs. Gerald Fiddlegarber.

I'll come right out and claim full responsibility for
bringing the Fiddlegarbers to Hernia. I met them in a
bush at a church retreat center in Goiter, Maryland.
More specifically, I was in a bush by *myself* when they
happened to walk by. Let it be said that I don't normally
spend a lot of time flailing about in bushes, either my
own or someone else's. At any rate, the reverend was
between jobs, so to speak, and Hernia had just lost its
most beloved preacher to the murdering hand of my
brother-in-law. I gave Reverend Fiddlegarber a one-
question interview, and when he passed it with flying
colors, I hired him on the spot. Since *I* and *myself* are
two-thirds of the search committee, it was my right to
do this. The third person on the committee is *me* who, I
suspected, would put up very little resistance. The question, by the way, had to do with interfaith marriages.

But back to Wanda and the cash cows. She knew that
roping in a minister and his wife could, potentially, be
important to her business. A favorable mention of her
establishment during the sermon, or even just at coffee
hour, might well convince the holdouts at Beechy Grove
Mennonite Church that dining at the Sausage Barn was
not tantamount to taking supper with the Devil. Wanda,
you see, belongs to the *other* Mennonite church in town,
and has at times made disparaging remarks about our
lack of progressiveness. Mrs. Fiddlegarber, however, had
no intention of being roped into anything.

"Is the rabbi here yet?" she demanded.

"Rabbit?" Wanda asked. "We used to serve rabbit,
but some of the customers complained. Said food ought
not to be cute."

"Not rabbit," Ida growled. *"Rabbi."*

"I'm not sure we serve that either," Wanda said sadly,

her dreams for expansion going down the drain. "Does it go by another name?"

"Oy boy," I said to let everyone know just how ecumenical I was.

"It's like a Jewish minister," Reverend Fiddlegarber said, a twinkle in his eye. For the record, he is a warm, considerate man, not at all like his wife, Petunia. Then again, what can one expect from a woman who works as a freelance writer of instructions for enema boxes?

"I don't think there are any Jews here," Wanda said, after scanning the room. "Except for youse two."

No sooner had the last word exited her mouth than a tall man with curly blond hair stood up near the back of the main dining room and waved. Gabe waved back.

"Now there's three," he said.

7

Rabbi Jay Feldman from Pittsburgh was both friendly and likable, which meant, of course, that Ida Rosen and Petunia Fiddlegarber were immediately united in their intense dislike of the man. They began by tag-teaming him with trivial questions but soon turned on each other in a heated theological debate, for which neither of them was remotely qualified. It soon became clear that unless I managed to separate them, the reverend and the rabbi were not going to have a productive conversation.

"Ida, dear," I said, manufacturing enough charm to strangle a bracelet, "I'm going to the ladies' room. Would you like to come along?"

"No."

"You sure?"

"I don't have to go."

"Come anyway."

"Vhy should I vant to see you make pee-pee?"

"We need to talk," I hissed. Yes, I know, one can't hiss without an *s,* but if people in books can do it—books that have made it to the *New York Times* bestseller list—why can't I?

Ida wouldn't budge. "So, vee talk here."

I kicked Gabe under the table. Alas, I may not have hit my mark on the first try. The rabbi's blue eyes widened and he gripped the table with both hands.

"Gabe," I hissed, kicking again, "do something."

"Ma," he moaned, "just go with Magdalena. Please?"

"All right, so I'll go already. But you make sure that this goy pretending to be a *rebbe* doesn't make a Christian out of you."

"I resent that, Mrs. Rosen," the rabbi said hotly. "I'm as Jewish as you are."

"There is nothing wrong with being a Christian," Petunia roared.

I grabbed Ida's arm and dragged her to the ladies' room. It was not a pleasant place to be, seeing as how Wanda keeps it only slightly more hygienic than she keeps the kitchen. I resolved not to touch anything and got right down to business.

"Ida, I'm so glad you agreed to this pleasant little chat."

"Nu?"

"What's new? Well, funny you should ask." I smiled at my reflection in a mirror so smudged, some wag had taken to carving her initials on it. "Do you think I'm pretty?"

"Vhat?"

"You know, attractive?"

"For this you make me leave my Gabeleh?"

Mama always said it was easier to catch flies with honey than with vinegar. When I asked what she planned to do with the flies, she stuck a bar of soap in my mouth. But I think I know what she meant.

"Ida, you are a very attractive woman."

"Yah?"

"Very."

She stood on her tiptoes to peer in the mirror that hung above the sink. Unable to get a satisfying image, she tugged at the bodice of her dress.

"You think this *shmatte* doesn't make me look fat?"

"Not in the least."

"So, it's a *shmatte,* then?"

"No, it's a beautiful dress, every bit as lovely as you are. You're stunning, Ida. Everything about you is gorgeous. Now, let's get back to talking about me."

"How long have you known?"

I smiled modestly. "That I was beautiful? Believe it or not, it wasn't until this morning—"

"Enough of this silly talk. How long have you known about this gay ting?"

"What gay ting?"

She waggled a sparse eyebrow. "You, me. Zee horizontal hoochie-hoochie."

"*Excuse* me?"

"For you, maybe I understand. Because, as you say, I am a real looker. But for me—vell, you are not such a hot potato."

"Potato?"

"So, tell me, Magdalena, does my Gabe know you shving both vays?"

"I only shving one way," I wailed, "and I haven't shvung for a very long time!"

"The goyim and their riddles," Ida muttered and charged out of the ladies' room.

I waited until a respectable amount of time had passed before trying to sneak out of the ladies' room and, ultimately, the restaurant, unnoticed. My wedding plans would have to be made without me. Perhaps it was just as well, since large chunks of my marriage would undoubtedly be scripted without any input from me.

I'd forgotten; there is no sneaking out of the Sausage Barn. Wanda's talons found the collar of my dress just as surely as they would have found a fleeing hare.

"Pay up, Magdalena."

"Pay what?"

"The bill. Just because you're chief of police in absentia doesn't mean you can't be arrested. I'll issue a citizen's arrest if I have to."

"Look, as far as I know, they haven't even ordered yet, much less gotten their check. Just put whatever it turns out to be on my tab. Have I ever not paid you, Wanda?"

Her stare softened. "Unfortunately, I have to hand it to you on that score. Of course, *you* can afford to pay your bills on time."

"I am indeed blessed. Now, if you'll excuse me— Hey, what did you mean by 'in absentia'?"

"Everyone knows Cornelius and the chief of police were involved. One can only assume that she would go into mourning for a few days. Has she left town? My cousin Herbert in Peoria just opened a Sausage Barn—"

"What do you mean 'everyone' knows?"

"Must you always interrupt—"

"Apparently. And what exactly *is* it they know?"

"Magdalena, surely you jest. And here I thought you had a bat's radar. I bet there isn't a soul in Hernia over three years of age that hasn't been gossiping about the chief of police doing the tarantella two-step with the town's most eligible bachelor."

"No, no, no! You're not getting it right; you've got two dances in your metaphor. You're supposed to have one dance and one bed item— Just a minute, I'm over three, and I haven't been gossiping."

"You see? You even interrupt yourself. How annoying is that?"

"I'm not the least bit annoyed with myself. Now, pray tell, who was your source for the rumor?"

"It isn't a rumor. And if you must know, I heard it from Alice Troyer."

"The same Alice Troyer who is a very intelligent and somewhat amusing woman, but who, and I say this lovingly, has a nose that resembles a garden root?"

"Yes. She seemed almost jealous."

"I don't doubt she was."

"Pardon me?"

"Of course, dear." I clutched my purse tighter to me and barreled out the door.

Alice Troyer lives in a gingerbread house. She is not a witch, although she does own one. Her spacious Victorian is dead smack in the middle of Hernia's historic district and boasts some of the finest craftsmanship of the late nineteenth century. In summer she hangs baskets of ferns and flowering vines from the porch roof. In the fall she piles baby pumpkins on either side of the front steps, and a lifelike witch guards the door. In winter plastic icicles cling to the eves, reflecting the myriad of tiny, tasteful lights that twinkle on every bush and tree. Tourists invariably stop to admire Alice's decorations, and it is said to be the second most photographed house in the county. Alas, the most photographed would be mine, due to the large number of untimely demises that have occurred on my property.

Since it was late spring, the flower beds on either side of the walk were a riot of color and too many other clichés to mention. The fern baskets were up again, and guarding the door was a life-size ceramic goose decked out with a pink cloth bonnet and a matching bow for its neck. If you ask me, anyone who has enough time to spruce up a goose, even a fake one, has enough time to play with the Devil.

Alice answered the door with a look of utter shock on her face. She tottered backward, and for a second I thought she would faint. Then, lurching forward, she grabbed the door jamb and steadied herself.

"Land o' Goshen! Won't wonders ever cease?"

I glanced around. "What wonders?"

"You, Magdalena. This is the first time you've ever darkened my doorway."

"Very funny. I thought something was wrong. Do you always greet your guests this way?"

"You're a guest? Wait right here while I change the soap and put out a cute little towel."

"Nonsense. I'm here on police business."

"Honest, officer, I didn't mean to do it. He made me do it. But I promise to be good from now on. Just let me keep the money."

"*Excuse* me?"

"Gotcha, Magdalena. Come on in."

I followed her into a pleasant enough room, but when offered an armchair, I checked it carefully for a whoopee cushion.

"What are you doing," she said, "looking for loose change?"

"Yes, and I found a twenty-dollar bill." My backside was toward her, so I pretended to stuff something down the front of my dress.

"No way! Let me see."

"Too late. Finders keepers, losers weepers." I plopped my shapely patooty on the cushion, which was really quite comfortable, by the way.

"You didn't really find any money—did you?"

"Maybe."

"If you did, it's mine."

I screwed my face into what I hoped was a smug smile. That old saw about a smile taking fewer muscles than a frown was undoubtedly thought up by some annoyingly cheerful person on a sugar drip. Not only do my smiles require a great deal of facial exertion, but they can be downright painful at times. This was a particularly excruciating one.

"Magdalena, do you have to use the bathroom?"

"No. I'm trying to be pleasant."

"Never afraid to try a new thing. That's what I like about you."

Consider the source, Mama always used to say. But she never had to interrogate a professional comedienne. I prayed for a Christian tongue.

"Alice, dear, I'm here to ask you some tough questions about your relationship with Cornelius Weaver."

Her expression was worth any amount of annoyance. "*What* did you say?"

"Did you love him?"

Her face darkened. "That's none of your business."

"Then, you did. In that case, I'm sorry for your loss."

"If you must know, we were going to be married."

"But I thought he was engaged to Priscilla Livingood."

"Cornelius promised to break it off with her just as soon as he could think of an easy way to let her down. He took me into Pittsburgh, to a high-end jewelry store, to choose the ring. It was a knockout. Over two carats, and clear too; not like the ones sold in the big chain stores at the mall that are so included you swear there's a fly trapped inside. Anyway, they had to size it, so we left it there for a few days. That was okay with me, because our engagement party wasn't for another two weeks. Then the night before the party he calls and tells me—*over the phone*—that the engagement's off, and that he's always loved Priscilla Livingood."

"You must have been heartbroken."

"Heartbroken, my asphalt road! I was livid. I would have strangled Cornelius with the phone cord, except that he was at the other end. After I'd cooled off some, I called him back and asked him what she had that I didn't have. 'A good body and a bigger bank account.' That's an exact quote. Not a *great* body, but a good one. That implies mine isn't even good. How mean is that?"

"Very, but I might be able to top that. My pseudo-ex-husband, Aaron Miller, dumped me for a woman he'd already been married to, and then had the chutzpah to ask me to raise their daughter." Chutzpah is not a Pennsylvania Dutch word, by the way, but Alice seemed to know it. No doubt it was her showbiz connections.

She nodded. "So we have that in common; we've both been dumped. At least you're beautiful. All I have is funny, and men don't like it when I'm funnier than they are."

"You really think so?"

"Unfortunately, yes."

"No, I mean the part about me being beautiful."

It was the wrong question to ask a woman who was so homely that her parents had to rent a baby to take to church. She frowned hard enough to make her bangs brush the tip of her radish nose.

"Just what the heck are you doing here anyway? My relationship with Cornelius Weaver is *my* business. It's not your business, and it's certainly not police business. Color me stupid, but I thought you were here to offer your condolences, not to give me the third degree."

"I said I was sorry for your loss, and I meant it. But you're wrong; this is police business. You see, the coroner has ruled that there are suspicious circumstances surrounding the death of Cornelius Weaver."

She seemed less shocked now than she had been to see me at the door. "What strange terminology you use, Magdalena. How can circumstances surround anything?"

Gritting one's teeth can wear down precious enamel. I chose to glower, which is much kinder to one's person, forehead lines excepted.

"He may have been murdered. But you don't seem surprised by this news."

"*News?* I would be surprised if he wasn't murdered. You couldn't swing a cat in Hernia without hitting one of his dumped lovers."

"You don't say—no, please, do say!"

"What do you want? Names?"

"Now we're cooking with gas. Spill all, dear."

8

"Well, I only know one name."

"Who is the skunk?"

"I think you mean skank. Anyway, that would be Caroline Sha."

"But she has no hair!" The horrible, judgmental words just slipped out of my mouth. I blame that all on Mama and the cod liver oil she made me take. How can one be expected to exercise restraint with a slippery mouth? At any rate, Caroline suffers from alopecia areata. She is completely bald, lacking even eyelashes. In a predominately Amish and Mennonite community such as ours, having this disease is ironic, given that so many of us, thanks to the Apostle Paul, believe that hair is a woman's crowning glory. Mama never cut her hair until she was in her forties, and that was a misguided attempt to bond with my younger sister. My hair has never been cut—well, I do have my split ends trimmed, and once I had to have a chunk hacked out in order to remove a wad of gum. I must hasten to add, lest one waste too much time feeling sorry for Caroline Sha, that she has the most beautiful face I have ever seen.

Alice shook her head, no doubt commiserating to herself that I was wasting her time by just stating the obvious. "Of course she has no hair, but that doesn't stop her from being drop-dead gorgeous."

"I wouldn't say she's all that pretty."

"Any other woman, given her condition, would wear a scarf, or a wig, but Caroline knows that this would detract from that flawless face of hers."

"Flawless is stretching it a bit, don't you think?"

"Come on, Magdalena, admit it. You're a beautiful woman, but Caroline is downright stunning."

I sighed. "Okay already, she's a looker. So Cornelius was seeing Caroline as well. First, how do you know that?"

"Ha! I caught them—well, how shall I say this so as not to offend your tender ears—I caught them engaged in the act."

"For your information, my ears are not so tender."

"Magdalena, you're a prude. Don't deny it."

"Just because I'm not a tramp, like some people I know."

"You're a rude prude."

Sometimes it pays to swallow one's pride, no matter how bitter the taste. "Whatever you say, dear. Can you think of any reason that Caroline might want her lover dead?"

"They weren't lovers, for goodness' sakes! Their relationship was purely physical."

"How do you know?"

"Because Cornelius told me so."

"He did? When?"

"The night he broke off our engagement. I think he was trying to let me down as easy as possible—at least from his point of view. He said I shouldn't feel bad because I wasn't the only one he'd been stringing along. There were plenty of others that would be getting the same news and feeling the same way. He wanted me to comfort myself with the knowledge that he'd actually loved me. The others, like Caroline Sha—that's when he mentioned her name—were just notches in his belt."

"That's disgusting!"

"That's Cornelius in a nutshell."

I thanked Alice for her time, and gently pointed out

that my visit might have been a tad more pleasant had she offered me some refreshments. Alice, who supposedly has a great sense of humor, was not amused.

Having skipped brunch at the Sausage Barn, and not getting even so much as a brownie from Alice, I was starving. Thank heavens there is always one place where they have to feed you, and that, of course, is home. I could smell yeast rolls baking the second I opened the kitchen door. Freni was standing at the table, her back to me, brushing shortening on a pan of rolls to make them glisten.

"Yoo-hoo," I called pleasantly. " 'Tis I, your comely, and clever, cousin."

Freni paid no attention to me.

"Lost in thought, are we, dear?"

Still no response.

I walked over and tapped her on the shoulder. "Earth to Freni—"

That's when my dear cousin left the earth. Freni jumped so high that, had she been a good three feet taller, she would have connected with my eight-foot ceiling.

"Ach, *du lieber!*" she gasped, after several gasps that were solely for oxygen intake.

"Relax. It's only me, your very own Magdalena, as big as life and twice as ugly—no, make that beautiful."

"For shame, Magdalena. I think maybe you use seven of my lives, yah?"

"That's what you said the last two times I scared you. That puts you twelve lives in the hole."

She appeared to be staring at my mouth. "And now the tricks," she said.

"Tricks?"

"It is a child's game, Magdalena. You move the lips only, but I know you say nothing. I have been around the blocks; I am not such a spring pullet."

"Blocks? Chickens? What on earth are you talking

about?" A split second after saying that I noticed the huge balls of dough protruding from her ears like heads of cauliflower. That just goes to show how little attention we pay to people we see on a daily basis. At any rate, I grabbed the dough ball on the left and eased it from her ear. I did the same to the one on the right.

Freni looked at me as if I were a magician and had just pulled a pair of rabbits out of her head. "Ach! What do you do now?"

"Is this the same dough that you plugged your ears with on Monday?"

She flushed, her memory coming back to her along with the ability to hear. "No, I don't think so."

"What do you mean by 'I don't think so'? Is this something you do on a regular basis? And if so, why haven't I noticed? Somewhere there is a village missing its eccentric."

She gave me a pitying look. "Always the riddles, Magdalena. If I live to be one hundred, I will never understand the English." To the Amish, anyone not of their faith is "English." Because I am her kinswoman, and our denominations share some history, to Freni I am marginally English—depending on her mood. But an Amish woman from London (I'm pretty sure there aren't any) would not be English, whereas a Buddhist from Japan would most definitely be English.

"Freni, I wasn't asking you a riddle. I was merely inquiring whether or not sticking bread in your ears was a habit. By the way, how are the guests doing? Any complaints you need to pass on? Silly me, how could you have heard what they were saying?"

She shrugged. "Yah, but yesterday there is a complaint."

"Oh? From whom?"

"The woman from Charleston, the one you say is uppity."

"I did not say—let's move on, shall we? What did *she* say?"

"She ask me how many threads there are in the bed-sheets."

"What did you tell her?"

"I tell her 'enough.' "

As Freni spoke, she calmly brushed melted shorten-ing on the two rolls rescued from her ears, and plopped them in a baking pan along with some others. Waste not, want not. Freni is a woman after my heart. As for the bedsheets in my guest rooms, the thread count is low because I believe in being thrifty. Besides, coarse sheets serve to exfoliate dead skin as my guests toss and turn on their lumpy mattresses. If you ask me, folks should pay extra for the privilege of having their bodies buffed while they sleep.

"You did fine, Freni."

I started for the door to my suite, which opens off the opposite side of the kitchen from the back door.

"Magdalena?"

"Yes?"

"How did it go with the Jewish preacher?"

"The rabbi? He seemed very nice, but I really didn't get a chance to talk to him."

"Yah?"

"Her."

Freni nodded. Given the fact that she virtually lacks a neck, it looked more like a hiccup.

"I do not know which is worse, Magdalena: your mother-in-law, or my daughter-in-law."

"She's not my mother-in-law yet! Besides, your Bar-bara is the salt of the earth."

"Too much salt makes high the blood pressure, yah?"

I laughed the laugh of a doomed woman. Several months prior I had oh-so-cleverly palmed the Babester's mama off on Doc Shafor, a randy octogenarian friend of mine whose libido has been stuck on high for as long as I can remember. I thought it was love at first sight, and I believe they did as well. As insurance I sent them on an all-expenses-paid trip to Bora-Bora in French Polynesia, which is as far as one can get from Hernia without cooperation from NASA. But alas, twenty-six hours on an airplane, in economy class, was too much for the budding romance. The fact that they haven't taken contracts out on each other is only because neither of them has any money.

"Just think, Freni," I said meanly, "if she moves in here with me, you'll have her *and* Barbara."

"Ach!"

"Ach, indeed. I think you'll soon find that your daughter-in-law is a picnic compared to Ida Rosen."

"A picnic with low-salt food, yah?"

We laughed.

"Magdalena, I think maybe your *maam* would have been proud of you. But not so proud that it is a sin, yah?"

"Thank you, Freni." I walked back to where she was standing and, bending at the waist, kissed the top of her head, just in front of her prayer bonnet. Her ears still smelled of yeast dough.

"Ach," Freni squawked. Such overt displays of sentiment are practically unheard of in our culture, and limited to Baptists and Presbyterians, who appear to be prone to excess of all kinds. It is a little known fact that nearly seventy-eight percent of all Amish, and probably sixty-three percent of all Mennonites, lack the demonstrative gene. (Then again, since 61.2 percent of all facts are mostly made up, this statistic may be somewhat inaccurate.)

At any rate, I kissed her again.

Once in my suite, I headed straight for Big Bertha. Friends may come and go, but the pleasures of a thirty-two-jet whirlpool bath are forever. Yes, it is a sin to bathe in the middle of the day, but I was a fallen woman. Just ask any proper matron in Hernia what she thought of Magdalena Yoder's morals. The answer, thanks to

Aaron Miller, would not be pretty. Having succumbed to the pleasures of the flesh with a pseudo-husband, what more did I have to lose by releasing tension with thirty-two swivel heads?

I poured a lavish amount of gardenia-scented bubble bath into the tub and let the froth grow until the surface of the pool was covered with a meringue of bubbles two feet high. I was about to step into this earthly slice of heaven when the telephone beside my bed rang. This is my private line, and besides family, only a select few have access to me through it: Babs, Mel, Charlize, Katie, Oprah, Ben—you get the picture.

I eschew caller ID. If the Good Lord had wanted us to know who was calling, he would have made us all mind readers. "Hello?" I said in my pleasant voice.

"Ma'am, we have reports that basements in your area have been flooding. We here at Squanderyore Savings can come out and give you a free damage assessment, and if your house qualifies, we can put on a complete waterproof seal for only six easy payments of ninety-nine ninety-nine. May I schedule a visit from one of our water-damage experts?"

I sighed. "I'm afraid my house won't qualify. I've been nagging it to study for the last twelve years, and all it ever does is make excuses. I've even resorted to threats. 'If you don't get good grades, you're not going to have a lock on Yale,' I tell it. 'And what if you can't get into any college? What are you going to do then? Live in a trailer park? Or worse yet, live on the street as a tent?' And wouldn't you know, my house doesn't even have the decency to answer."

"Excuse me, ma'am? Are you all right?"

"Fine as frog's hair—which is pretty ding-dang fine. Most folks don't even know frogs have hair; that's how fine it is. While we're on the subject of amphibians, why would anyone in their right mind fall in love with a big blue frog? That's almost as bad as falling in love with a muskrat—not that I've done that, mind you.

Aaron was only a rat. But *muskrat* love? What's up with that? Have you ever smelled a muskrat up close? There's a reason for the *musk* part of their name. The *rat* part too."

"Ma'am, I'm sorry, but I'm going to have to go now."

"Oh, no you don't. You called me on my private line, so you're just going to have to hear me out. Are you married?"

"Uh—I just got engaged." The caller was a man, but the excitement in his voice was almost palpable.

"Where's the honeymoon going to be?"

"That's just it. My fiancée is planning the wedding, but I'm supposed to plan the honeymoon. I thought the bride was supposed to plan everything."

"Would you like me to help you?"

"Nah—okay, I'll bite. How?"

"Well, I know this charming little inn down in Amish country, in the mountains of southern Pennsylvania. The ambience is supposed to be out of this world. Sometimes movie companies even go there to shoot."

"Yeah? Who am I kidding, I could never afford a place like that."

"Don't be so negative. I know the owner quite well, and I'm pretty sure I could talk her into arranging a special price for you. It's not going to be cheap, but then quality never is, is it?"

"I guess not. How much will it be for three nights?"

"With or without ALPO?"

"Excuse me?"

"That stands for Amish Lifestyle Plan Option. For just fifty measly bucks more a day you get the privilege of living like a real Amish person. By that I mean you get to make up your own room, feed the chickens, milk the cows. You know, all that fun stuff."

"Cool! But how much?"

"Just a minute, let me calculate." I made pinging noises with my mouth. "Well, well, well, what a coincidence; you're never going to believe this, but it comes out to exactly ninety-nine ninety-nine times six easy payments."

"Fantastic! How do I sign up?"

I took a credit card number before heading back to the warm, welcoming spigots of Big Bertha. I settled into the lather with a groan of sinful pleasure, and that's when the Devil grabbed me by a foot, and pulled me under. I mean that literally.

9

There is nothing more frightening than Satan trying to drown you in an oversized whirlpool tub. I fought back mightily, tooth and toenail. I bit, I slapped, I scratched—all things a proper pacifist would never dream of doing. But if, indeed, all things are fair in love and war, then surely they are fair in mano a mano combat with the Prince of Darkness.

I wasn't surprised that the Devil had chosen to attack me physically while in a corporeal form; I've been a wicked woman. What surprised me is that His Evilness had taken the form of a woman.

"Stop it, Mags," she shrieked when it was clear I had finally bested her.

The fact that the Devil was using my sister's voice was unconscionable. Of course, the Devil doesn't have a conscious, and can't really be bested by a mere mortal, but I had soap on the brain. While my thoughts struggled to keep up with me, I gave Lucifer another good whack, this time with a Lifebuoy bar.

"Ouch! That hurt, darn you."

"*Susannah?* Is that really you?"

"No, I'm somebody else. Of course it's me. You're really weird, Mags, you know that?"

"The pot calling the kettle," I said, glowering at the only other human being to form in my mother's womb, and then not until a full eleven years since I'd called that uterus home. "What in tarnation are you doing in Big—bathtub? You weren't in it when I filled it."

"I spoke to you when I came into your bedroom, but you were on the phone and didn't hear me. I guess you didn't see me either. So when I came in here to use the toilet, and saw those bubbles—well, you can't blame a girl for not wanting to see them go to waste. And it's not like I have a setup like this at home."

"So you sampled my bubbles. Now, get out. Please."

"Why can't I stay? We used to take baths together all the time when we were little."

"We were never little together; I was thirteen, and you were two. The only reason I bathed with you is because Mama forced me to, in order to save water. Then came the notorious day of the floater—never mind. Just am-scray."

"Fine, if that's the way you're going to be. Kicking a poor widder woman out into the cold."

"You're not a poor widder woman. I give you an allowance large enough to support a small kingdom, and your husband is not dead. He's a cold-blooded killer who will spend the rest of his days behind bars."

Susannah stood, the bubbles sliding in gentle avalanches. "You don't have to be so mean. I didn't know Melvin was a killer when I married him."

"Yes, but everyone told you he was a—" I clapped a soapy hand across my mouth. There was nothing to be gained by reminding my sister that she had chosen to spend the rest of her life with a loser. Anyway, I had done the same thing. The only difference was that my loser has yet to kill anyone. Of course I'd married an extremely handsome man, not a giant praying mantis. And furthermore, everyone in Hernia had thought the world of Aaron Miller, whereas only Zelda Root, my half sister, and her merry band of Melvinites thought well of Melvin. Even his mother didn't have such a hot opinion of him.

Susannah reached for one of my large, fluffy towels. They are one of the few luxuries I indulge in. (I thoughtfully provide my guests with the rough, cheap variety; yet another way for them to exfoliate.)

"You're right," she said.

"*Excuse* me?"

"I was an idiot. A fool. What am I going to do, Mags? No one in their right mind would marry me now."

"That's because you're still married."

"Besides that. You know what I mean."

"There is no 'besides that.' Don't you think that divorcing the murdering mantis would be a place to start?"

"I thought you were against divorce."

"I am—in theory. In practice, sometimes it's the only option. That said, I do think divorce is way overrated. Believe me, dear, it's not gay marriage that is going to ruin the institution; it's divorce, and contributing to that, the ease with which one can get married in this country. Consider the fact that one has to be tested in order to get a driver's license, but not to get a husband license. Believe me, husbands are a lot harder to handle than cars."

"You're preaching to the choir, Mags. I agree with everything you say."

"You *do*?"

She nodded, flinging clusters of bubbles dangerously near my eyes. "Like I said, I'm a fool. Because of that, I'm ruined."

There is nothing more heartbreaking than having a worthy opponent capitulate because of a broken heart. I wanted to hug Susannah, but we can barely do that while wearing clothes. I would try to compensate with a platitude.

"Just think of poor Priscilla Livingood. Now, there is a woman who won't be able to hold her head high in Hernia much longer. She was engaged to the male version of a slut—wait just one ding-dang minute. How come there isn't a word for the male version of a slut?"

"There's *lothario*."

Frankly, I was surprised Susannah knew the word. "Nope. *Lothario* doesn't have the same moral connotation. Now, where was I?"

"You'd just called Cornelius a slut. You must have found out about Thelma Unruh."

"Huh?"

"I told Thelma she was kidding herself, but you know those Unruhs; they're more hardheaded than us Yoders."

Never complain, never explain, a wise woman once said. And really, when it came to push versus shove, what did it really matter how much I knew, versus how much I was about to know? Withholding information isn't exactly a lie, is it?

"Poor, poor, Thelma," I said,

"She's a natural blonde, you know. You've got to watch those natural blondes; they're sharper than you think. It's the brunettes who dye their hair and try to pass themselves off as blond—they're the ones missing a few marbles. Like, please, who do they think they're kidding with those dark roots and sallow complexions? Besides, their boyfriends will find out soon enough, when the cups don't match the saucers."

"What does dying one's hair have to do with dishes?"

My sister rolled her eyes. "The drapes won't match the rug."

My brain is dense, not impermeable. "Susannah! How crude."

"I'm not being crude, merely stating a fact. Anyway, like I said, it's the natural blondes you have to look out for. Cool as cucumbers, some of them. I told Thelma she was too smart to be messing around with Cornelius, but do you know what she told me?"

"Spit it out!" I said, spitting out soapy water.

"She told me she didn't care that Cornelius was engaged to Priscilla, because she had a surefire plan to bust them apart. I asked her what, but she wouldn't say. She said that in the meantime it was kind of fun to be the other woman and sneak around. So I asked her if she at least cared if what she was doing hurt Priscilla."

"And?"

"She said that it was Priscilla's fault, not hers. If Priscilla was too stupid to hang on to her man, she deserved what she got."

A shiver ran up my warm, sudsy spine. "Who knew Thelma could be so cold?"

"You've got to be kidding, Mags. That woman is a conniving skank. I wouldn't trust her with yesterday's garbage. Like I said, it's the natural blonde in her."

Both Susannah and I missed being blond by a hair. We share the same light brown color that is as close to dark blond as one can get without crossing the line from mousy to dishwater. Just a couple of highlights would put me over the great divide, while robbing me of at least twenty IQ points. Susannah has gone the other way, dying her hair an impossible shade of auburn that has strong purple undertones.

"I didn't realize you knew Thelma so well," I said, reaching for a towel. I wrapped it tightly around me as I stood, so that Susannah couldn't even peek at my birthday suit, had she been so inclined. It's not that I was ashamed or bashful; I didn't want her to be envious of the bounteous booty—I mean, beauty—the Good Lord had bestowed upon me—just in case she hadn't already noticed it.

Susannah didn't question the towel. "Thelma and I are the same age, Mags. We were in school together, all the way through twelfth grade."

"I don't remember that."

"Jeez, are you losing your memory? She came to practically all my sleepovers."

That explained it. My poor overtaxed brain has graciously deleted most memories involving childhood inequities. Mama was as high-strung as a two-tailed kite on a windy day, and her first time through raising a child—that would be me—she ruled with an iron fist and a concrete mind. I wasn't allowed to have any friends visit the house lest they observe some minor imperfection in her housekeeping and report it to their mothers. By the time Susannah came along, Mama had begun a slow trend toward both moderation and modernization, which peaked, wouldn't you know, after I'd turned twenty-one and was officially no longer her responsibility.

Someday, when I get to heaven, I'm going ask the Good Lord why He picked me to be Mama's guinea pig. Life is so not fair. Why is it that the odds appear to be stacked against me, and not against ne'er-do-wells like Susannah? That woman breezes through life, swaddled in fifteen feet of filmy fuchsia fabric, with a dog in her bra— her *dog*! Where was that mangy mutt now that she was naked? It never left her sight. Ever! The cantankerous little rat even piddled in her bosom when she smuggled it into the movies.

"The rat," I shrieked. "Where's the rat?" I had a nightmarish vision of having to give mouth-to-mouth to a three-pound dog that is two-thirds sphincter and one-third teeth. What if I blew on the wrong end?

"A rat?" Susannah shrieked as well and jumped up on the toilet lid, which, fortunately, was in the down position.

"Not a rat, *your* rat. The malicious mongrel that inhabits your Maidenform."

Susannah jumped down. "His name is Shnookums, and you know perfectly well that he isn't a mongrel; he's a purebred Russian toy terrier. And if you must know, he's up in Johnstown doing his studly thing."

"His what?"

"I've been renting him out for stud service, to generate a little more income—one that I can spend as I please. I told you. You see, you *are* losing it."

"People actually *pay* to have that thing do the terrier tango with their dogs?"

"A thousand dollars a pop, or pick of the pups. I always take the money, because I could never love another dog as much as I do my Shnooky-booky."

Thank heavens there weren't any flies hovering over the tub, because I might have inhaled them. "A *thousand* dollars for *that*?"

"He has impeccable lines, Mags. Besides, he was third runner-up in Best of Breed last year. His kennel name, by the way, is Volga Mist's Prince Shnookums."

I heard her words, and understood their meaning; I just couldn't comprehend them. "I'm afraid you've lost me, dear. Did you say he has a title?"

"Think of it as a beauty contest for dogs, but it's much more than that. You see, they have a breed standard, to which the dogs have to conform—oh, never mind, you're not going to get it, so why should I even try to explain?"

"But I *am* interested. Did you just say Shnookums has a title? Should I have been calling him Your Royal Highness?" Sometimes the Devil just has to insert a bit of sarcasm. I try to fight it, I really do.

"He has lots of show titles, but Prince is just a name I gave him."

My nose itched, which is always a signal that I'm about to have a moneymaking thought. "Hmm. If an ugly beast—and I mean that kindly—can make a thousand dollars a pop for doing something he likes to do against my leg for free, how much money could one make with a good-looking dog? You know, like a golden retriever or a lab?"

For some strange reason, Susannah was miffed. "I take that back, what I said earlier. You're not losing it; you've never had it."

"At the risk of sounding proud, may I remind you that I made straight As in college?"

"I'm not talking about intelligence. You have guests coming here from all over the world, but you're still a country bumpkin, and you're the greediest woman I've ever met."

I reeled in shock, which is a dangerous thing to do when standing in a soapy bath, especially one with thirty-two powerful jets. "I am most certainly not a country bumpkin!"

"Yes, you are. I bet you didn't know there was such a thing as a dog show until just now."

"Of course I did; you've mentioned them before. I just didn't know there were bucks to be made in the barking biz."

"That's just like you; all you ever do is think about money! And what for? You have oodles, but you never spend it. You're the cheapest woman in the universe, you know that? You can pinch a penny till it screams."

"Not only that, but I once made a nickel beg for mercy."

"And that's the other thing you do that drives me up the wall."

"What? Squeeze my dimes so hard I stunt their growth? I always wondered why they're the smallest coins."

"You're always sarcastic, that's what. I hate it, I hate, I hate it!" My sister stomped from the room, leaving soggy footprints on my bathroom carpet. I shook my head in shame. When I had the inn restored, after the devastating tornado that flung me facedown into a pile of cow manure, I should have sprung for tile, or at least a good-quality linoleum. Susannah was right; I am cheap. But waste not, want not, right? One must save for the proverbial rainy day—or string of rainy days, given how inaccurate weather forecasts generally are. Besides, what Susannah didn't know is that I've saved up a hefty amount of money for her retirement. She is never, ever, going to be truly in need. Neither is anyone else I love, including my pseudo-stepdaughter.

"You can thank me later," I hollered after her.

Immediately my words came back to haunt me.

10

Lamb Curry

Ingredients

1 cup yogurt
¼ teaspoon turmeric
  powder
1 teaspoon cayenne
  pepper
1 teaspoon cumin powder
1 teaspoon coriander
  powder
Salt to taste
1 pound lamb, cleaned
  and cubed
1 tablespoon oil
3–4 medium onions, finely
  sliced
4 bay leaves (whole)
4 cloves (whole)

5 cardamoms (whole)
2–3 teaspoons ginger-
  garlic paste
3–4 medium tomatoes,
  finely diced
1–2 tablespoons tomato
  paste
2–4 green chilies slit down
  the middle, but kept
  intact with stem to make
  it easier to remove from
  curry after cooking.
1 teaspoon garam masala
¼ cup coriander leaves,
  finely chopped, for
  garnish (optional)

YIELD: 4 SERVINGS

Preparation

1. In a bowl mix yogurt, turmeric powder, cayenne pepper, cumin and coriander powders, and salt. Marinate lamb in this mixture for ½ hour or more—the longer, the better.

2. In a heavy-bottomed pan, heat oil over medium-high heat and sauté onions, bay leaves, cloves, and cardamoms till a light golden brown.
3. Add ginger-garlic paste and fry for a few minutes.
4. Add tomatoes, tomato paste, green chilies, and garam masala and mix thoroughly. Add a little warm water now and then if mixture gets too dry or starts to stick.
5. Add marinated lamb mixture. Mix well. Let lamb cook 15 minutes. Add a little warm water. Mix. Cover, lower heat, and cook till tender (approximately 45 minutes) and oil separates.
6. Garnish with coriander leaves. Serve with rice or naan bread, accompanied by a nice salad and raita.

Notes

- Work with chilies carefully and wash your hands immediately after. The heat is in the seeds, so you may remove them before using the chilies. Chilies and cayenne pepper may be adjusted to taste and other peppers may be substituted, but sparingly. It may be safer to start with 2, taste along the way, and adjust. The curry will marinate with the green chilies, so remove them from leftovers to prevent further spiciness.
- Beef, chicken, or both may be substituted as well.
- For a variation, just add cut pieces of eggplant in step 4. If using potatoes, add them to step 5 to avoid ending up with mashed potatoes!
- Discard whole spices, that is, cloves, cardamom, and bay leaves, before eating.
- In step 5, when adding water, adjust it accordingly: more water if you want a slightly soupy curry to enjoy with rice and bread, or less water to keep it a bit on the dry side. Your choice.
- For a special regal flare, after step 5 you may also add ¼ cup heavy cream, a pinch saffron that's been soaked in 2–3 tablespoons of water, and ¼ cup blanched almonds that have been ground. Allow to simmer for about 10 minutes and enjoy Shahi Korma!

- You could also forgo the yogurt and still have a delicious curry. In that case, after sautéing the onions till golden brown, add the ingredients in step 4, then the meat, then all the spices, allowing cooking time of a few minutes in between each addition. Let the flavors cook and blend together for sufficient time; this will prevent a raw spice flavor. Add desired amount of water, mix, cover, lower heat, and cook till meat is fork tender.

11

"What's Auntie Susannah so mad about, and whatcha want me to thank ya for?"

Alison Miller, my fourteen-year-old charge, had somehow managed to slip into my room on cat's feet. Normally the child clumps around like a drunken elephant, not that I've seen a whole lot of those with which to compare her. At any rate, she'd propped herself against my bureau for support, since like most adolescent children, she seemed to lack a working spine.

"At what point did you come in?"

"Just when she ran out."

"And you're already too tired to stand up straight?"

"Sheesh, Mom, all ya ever do is pick on me. I'm a teenager, in case ya haven't noticed."

"Trust me, dear, that observation has not escaped me."

"So, ya gonna tell me or not?"

"Not. It isn't your business."

"It is, if I gotta thank ya."

"I've changed my mind. But I do want to know why you're home from school so early."

"Half day, that's why. Something to do with a ballgame all the way over in who-knows-where. Ya know I don't like sports. Anyway, it was in the flyer I brought home the other day. Didn'tcha read it?"

"Don't be silly, dear."

"That means ya didn't."

"But I was going to," I wailed. I know, I've promised to lay off the wailing, but sometimes I have no choice.

Alison regarded me with eyes the color of her father's, my erstwhile bogus husband. They are a bewitching blue, and I think there should be a law against them.

"So, can I go over to Jimmy's?"

I cleared my throat several times. It's a trick I learned, after becoming a pseudo-mom. It gives me a little extra time to think.

"Jimmy? I thought we settled that. I mean, I thought he—uh—was interested in someone else."

"Yeah, but he dumped her, and now he wants to date me again."

"You are too young to date. And Jimmy is too old for you. Alison, we've been through this a million times."

"Okay, no need to get your panties in a bunch. Can I go with ya, then?"

"Too late, dear, I'm engaged. You should have asked sooner."

The beguiling blues widened for a second, and then she burst out laughing. "Good one, Mom. No, I want to go detecting with ya."

"*Excuse* me?"

"Auntie Freni says you're working your *tuchas* off on a new case, and since I don't have school this afternoon, I want to come with ya to watch ya grill your suspects."

"Freni actually said *tuchas*? Where did she learn that?"

"Same place you did: Grandma Ida."

"She is not your grandmother! Not yet, at any rate."

"So, how about it? Can I come?"

To tell the truth, I was immensely flattered. From what I've heard, most fourteen-year-old girls wouldn't be caught dead hanging around their mothers. Perhaps I was doing a better job than I thought.

"I don't grill anyone; I merely put the screws to a few deserving individuals—oh, all right, you can come. But you have to be quiet. No interrupting me with questions, or touching their stuff."

"Deal."

"And try not to lean against their walls either, and if they ask you to sit, don't throw yourself on the chairs or couches. Lower yourself properly, like a lady."

"Yeah, yeah, whatever. So who are ya going to screw over first?"

"*Excuse* me?"

"Them's your words, Mom, not mine."

I was in for a long day.

Thelma Unruh, the natural blonde, lived the closest, but I decided to pick my victims alphabetically. Besides, Caroline Sha lives on the tippy-top of Buffalo Mountain, where the views are stunning. Hopefully, a drive up the mountain would lift my spirits. Who knows, I might even burst into a spontaneous rendition of "Climb Every Mountain," one of the few secular songs to which I know the words.

As we twisted and turned up the narrow road that led to the old Sha homestead, I had a field day sharing the sights with my foster daughter. The fact that Alison seemed genuinely impressed was an unexpected blessing.

"We don't have nothing like this in Minnesota," she said. "At least not where my parents live."

"This is where our ancestors lived for generations, dear. This land is your land. See the valley there? Your great-great-great-great-great-grandfathers and grandmothers settled it almost two hundred years before you were born."

"Did they chase off the Indians?"

"Of course not, dear; they were pacifists. They let others chase them off. A generation earlier, two of your direct ancestors were captured by the Delaware tribe and adopted as full-fledged members."

"Cool. Can we see our place from here?"

Our place? What music for my soul!

"Yes, dear, our place is over there to the left. You can just barely see the inn through those big maple trees."

"Who owns that big farm there, Mom?"

"Which one?"

"The one with them blue silos—I think that's what ya call them."

"Very good, dear. That belongs to Amos and Wilda Bontrager. They haven't any children, so someday it will be for sale."

"Can we buy it?"

"Would you really like that, dear?"

I could hardly believe my ears. It warmed the cockles of my heart just to think about my dear, if somewhat aggravating, pseudo-stepdaughter and her future family living on a farm near Hernia. I would have pseudo-step-grandchildren to play with, and when I finally became infirm, either Alison or one of her daughters would feed me with a silver spoon and escort me to the privy. What more could one ask of a life well lived?

"Heck yeah," Alison said, excitement rising in her voice. "We could tear down that stupid barn and them nasty silos, and build us a great big shopping mall. And 'cause we'd own the mall, we could get all the stuff from it for free. Man, I'm going ta build me a tunnel that goes straight from the Gap to my bedroom."

Disappointment is a bitter pill to swallow, but I managed to choke down most of mine before turning onto the gravel lane that dead-ends at Caroline's drive. An enormous white dog appeared out of nowhere, barking loudly, and escorted us the rest of the way to the house.

"Alison, you're not afraid, are you?"

"Heck no, I ain't."

"Good. The dog's name is Cujo. He's really a sweetheart, unlike your Auntie Susannah's little mutt."

"Hey! I like Shnookums."

"But you can't—never mind. Do you know what alopecia is?"

"Yeah. A girl in my class has it. It ain't fair, if ya ask me."

"We're not meant to understand everything in this life, dear."

"That don't mean I gotta like it. Trish don't have ta worry about fixing her hair at school, or getting it all messed up during gym."

"Wait a minute. You're jealous of Trish?"

"Who wouldn't be, Mom? The boys think its sexy, and she's got this cool sticker for her locker that says, 'Bald is beautiful.' Amanda Brinkwater's mom let her shave her head, but the principal expelled her. He don't say nothing 'bout Trish. It ain't fair, just like ya said."

"You said that, not me."

The door to the house opened and out swept the most beautiful woman in all of Bedford County. Caroline was draped in a red and gold sari, no doubt something she'd picked up on her recent trip to India. The woman gets around more than a bad pun. It's a wonder she had the time to have an affair with Cornelius Weaver.

"Welcome, visitors!" she said as she bowed low to the waist.

"Having a condition doesn't stop her from being a fruitcake," I said, charitably under my breath.

I could have said much worse, mind you. Carolyn Sha is an artist—Buffalo Mountain seems to be awash in artists—and gives new meaning to the word *eccentric*. The stone facade of her spacious home gives no hint that the interior walls are made of paper. I mean that literally. They are double-sided panels that slide along tracks, an idea she claims to have gotten while visiting Japan. Her furniture consists of nothing more than colorful cushions, and her bed is just a mat, for crying out loud. Even invited guests are required to remove their shoes before entering the house, and don't expect to consume a proper meal, unless you count soy as at least two food groups and are adept at eating with chopsticks.

While Alison played with the wolf in a white dog's clothing, I explained the nature of our visit to Caroline.

Other than a trembling vein near her right temple, she displayed no change of emotion.

"Certainly," she said, and led me into the main room, which at the moment pretty much included the entire house. "I'm letting the chi settle a bit," she said as if it were an explanation. "Sometimes there is just too much motion for me to think."

"That's nice, dear. An overactive chi can lead to chikiness, and we certainly don't want that."

She motioned to an array of beautiful, brightly colored, silk-covered cushions scattered about the floor. I knew that Caroline had designed the fabric herself and that this, in fact, is what she did for a living.

"Have a seat," she said. "Sit anywhere you like."

I piled three flat cushions so that they formed a low seat. Meanwhile, she sat cross-legged on a single cushion and, despite the fact that her sari was hitched up almost to her knees, still managed to look both modest and graceful.

"How's things?" I said, borrowing from Alison's lexicon. Caroline was, after all, closer to Alison's age than she was to mine.

"Things are wonderful, thank you. I just finished designing the bed linens for the Taj Warhol Hotel in New Delhi. That was a bit more of a challenge than I'm used to, so I'm glad to get it out of the way."

"Pardon me, dear, but didn't you mean to say the Taj *Mahal* Hotel?"

Her laughter was like the chimes I often play with when I find myself alone in the garden section of Home Depot. Sometimes I get as many as a dozen chimes tinkling at the same time. If any employees dare give me the evil eye, I point to the nearest child and shrug. Technically, this isn't lying, because the child *would* have started the chimes playing, if only he, or she, had thought of it. Now, where was I? Oh, yes.

"No, you heard right," Caroline said. "The owner is a big Andy Warhol fan, but his wife wanted a Taj Mahal theme, so they compromised. Would you like to see the sketches?"

"Uh—well—perhaps on another occasion. I'm here to ask you a few questions about Cornelius Weaver."

Her beautiful features turned as white, and hard, as alabaster.

"You were aware of his death," I said, "weren't you?"

"Miss Yoder, I'm so sorry, but I completely forgot that I'm expecting a call from Dubai this afternoon. You see, a sheik's son is getting married, and all fourteen of his current wives want matching outfits for under their abayas—"

"In a pig's eye, dear."

"I beg your pardon!"

"You heard me. I know quite well that you and the late Cornelius were having an affair. Spare me the sinful details, but other than that, I want to know everything about the relationship. Where and how often you two met. Did the others know? When was the last—"

"Others?"

"The rest of his harem, so to speak. Surely you ran into each other, coming and going. Or did you use the back door?"

It is easy to tell when a bald woman is livid. Especially if she picks up the pillow she is sitting on and not only hurls it at you, but catches you off guard, hitting your left eye with one of the corners. To be sure, I squealed like a nine-year-old girl. To be fair, I squealed even louder.

"Miss Yoder, I'm so sorry! What can I do to help?"

"Ice! Bring me an ice pack."

"I'm sorry, but I don't believe in ice."

"Say what?"

"It not only bruises the water; it slows down the chi."

I kept my left hand over the injured eye while I jiggled my right pinky in the corresponding ear to make sure it wasn't clogged with gunk. "Did you say it bruises the water?"

"Yes."

"But you don't think some trees were pretty badly bruised in order to make your paper walls?"

"I knew you'd say that. Everyone does. But you see, the paper was already made when I bought it. Freezing water, on the other hand, is totally under my control."

"Do you ever boil water?"

"Of course. I could make you a cup of chai. That might help with the pain."

"Chai with chi?"

"Now you're mocking me."

"Sorry, dear, my tongue seems to have a life of its own. But if it's all the same, I prefer some hot chocolate. Never underestimate the healing power of a cocoa bean, I always say."

She uncrossed her legs and rose to her feet in a fluid movement that I would not have been able to imitate at any age. Maybe there was something to this chi business.

"Would you have any ladyfingers to go with that?"

"More mocking?"

"No, I seem to have skipped lunch."

"I have some nut and honey bars. Will that do?"

"Absolutely."

"How is the pain?" she called from the kitchen end of the vast room.

"It's died down a bit. I think I'll survive."

"Good. Then you can grill me now, right?"

"Excuse me?"

"Your reputation precedes you, Miss Yoder."

12

I didn't know whether to feel flattered or insulted. If my reputation pegged me as relentless, ending an interview only when I had the desired information, that could be a plus. In any case, whatever I could do to enhance my reputation would make my job all that much easier.

"I'll need a nice flat surface for the thumb screws, but I forgot the bamboo splinters. You wouldn't happen to have any shish kebab skewers, would you? They'll do in a pinch—all puns intended. Oh, and I brought my own stretching rack. It's portable, and I can set it up just about anywhere. I had to leave the iron maiden behind, as it's currently in use."

She made no comment until she returned with the snacks. "Miss Yoder, either you have a very dry sense of humor or you are a very sick woman. Possibly both."

"Definitely both." I took a bite of honey bar. It wasn't nearly as sweet as I would have preferred. Neither was the hot chocolate, which wasn't even chocolate, but made from carob powder. I didn't have to ask about that; you can't fool a real chocoholic.

"So ask away," she said, just as calmly as if she was inviting me to inquire about a vacation to the Poconos.

"How long were you and Cornelius involved? More specifically, were you two still an item when he proposed to Priscilla Livingood?"

"Priscilla," she hissed. "Don't say her name again.

Words have power, and I don't want that word imprinting on these walls."

"But you just said—oh, never mind. Please answer my question."

"Yes, we were an item, as you put it, when he gave her that vulgar ring, but they were never truly engaged. Not to be married, at any rate. You see, Cornelius had a roving eye, and that woman thought she could tame him by tricking him into marriage, but it wasn't going to happen. He would have balked, sooner rather than later. The minute she started talking about guest lists and menus, he'd have come to his senses."

"But she must have talked about those things; they were three days away from tying the knot."

"Are you *sure*? Were you invited?"

"No, I was not invited, and I wouldn't have gone if I had been invited and the wedding was still on. With all the bed-hopping Cornelius engaged in, I might have been seated next to Beelzebub himself. Sitting next to Satan on a Saturday is not my cup of chai."

"Well, *if* there really was going to be a wedding, it's only because she tricked him."

"Tricked him?"

"There is no other way to explain it. That woman has less personality than a boiled rutabaga, and not one bit of her is real. She had the nerve to brag to me that they went on a ski trip together to Aspen in February. He supposedly popped the question when they were sitting in front of a cozy fireplace. Oh, please, give me a break. That woman can't sit within twenty feet of a fireplace, for fear of melting."

"Miss Sha, a less judgmental woman than myself might offer the opinion that you sound bitter."

"Bitter? About what? You don't honestly think I would have wanted to marry Cornelius, do you?"

"Who wouldn't have—except for myself, of course. I am, as you may have heard, engaged to an exceptionally handsome Jewish doctor, who will someday be a famous novelist."

"Ha. I think you should be the one writing the books, given your vast imagination."

Pride is one of the gravest of sins, so I work hard to eradicate it from my life. I think I have made remarkable progress, even to the point that I can finally say that I am proud of my humility. But today the Good Lord must have been testing me, for not only had I been informed that I was beautiful, but apparently I had a vast imagination as well. Glory hallelujah was all I could say at a time like this.

Caroline smiled pleasantly before continuing. "Your fiancé is retired from medicine, is not even published yet, and from what I hear, he's bolted to his mother's apron with three-inch chains. Yet somehow you see this as positive. Miss Yoder, I've got to hand it to you; you're even more positive than Norman Vincent Peale."

I jumped to my feet. One of the advantages of wearing size-eleven shoes is that it's easy to land on them. Sometimes, however, my tootsies can be quicker than my brain.

"Oh, yeah?" I retorted. "Well, this isn't even real hot chocolate."

"Of course not. I'm a vegetarian."

"And where do you think cocoa beans come from, a cocoa cow?"

"Well, chocolate milk—" Her blush seemed to flow across her scalp like a red tide. "Miss Yoder, I would appreciate it if you'd leave."

I opened my pocketbook and pretended to speak into it. "For the record, are you throwing me out?"

"No, I'm not—yes, I am! You are the rudest woman I've ever met, and I've met some real doozies, including your soon-to-be mother-in-law."

"You've met Ida?" I asked in astonishment.

"I went to Bora-Bora a while back. She and Doc Shafor were coming back on the same flight. They weren't speaking to each other, but they both had plenty to say to me."

"Do tell," I said, and threw myself back down on my makeshift chair.

"Don't get too comfy, Miss Yoder. There isn't that much to tell."

"No need to use the C word dear; a bed of nails would be more relaxing. But enough about furniture, or the unfortunate lack thereof. What did the battle-axe have to say?"

"What *didn't* she say? If Miss Yoder could only hear Mrs. Rosen talking, I thought to myself, she'd take a one-way flight to Kuala Lumpur and never look back. Malaysia produces some lovely textiles, incidentally. The batiks are simply gorgeous. And KL, as we in the know call it, is a fascinating city in its own right, what with the mix of cultures—Malaysian, Chinese, Indian. You should see the Batu Caves on the edge of town. There is a Hindu temple—"

"Enough with the travelogue, already. Let's talk about me. What did that obnoxious woman have to say about *me*?"

"All right, if you insist."

"I most definitely do. And I promise to leave your paper house the second you tell me."

"Deal. Well, Mrs. Rosen said that she'd rather her son marry a homely woman with a brain than a knockout beauty like yourself, who wouldn't know her elbow from her knee if she didn't have it labeled with indelible marker."

"That was a joke! I did it to amuse Alison."

"She also said that it was a good thing she was moving in with you, or her poor son would starve to death."

"But Freni is an awesome cook."

"I'm sure she is, but Mrs. Rosen seemed to be under the impression that Freni Hostetler would be given her walking papers."

"*What?*" That hiked my hackles so high, I was back on my feet again.

"Oh yes," Caroline said calmly, although a wicked grin played at the corners of her mouth. "It was quite clear that Mrs. Rosen has every intention of taking over the PennDutch Inn. She even went so far as to give it a new name: Rosen's Roost."

"We'll see about that," I growled and swept from the house on a tide of righteous wrath.

Alison, who was having a ball with the enormous white dog, did some growling of her own. I had to remind her several times that it is I who spring for her allowance, and not that ne'er-do-well father of hers up in Minnesota (that part I left out, although I did think it). It wasn't until she smelled Ida's blood in the air that she agreed to go. Then, all of a sudden, she couldn't wait.

My ancestors became pacifists under the tutelage of Menno Simons, the founder of the Mennonite sect. This occurred in the late fifteen hundreds. But Menno and his minions were not strict enough for my people, who switched over to the teachings of Jakob Amman, founder of the Amish church about a century later. They also followed the pacifist way of life, and many of them were tortured—drowned, burned at the stake, and so forth—by the state-established church in Switzerland. After several generations in America, my family became Mennonite again. I say all this to prove that I have four hundred years of pacifist blood running through my veins and must think at least twice before stepping on a cockroach. Now, Ida Rosen, a tiny little woman from New York City, was about to undo centuries of careful inbreeding. Whoever started the saying that "good things come in small packages" should be whipped with a generous length of high-quality wrapping ribbon.

Fortunately for my blood pressure, I didn't have to spend much time looking for the bane of my existence. She was right where I'd expected her to be, ensconced on the Babester's Italian leather couch, giving instruc-

tions to another diminutive woman, Judge Judy. Since
Green Acres went off the air, I don't watch television,
but if I did, I'd definitely watch *Judge Judy*. I'm all for
giving what for to those who deserve it—but not vio-
lently, of course. Yes, I know, the Bible says to turn the
other cheek, but it says plenty else too. In fact, there is
an entire book called Judges. Should I ever lose the inn,
heaven forefend, or retire, I would seriously consider
becoming a judge. The robe is certainly modest enough
to suit my needs, plus I could sit down, and while it
might come as a surprise to some, I'm quite good at giving others a piece of my mind.

I have my own key to Gabe's place, just in case I
need to turn off the stove or, to be entirely truthful, am
overcome by the desire to snoop. Anyway, this is how
I managed to catch itsy-bitsy Ida shouting orders to
the boob tube. So engrossed was she, that I must have
stood there for several minutes before she noticed me.
When she did, she let out a throaty yelp and clutched
her ample bosom with both tiny hands. It then took her
several tries to produce a coherent sentence.

"Vhy you vant to give an old voman a heart attack?"

"I want no such thing—well, maybe a very mild attack, one that didn't hurt too bad, or do too much damage, but just strong enough to make you pack your bags
and haul your hiney back to Manhattan. Sorry for using
such foul language, but I'm a mite on the perturbed side
at the moment, and I promise to take a bar of soap to
my mouth as soon as possible. And of course that would
be the antibacterial variety of soap, which, I have discovered, will substitute for mouthwash in a pinch."

"Ugh," Alison said. "It tastes horrible. Believe me,
Grandma Ida, I know what I'm talking about, because
she made me eat a piece once when I said a swear
word."

I gave the ungrateful child a mild version of the evil
eye. "I only had you chew it; I didn't make you swallow.
Besides, most things that are good for us are unpleas-

ant, like broccoli, and lima beans, and hard benches at church. And for the umpteenth time, she isn't your grandma; she's merely your pseudo-grandmother-to-be, which, on Magdalena Yoder's Scale of Familial Connectedness, ranks a two on a scale of one to ten. Only ex-cousins-in-law rank lower."

Ida released her bosoms in order to throw her hands in the air. "You see?" she said, addressing the ceiling. "The voman is *meshugganeh*. Nothing she says makes any sense. Vhat am I to do, I ask you? Just sit back and vatch her marry my Gabeleh?"

I strode over to the TV. I've never used a remote control, so I don't know how those gizmos work, but with a bit of searching, my eagle eye eventually found an OFF button on the set itself. I punched it with enough force to knock over Arnold Schwarzenegger. Alison stared at me openmouthed, but I turned my full attention to my new nemesis.

"I have no problem with you just sitting back and watching—from a distance, of course. But what's this I hear about you taking over the PennDutch and renaming it Rosen's Roost? It isn't your inn, for crying out loud, and it's never going to be."

"Does that mean," Alison said, her voice rising with excitement, "that I get to inherit it?"

"Maybe," I grunted, "if you outlive your Auntie Susannah and her mangy mutt. Now am-scray, so I can ell-yay at the eadache-hay from ades-Hay."

Ida hauled herself to her feet and advanced toward me, her bosoms leading the way like a pair of giant, well-padded battering rams. She didn't stop until there were only a few inches left between her chest and my navel. Then she threw back her head and allowed her gaze to climb slowly skyward, until her beady eyes finally locked onto mine.

"*Nu*, so I don't speak Hebrew, so vhat?"

"*Hebrew?*"

"For your information, my Gabeleh doesn't speak it

either, so you learn it for nothing. Now Yiddish, that's another story."

"That wasn't Hebrew," Alison gushed. "That was—"

My hand found my young charge's mouth, which I gently covered. It was obvious the old woman didn't know about pig latin, a fact that could come in mighty handy at some later date.

"You seem to have a knack for changing the subject, Mrs. Rosen. I still want to know what made you think you could possibly take over the PennDutch Inn."

"You vant to know so bad? I tell you! Because vhat belongs to my son is also mine, yah? I gave birth to my boy, I changed his diapers a million times—such a poopy boy you never saw. Vhen he vent to school I verk sewing *shmattes* for ten hours a day. I verk my fingers to the bone, for that my Gabeleh should become a doctor. And now he vants to give his poor ma something nice, but his rich girlfriend, she can't be bothered."

"Rich *shikse* girlfriend."

She shrugged. "So maybe that too. Is it a crime for a mother to vant the best for her son?"

"Not at all," I said agreeably.

"Think again," a male voice said as the love of my life entered the room.

13

"Hon," Gabe said to me, "I'll take it from here."

"Uh—take what?"

"I'll handle Ma."

"Go easy on her, dear. This sweet little woman loves you so much. It's just heartbreaking to hear about all her sacrifices." My intended was standing behind me, so he couldn't see me stick my tongue out at Ida. Neither could Alison. And for the record, I stuck it out only a few millimeters. I'm capable of a good deal more.

"You see vhat she did?"

Gabe put his hand on my shoulder. "She gave you empathy, Ma. That's more than you give her."

Ida's tongue was remarkably long, and frankly, not nearly as pretty as mine. "There! I give her vhat she vants; plenty of empty."

"Ma! How could you?"

"Vhat? I should let her insult me, and not fight back?"

"She didn't insult you, Ma. And the word is *empathy,* not *empty.* I want you to apologize right now."

"Vhen Hell freezes over."

Both Gabe and Alison gasped, but I sighed piteously. "That's all right, dear. She needn't apologize. I'd feel the same way if a woman I didn't approve of was about to marry my only son."

"She'll apologize," Gabe grunted.

As we waited for the aforementioned Hades to freeze over, I let my tongue flick from side to side. Soon it took on a life of its own, playing along the perimeters of my lips.

"You see?" Ida sputtered. "She insults me again."

I sucked back my telltale tongue in order to speak. "Oh, my stars and heavens. I didn't mean to upset her so much. Alison and I will be going now. Say good-bye to your grandma, dear."

"But you said she wasn't my grand—"

I grabbed the urchin's hand and fled while the going was good.

"But, Mom," Alison said as we got in my car, "you were sticking your tongue out at that nice old woman."

"Whatever gave you that idea, dear?"

"The mirror."

"What mirror?"

"The one above the couch where Grandma Ida was sitting."

"Oh, *that* mirror. Oops." My face started burning just as hot as if I'd held it too close to a campfire. If Alison beheld my wicked tongue, then it was almost certain that Gabe had seen it as well. And to think that the dear, sweet man had chosen to take my side over that of the woman who still cuts his meat.

"That wasn't very nice, Mom, was it?"

"Perhaps—no, it wasn't." I hung my head in shame. Now that I'd finally grown a chin, I didn't have nearly as far to hang it.

"Does that mean ya're going to be grounded?"

"I beg your pardon?"

"If I stuck my tongue out at an old lady, ya'd ground me for years *and* take away my allowance."

"Not years; only months."

"Well?"

"Well—a deep hole in the ground used to collect and store water."

"Not funny, Mom. Ya're always yapping at me about right and wrong, but I guess it don't work the same for grown-ups, right?"

"Wrong! But you see, dear, we grown-ups live in a much more complicated world, one that often calls for complex solutions in order to expedite conflict resolution. Therefore it is incumbent on us to implement retaliatory measures judiciously, so as to avoid tertiary expenditures." I had no idea what I'd just said. Hopefully she didn't either.

"Haufa mischt."

"What did you say?"

"I said horse manure. That's how ya say it in Amish."

"I know what it means," I growled. To be honest, I was so proud of my young charge for picking up some "Dutch" that I was tempted to give her a high five. But of course I couldn't approve of such foul language. I gave my young charge the evil eye. "If you must swear, say 'chicken droppings.' "

"Yeah, whatever. My point is, Mom, that ya were just trying to confuse me with that fancy language. Ain't that right?"

"I plead guilty on all counts. From now on I will try not to taunt Gabe's mother, and to punish myself for the tongue business, I will ask Freni to make mashed turnips for supper, and I promise to eat as much as you put on my plate." The only thing worse than mashed turnips is fried liver with rubbery blue veins running through it.

"Really? You mean that?"

"Absolutely. Now, are you coming with me on my next interrogation?"

"Nah, I don't think so."

"Why not?" I couldn't help but sound disappointed.

"It's not as fun as I thought. Ya don't really turn any screws on your victims. I think I'll go over to Stephanie Burkholder's house and watch her parents fight. Sometimes they throw furniture at each other, but it's usually

just food. Steph says that the stairs landing is a good
place to see the action from, and we can run to her room
if things get too bad."

"That's an awful idea, and I forbid it!" Who knew the
Burkholders were having so much trouble in their mar-
riage? I was going to have to pay closer attention next
Sunday at church.

Alison slumped so far in her seat that if it hadn't been
for the belt, she would have slid to the floor. "Okay
then, I'll just hang around the inn and do nothing. Who
knows, I might even die of boredom."

"Or you could come with me, like I said."

"Nah, I'd rather die."

"Suit yourself, dear."

When I dropped Alison off at the inn she immediately
became engaged in helping Freni make *snitz* pies for
supper. I said a prayer of thanksgiving for elderly
cousins before resuming my quest to find Cornelius
Weaver's killer.

Thelma Unruh, my next interviewee, operates a
beauty parlor business out of her home on Poplar Street, in Hernia's beautiful historic district. The
rambling Victorian house with peeling paint, sagging
porches, and bulging balustrades is, quite frankly, an
eyesore. The town council has been trying for years to
get Thelma to spruce up her house, but she stubbornly
refuses. We have even gone so far as to fine her, but she
won't cough up a dime. As for the beauty shop, according to Ordinance 367, it isn't even allowed.

How does Thelma get away with this, one might
rightly ask? The answer is simple: Like me, Thelma is
descended from one of the founding families of our
fair town. Her great-great-great-great-grandfather, Leghorn Unruh, pounded the first property marker into
Hernia soil, claiming the freshly cleared land for God
and king—I wish. Leghorn appears to have been gifted
with remarkable foresight, looking out, as he did, for

generations of slovenly Unruhs. When the town was incorporated a few years later, and he found himself smack dab in the middle, Leghorn Unruh refused to become an official part of the community, unless he was permitted to do things his own way. After much palavering, the founding fathers granted the Unruh homestead semiautonomous power in perpetuity. In short, although his descendants must pay property taxes, and in turn are entitled to municipal amenities, there are to be no restrictions on what the family can do with either the house or the land.

Theoretically, Thelma Unruh can raze her ramshackle mansion and erect a ninety-story skyscraper, or, much more appropriately, go into chicken farming. Speaking of skyscrapers, Elias Unruh, Leghorn's grandson, attempted to build a circular tower that reached to Heaven. The Good Lord need not have feared an unwanted visitor, because Elias decided to be his own architect, and the tower collapsed when it was only three stories high. A circular remnant of this structure has been preserved within the walls of the crumbling Victorian. Unfortunately, this is not hearsay, as I have seen it several times with my own eyes.

At any rate, I gave Thelma a buzz, and when she didn't answer at her home number, I tried her business.

"Hello. Unruh's Unique Hair Designs."

"Hello. Yoder's unique PennDutch Inn. May I speak to the illustrious Thelma, please?"

"Magdalena, is that you?"

"As large as life, and twice as loud."

"What?"

"Never mind, dear, I need to drop by for a chat."

"When?"

"Now."

"No can do, unless you have an appointment."

"Then please let me make one—for as soon as possible."

"How does immediately sound?"

"Great!"

"Now, what do you want done?"

"Nothing, of course. Like I said, I just want to chat."

"Again, no can do. Magdalena, this is Unruh's Unique Hair Designs, not Unruh's House of Perpetual Chatter. You have to schedule a procedure."

"Uh—okay. Trim my ends. Some of them are undoubtedly split, but just some, mind you. I keep my hair well conditioned."

"That's what they all say. But in any case, that won't be enough. I have to design something. You know, do a little styling."

"Oh, all right. But it better be temporary. I've worn my hair in proper Christian coils my entire life. I better not come out of there looking like Betty Baptist, or heaven forefend, Patti Presbyterian. And before we go too far, how much will this cost?"

"A style with wash will be twenty-eight."

"Dollars?"

"Of course—oh, that's right, you do have a reputation for stinginess, don't you?"

"I prefer to think of myself as frugal. And just so you know, our Good Lord Himself was frugal. He *turned* the water into wine; He didn't bring it as a gift."

"I think that's blasphemous."

Alas, so did I. After whispering a quick prayer for forgiveness, I got back to business.

"So how much would it cost without the wash?"

"Don't be silly; I wouldn't cut someone's hair without washing it first. I tried that once with Wanda Hemphopple and was in for a nasty surprise."

I swallowed guiltily. "You found a hot dog?"

"Among other things. Did you know that an original menu from the *Titanic,* even one in bad shape, is worth a lot of money?"

"You found a menu in her beehive?"

"Heavens, no. But there were a couple of termites in there, which fell out, of course, and then escaped. Before I could have them exterminated, they got into my desk drawer and ate the *Titanic* menu. I bought it at a yard sale and was all set to take it in to the *Antiques Roadshow* when it came to Philadelphia."

"I promise I don't have any termites in my hair. Can't you at least shave off a dollar or two?"

"No can do, but I can shave off that mustache of yours. That would be on the house."

"I don't have a mustache," I yelled, "and I won't for at least another week." I slammed down the receiver. The nerve of that woman. She was going to get a piece of my mind, even if it was the last remaining piece.

14

I nearly broke my neck climbing up the rotten wooden steps that lead to the sagging and rotten porch, so it is quite possible that I rang the buzzer a few more times than was necessary. Therefore, I was a mite surprised that when she opened the door, Thelma appeared as calm as a setting hen. That's when I decided to ruffle her feathers—just a wee bit, and all in good Christian fun.

"My lawyers will be in touch with your people later on this afternoon. The injuries I have sustained from the bottom step alone should be worth a couple of mil."

"You need to go around to the back. There's a sign that says 'Business Entrance.' "

"I'll do no such thing. I risked life and limb to get this far."

"Then I'm afraid I'm going to have to cancel your appointment."

"I'll double your fee."

Even though Thelma wears glasses with a pale blue tint, her eyes appear a washed-out gray. Her brows are so sparse, she has to pencil them in, and it would be safe to bet the farm that she never has to worry about a mustache. But it is her crowning glory that makes her the envy of every woman in Bedford County.

The all-natural golden tresses cascade in waves below her shoulders because, unlike myself, Thelma is a member of the more liberal First Mennonite Church. No braids or buns for her. It has been noted, by the gossipers among us, that Thelma tosses her locks repeatedly whenever she speaks to a man. Long swirling hair is supposed to be attractive to men, but I can't for the life of me figure out why. After all, hair is nothing more than long strands of dead protein called keratin. In theory, at least, one would be just as successful by waving a bouquet of donkey hooves at a man. In practice, however—trust me—ix-nay on the ooves-hay.

Thelma tossed her mane in vain before responding to my offer. "Okay, I'll break my rule. We can chat without a procedure, but you have to pay up front."

I fished the money out of my well-worn purse. "Here you are, dear. Now, if you don't mind, let's move this show inside and get nice and comfy. Some hot chocolate would be nice, and some ladyfingers. Oh, and I prefer the mini marshmallows to the large ones."

"You're not getting refreshments, Magdalena, and we're not moving inside. We're going to talk here."

"Here where? There isn't even a rickety porch swing upon which to plunk my patooty."

"You just want to see the tower remnants, isn't that right?"

"No—not just. Anyway, I've seen them before. What I want is to talk to you about Cornelius Weaver."

The pale irises widened behind the tinted lenses. "What about Cornelius?"

"I understand you were—uh—seeing him."

"You mean having an affair, don't you?"

"Your words, dear, not mine."

"Who told you?"

"I'm not at liberty to disclose my source. Besides, this is a small town. One can't change toilet paper brands without hearing about it at Sam Yoder's Corner Market."

"You've stopped using corncobs?"

"I supply them only in the outhouse, and it's for my guests' amusement. Proper paper is available upon request. But speaking of gossip, you had to know that Cornelius was engaged to Priscilla Livingood."

"Of course I knew," she said with surprising vehemence. "I'm a *natural* blonde. And just because Cornelius gave Priscilla a ring doesn't mean that what we had together wasn't special."

"I'm sure it was. Thelma, I'm afraid I have some bad news. Preliminary autopsy reports reveal that Cornelius might have died under suspicious circumstances."

"I knew it!"

"You did?"

"Priscilla was just after his money, wasn't she? Ha, talk about irony."

"Indeed—I mean, yes, talk about it!"

"Well, everyone knows that Miss Silicon USA is up to her liposuctioned armpits in debt, just so that she can look like Barbie. I bet she could fit into Barbie's clothes too, although the shoes would probably be too small. At any rate, Cornelius told me more than once that all Prissy Priscilla could talk about was money. How expensive her procedures were. It was clear to me from the beginning that she believed Cornelius was stinking rich, on account of he lives in one of the big historic homes and comes from a solid family background. But he wasn't, you see. Rich. Tourists drive by and think we're really loaded on account of what they see, but boy, are they wrong. Name one person, one descendant of the founding fathers, who is really rich."

"Yours truly." I tried not to sound smug.

"Yeah—well, you made your own money. That's different. My point is that when those big-city folks come here and look around, they think we're wealthy. Do you know how much money I made last year?"

"No."

"Guess."

"Fifty thousand."

"What dreamworld do you live in?"

"Seventy thousand."

Even though they're penciled on, Thelma's brows can work themselves into a nasty scowl. "I wish. My gross was twenty-seven thousand nine hundred. And chump change."

"That's pretty gross," I agreed.

"I bet you made a lot more than that." The words were flung at me like bricks.

"Back to Cornelius, dear—"

"I'm not your dear, and I'll thank you to know that. Now, answer my question, Magdalena."

"I did."

"No, the one about your income."

"That wasn't a question," I wailed. Yes, I know, I wail far too much, but I felt like I was up against a wall covered with spikes, like the inside of an iron maiden. It is a device that, for some bizarre reason, has been much on my mind lately.

"I told *you*, so now you tell me."

"It wouldn't be right."

"It's the only way you're going to get me to share my theory of who killed Cornelius."

"You have a theory?"

"Quit wasting my time."

"Okay, but you're not going to like it." I closed my eyes. "Take your income, multiply by ten, and add another two percent for ALPO."

She was silent for far too long. "That much," she said finally. "Who knew? But it just occurred to me, given that the architecture of my house is much more interesting than an old farmhouse, and given that my place is within walking distance of Hernia's shopping district, not to mention the mystique of the tower wall, I bet I could double your business, maybe even triple it."

"What shopping district, for crying out loud? There's nothing in town but Yoder's Corner Market and Miller's Feed Store. And no offense, dear, but the architecture about which you boast is barely recognizable, seeing as how you've allowed this place to be run into the ground."

To my astonishment, and disappointment, my stinging remark failed to get her goat. "You're right, it could use a little sprucing up. But let's face it, Magdalena, with your personality, who needs sauerkraut? The way I see it, I've got you beat hands down in the public relations department. Hmm . . . what shall I name it?"

I had a brilliant idea. "How about Unruh's Roost? That would give a nod to your ancestor, Leghorn."

Pale gray eyes can appear quite steely when their owner is not amused. "I can honestly say it's been nice chatting with you, Magdalena. Your idea of an inn is fabulous. I'm going to get right on it. What thread count do you use?"

"What?"

"You know, for the sheets."

"One-sixty," I said proudly. "They have to pay ALPO prices if they want the burlap. There's no telling how much folks will pay for abuse, as long as they can view it as a cultural experience."

"Interesting. But you and I both know the Amish don't sleep on burlap sheets. That's just plain ridiculous. No, I'm going to go the other direction. I recently saw an ad for one-thousand-thread-count sheets in a magazine. That's what I'll get, and I'll import eiderdown comforters directly from Norway. My guests will feel like they're sleeping on butter."

"You can't do that!"

"Why not? You make your guests pay through the nose for shabby treatment. Mine will pay an arm and a leg for fabulous treatment. Whose inn do you think they're going to prefer?"

"Mine." I swallowed a mouthful of fear. "After all, I am an authentic Mennonite woman of conservative persuasion, and I have an honest-to-goodness Amish cook. I give them the cultural experience they crave."

She had the nerve to smile. "Have you ever been to Disney World, Magdalena?"

"No, but—"

"At Epcot you can sample a world of cultures, all of which have been re-created on the spot. If they can do it, so can I—on a much smaller scale, of course. But I can hire an Amish cook and Mennonite cleaning ladies. I can have a little blacksmith shop built out back, so the tourists can watch horses being shod. Oh, and a gift shop! One that sells homemade jams and pickled watermelon rinds, and traditional Amish quilts. Maybe even some Amish-made furniture." Her smile turned diabolical. "And of course, there is the *wall.* You're starting to get the picture, aren't you, Magdalena?"

"Indeed I am. It's a very expensive picture that is going to require a good deal of capital. Have you given that any thought?"

Thelma glared at me, a look that was made even more sinister by the tinted lenses. "I only just now thought of my inn. You don't need to rain on my parade."

"Your parade was going to run me out of business."

"Magdalena, I don't recall inviting you here. It's time for you to leave."

"But I paid double your hair-cutting fee just to speak to you, so I'm not leaving here until I've gotten my money's worth."

It was Thelma's turn to fish for the money, which she'd tucked in the pockets of her brown corduroy jumper. But upon finding the money, rather than hand it to me in a mature fashion, she had the nerve to thrust it under my perfectly shaped schnoz.

"Here. I don't want your money."

"Keep it; it's yours."

"Either take it or I'm dropping it."

I decided to call her bluff. "Do whatever you want, dear."

Lo and behold, Thelma was not bluffing. I stared in disbelief as the coins hit the porch floor and rolled in all directions. The bills, buoyed by a slight breeze, took longer to land.

What Thelma had done was totally un-American, possibly even illegal in several states. In my book, it was worthy of a one-way pass to the funny farm. It was also, I began to believe, evidence that the gal with the golden locks was not a gold digger.

"Toodle-oo," I said. "I left something on the stove and need to get back to the inn as soon as possible."

"Electric or gas?"

"What?"

"Your stove. What does it run on?"

I allowed my mind to visualize my most recent power bill. "Uh—gas."

"Ha! You're not cooking anything, except for another harebrained theory."

"I'll have you know I've solved a number of murder cases with this hare brain of mine. And for your information, missy, you were wrong about Cornelius not having any money. We share the same stockbroker and—never you mind. Suffice it to say, the man was loaded."

Poor Thelma, and I mean that literally, appeared stunned. "Are you sure?"

"As sure as I am that the sun will come out tomorrow."

"It's supposed to rain."

"It's a saying, dear. Trust me, the dearly departed had more dough than a string of commercial bakeries."

"In that case you really need to speak to Cornelius's mother."

"His mother is dead."

"His *step*mother isn't."

"Veronica Weaver? What does she have to do with the price of cheese in Amsterdam?"

"She had to loan him ten thousand dollars, that's what." She turned to go back into the house.

15

Palak Paneer

Ingredients

3 pounds spinach,
   thoroughly cleaned and
   roughly chopped
Pinch salt, plus salt to taste
½ pound paneer, cut into
   1-inch cubes
¼ cup oil
2 medium onions, finely
   sliced
2 medium tomatoes,
   chopped

2 green chilies, split in half
1 teaspoon ginger-garlic
   paste
¼ teaspoon turmeric
¼ teaspoon cayenne
   pepper (or to taste)
¼ cup heavy cream
¼ cup coriander leaves,
   finely chopped, for
   garnish (optional)

YIELD: 4 SERVINGS

Preparation

1. Bring a pot of water to a boil. Add spinach and pinch
   of salt and stir for approximately 5 minutes or till
   spinach is tender, but do not overcook. Strain spinach
   and keep ready.
2. Heat a little oil in frying pan and fry paneer cubes
   till lightly golden brown. Remove and drain on paper
   towels.

3. Heat oil and add onions. Stir-fry till light golden brown.
4. Add tomatoes, green chilies, ginger-garlic paste, turmeric, cayenne pepper, and salt. Thoroughly mix.
5. Let this mixture cook for 10–15 minutes. Add a little water if need be to keep from sticking or burning.
6. Add spinach and mix well.
7. Add heavy cream and stir. Then add paneer cubes and mix.
8. Cover pot and allow to cook on low heat for 5 minutes.
9. Garnish with coriander leaves and serve with naan or rice.

Notes

- You can find paneer in the refrigerated section of any Indian or Pakistani grocery store.
- Some like to leave their spinach just as is, while others like to blend it to a paste. The choice is yours. You may also substitute tender spinach leaves.
- Substitute 2 cups peas for the spinach to make Mattar Paneer.

16

"Wait just one Mennonite minute!"

"Now what?" she snapped. If you ask me, only mothers of teens have a right to sound that exasperated.

"Did you mean it when you said I could have this money?" I pointed at a nice, crisp dollar bill with the toe of a much-worn brogan.

"Yes. And for the record, you're impossible." The door slammed behind her.

I may be a weensy bit greedy from time to time—I'm only human, after all—but I am certainly not impossible. It was an honest question, a thoughtful one even. For all I knew, she'd changed her mind. Besides, it really was my money in the first place, and we hadn't even mentioned hair.

Greedy is not necessarily stupid, so before I left the premises I chased down every cent except for one. That penny lies beneath a hole in the porch, one that is guarded by a spider so large that, at first glance, I mistook it for a discarded hairbrush.

Having recovered my loot, I headed for the hills.

Veronica Weaver never quite recovered from the 1970s. Or would that have been the late sixties? I seemed to have missed out on the whole "make love, not war" movement. For me the "summer of love" was the summer I married Aaron Miller, and it was not so much a *summer* of love as it was a string of three-minute interludes.

At any rate, Veronica Speicher was a hippie who married Latrum Weaver, father of the late Cornelius. (Latrum's first wife, Willetta, choked to death trying to eat a ham sandwich while singing along to a Mama Cass recording.) Cornelius was only a lad of three when he acquired a stepmother and took to her like dust to a refrigerator top. By all accounts it was a happy marriage, ending only when Latrum succumbed to periodic bouts of increased heart rate—also due to three-minute interludes, or so I am told.

After her husband's death, Veronica purchased a three-bedroom mobile home and had it hauled up to Speicher's Meadow, a grassy knoll that had been in her family for generations. Veronica seemed perfectly happy up there—sometimes even too happy, like the time she was busted for growing more than an acre of marijuana hidden only by a border of sunflowers.

It was a miracle that I didn't wreck the car while driving up to Speicher's Meadow, given that I was also wrestling with the Devil the entire way. Sometimes Satan pops an idea into my mind that I can't seem to get rid of. I am ashamed to say that sampling marijuana was a particularly persistent thought.

But let's face it, what harm would there be in trying it only once? Just *once*. After all, it isn't like crack or cocaine, in which case once can be one time too many. And it isn't a manufactured drug, like LSD. Marijuana is a natural herb, like oregano, or basil. And in the Bible the Good Lord Himself gives us permission to eat every herb He created. Take Genesis 1:29, for example: "And God said, 'See I have given you every herb that yields seed which is on the face of the earth, and every tree whose fruit yields seed; to you it shall be for food.' " There is no exclusion for marijuana, a seed-bearing plant, just as there is no exclusion for wine-producing grapes, another seed-bearing plant.

Seedless grapes, on the other hand, might be problematic.

And if the Good Lord's endorsement isn't enough, then look to our nation's leaders. Bill Clinton and George W. Bush, the two most intelligent men who ever lived, both admitted to some youthful experimenting. Just because my youth was spent toeing the line in my sturdy brogans, does that necessarily mean that I will have to die with a virgin's nostrils? (In a manner of speaking, that is.)

Still, I know it was a sin to think like that, because just the thought of taking a puff or two got my blood to racing. "If it feels good," Mama used to say, "then it's wrong." That's why Mama was into hard, uncomfortable furniture and bland, tasteless food. Although Mama never wore a hair shirt, I once saw her tuck a burr into the waistband of her Sunday skirt, lest she derive too much pleasure from the hymns sung by a visiting choir.

One thing for sure, Mama would not have experienced a speck of pleasure from viewing Speicher's Meadow in early spring. The flowers and grasses that made it such a delight in the summer had yet to resurrect. The lane that led back to the trailer was muddy and riddled with potholes. The trees Veronica had planted years ago remained spindly and were, of course, still bereft of leaves. Even the mobile home looked tired and weather-beaten, as if biding its time until it could be hauled off to early retirement in a junkyard.

Much to my disappointment, there wasn't an automobile in sight. Whereas my mind is like a steel trap—rusty and illegal in thirty-seven states—it does work, if given enough notice. I hadn't called ahead because I knew that Veronica Weaver, like the Amish, did not believe in owning a telephone. This is not to say that Veronica is Amish; she is far from it. Instead, she subscribes to the notion that telephones, rather than bringing folks closer together, actually create distance, as they make face-to-face interaction no longer a necessity. This is, in my humble opinion, ironic coming from a woman who has chosen to live out in the tulle weeds, where the only faces she encounters on a daily basis belong to deer and raccoons.

The knowledge that I was quite alone gave me an idea that was borderline sinful. You see, many years ago, during my rebellious college days, when I wore dresses that came down only to my knees, and sandals without socks, I allowed myself to be talked into seeing a movie. I'm not referring to a home movie produced by a lonely missionary in some far-off place like the Congo; I'm talking about a real Hollywood movie.

It was one of only two movies I've ever seen; the other being *Eleanor Does Washington,* which I'd been led to believe was a political documentary, and which it would have been rude to walk out of, seeing as how I was seated in the middle of a row. It was, incidentally, an incredibly boring film. Anyway, *The Sound of Music* was the name of the other movie, the one I enjoyed. At the beginning of this film, Julie Andrews runs up over the crest of a hill, singing with joy. It is an image I have carried with me over the years, and from which I have drawn a measure of comfort during some difficult times.

While I do not claim to sing on par with Miss Andrews—oh, who am I kidding? I might well be the world's worst singer. Papa always told me to be the best I can be, and surely being the best *worst* singer is an accomplishment of sorts. I am unaware of a contest for this negative skill of mine, but the fact that I am guaranteed to put the hens off laying and curdle the milk in dairy cows six pastures away ought to count for something. One Sunday, during a particularly rousing rendition of "Joyful, Joyful, We Adore Thee," a pack of stray dogs burst into our little church and attempted to have their way with me.

Nonetheless I have enjoyed some musical moments

in the privacy of my own home, safe within the soapy embrace of Big Bertha. That I have never tried singing the opening song of my favorite movie whilst cavorting in a meadow is due only to the lack of suitable meadows in the Hernia environs. Our landscape consists of wooded ridges and narrow, cultivated valleys. To my knowledge, Speicher's Meadow is the only grassy sward between the turnpike and Maryland, across which one dare not venture without stocking provisions.

But I have digressed. My point is that I found myself quite alone in a meadow setting, and was overcome with the urge to exercise my lungs. Flinging my purse to the ground, I spread my arms, twirled several times, and then ran to the top of a low rise, all the while braying the words to the opening song of *The Sound of Music*. Upon ending the song, I cocked my head and pretended to hear the sound of bells clanging in the abbey below.

"Brava! Brava! Encore!"

One can imagine my shock and horror to discover that just below the rise was the supine form of a woman. The nerve of her! Who in their right mind lies down in a meadow like a tired sheep?

"Veronica Weaver!"

She stood slowly, brushing blades of dead grass from a bohemian-style skirt and blouse. Around her neck hung a tangle of brightly colored beads, a few of which matched the silk flower that was tucked affectedly behind her right ear. Except for the flower, which is fresh when in season, Veronica looked exactly the same as she did three years ago, the last time I saw her.

"Don't stop now, Magdalena. Sing 'Climb Every Mountain.' "

"You don't have to be mean."

"Mean? I don't get it. I love hearing you sing."

"And I love boiled turnips and fried liver—not!" Sometimes Alison's slang comes in handy.

She stared quizzically at me. Her blue-gray eyes are paler than mine, although perhaps they just appear that way thanks to the shaggy dark brow that stretches, uninterrupted, from temple to temple.

"I'm afraid you've lost me," she said.

"And I think I'm about to lose my temper. Enough is enough, Veronica. I know I'm a lousy singer. You don't need to rub it in."

"But I—you think I'm teasing you."

"Tormenting, is more like it."

She clapped her hands. No adult woman deserves to have hands that small, if you ask me. Even a Cracker Jack ring would be large on Veronica, which probably explains why I'd never seen her wear a wedding band, even when Latrum was still alive.

"But I'm serious. You may be untrained, but you have one of the most beautiful voices I've ever heard."

It was my turn to stare. "Are you nuts, dear?" For the record, I said that kindly, couched in Christian love, on the off chance the woman was telling the truth.

Veronica laughed pleasantly. "You're so frank, Magdalena. That's what I've always liked about you. You never beat around the bush."

"Only in private. Do you really like my singing?" I jiggled my pinkies in both ears to make sure they were in working order. They seemed to pass inspection.

"Like it? I love it. If you'd been trained, I bet you could have had a career as a singer."

"But I bray like a donkey!"

"Says who?"

"Mama. She used to bribe me with a molasses cookie if I kept my trap shut in church."

"No offense, Magdalena, but I knew your mama well. There never was a harder, more cynical, more bitter woman than the one whose womb gave you shelter for nine months."

"She wasn't that bad," I wailed in Mama's defense. "If I forgot and started to sing, I still got to lick some cookie crumbs that she'd shake loose from the bottom of the jar. Mama—now there was a woman who loved to sing."

"You see? She was jealous; that's all there was to it."

If the truth hurts, think of something else. "What were you doing lying on the ground, and where is your car?"

"One, my car's in the shop, and two, I was trying to hear buffalo hooves."

"Aha."

"Don't you 'aha' me. You think I'm nuttier than a Payday, and you're entitled to your opinion. But as it happens, I was taking a walk and started thinking about what this land must have been like in precolonial times. I'd read somewhere that there were so many buffalo—bison, actually—that just by putting one's ear to the ground, it was possible to hear an approaching herd from miles away."

"And did you?"

"Now who's mocking who? Of course I didn't. I just wanted to see what it was like. I did, however, hear you drive up. What gives, Magdalena? Why the visit?"

"It's about Cornelius. Your stepson."

Her round, hirsute face darkened, although no cloud passed overhead. "I still can't believe it. He was so healthy—his arrhythmia aside. I thought it was being controlled through medication. I had no idea it posed such a grave danger."

"Who might have known?"

"Pardon me?"

"I knew that Cornelius didn't work because of heart issues—I think everyone in Hernia knew—but who might have known just how bad it was?"

"Well, you'd think I'd have known, being his stepmother. In my defense—no, I take that back. There really is no excuse for me not knowing. But the reason I didn't is because I didn't want to know. I've always thought of Latrum's son as my own. After having lost his father, I couldn't bear to think that I might lose him as well."

"I understand. She isn't really even my stepdaughter, but I couldn't bear it if something happened to Alison." I took a deep breath before plunging on. "Veronica, I hate to have to be the one to tell you, but—"

17

She gasped. "Cornelius was murdered, wasn't he?"

"Yes. How did you know? I mean, I'm awfully sorry."

Tears filled her eyes. "Magdalena, I don't mean to be unkind, but why else would you be here?"

"To offer my condolences?"

She shook her head. Her hair, which was long and somewhat stringy, swung in clumps.

"You're not a bad person, but neither are you pastoral. It's like you have a vulture perched on your shoulder. When you show up it either has to do with money or murder. Silly me, I'd forgotten about that. Well, as you can see, I don't have any money, so it has to be murder."

"That is so unfair! True, perhaps, but nevertheless unfair. I can't help it that I have experience in these matters, so the police come to me."

She continued to shake her head. "How did he die? How was he killed?"

"Amitriptyline. It's a drug used to treat both pain and depression. But it can interact with the heart."

"Who? Why?"

"That's why I'm here. To gather as much information as I can. Just investigating all the women your stepson was involved with—well, it has to be a record of some kind."

"Just like his father."

"What? I thought you and Latrum had the ideal marriage."

"Ha. The ideal marriage is one woman and six husbands to support her, and wait on her hand and foot. But as far as traditional marriages go, ours wasn't even close. Or sadly, maybe it was. I loved Latrum until the day he died, and I have no doubt he loved me just as fiercely, but the man got around as much as Johnny Appleseed. I made the decision to stick with him early on. There was a price to be paid for that, but it was worth it. In his own way, Latrum loved me just as passionately."

"As passionately as a rabbit," I muttered under my breath.

"What did you say? Something about a rabbit?"

I sought desperately for a word that would sound the same but wouldn't upset her. "I'm sure you wanted to stab it" was out. "He was a nasty old habit" wasn't much better. I cleared my throat to give me time.

"When happiness comes, grab it," I eventually said.

"Magdalena, you are a wise woman, you know that?"

"Indeed. Tell me, Veronica, do you know the names of all Cornelius's—uh, for want of a better word, lovers?"

"Well, there was Alice Troyer—*that* one puzzled me."

"She may be no beauty, but she is definitely very smart. Funny too."

"If you say so. Priscilla Livingood, now there was a beauty."

"A veritable walking advertisement for petroleum parts."

"Oil?"

"Exactly. That's where silicone originates."

"You don't say. Caroline Sha is another beautiful woman, and all natural, I'd say. Such a shame about her condition."

"I think her bald head is stunning, so you must be referring to her spiritual values. All the talk about chi and chai—throw in some cha-cha, and you've got the Devil's playground."

"You may be wise and have the voice of an angel, Magdalena, but you're as weird as they come."

"Thank you for the superlative. I was just remembering how Papa always said that I should strive to be the best at whatever course I choose."

"Case in point. Which brings me to Drustara Kurtz. I just saw her on *Oprah*."

"Oh my, I didn't think Oprah swung that way—not that I'm judging, mind you."

"On Oprah's *TV* show, you ninny! Sorry, Magdalena. It's just that you can be so literal."

"Again, thanks for the compliment, dear. A lot of folks think they can get away with reading the Bible through a twenty-first-century lens. They say it wasn't meant to be taken literally, but rather as an account of mankind's journey into faith. Well, poppycock and nonsense! The Bible itself says it should be taken literally, so who are we to argue?"

"You're not sucking me into a religious argument, Magdalena. Don't you want to hear about Drustara Kurtz?"

"Do tell."

"If you give me a chance, I will. Like I said, she was on *Oprah*, discussing her new book, *The Dark Side of Heaven*. Have you read it?"

"Not yet. It's on my to-be-read pile, just under George Carlin's *When Will Jesus Bring the Pork Chops?*"

"Somehow I think you're serious. Be forewarned; George Carlin's book is not the devotional you think it is. Anyway, Drustara admitted that the town of Heaven in her novel is a rather thinly disguised Hernia."

It was either heart palpitations I felt, or my bosoms were off on yet another growth spurt. Clutching my chest, I sat down heavily on the winter-dried thatch of Speicher's Meadow.

"Am I in it?" I asked weakly.

"Magdalena, *dear,* life isn't all about you. There is a throwaway line about an inn that caters to wealthy tourists, but nothing about you per se."

"Are you sure?"

"Positive."

"Will disappointment never cease? I mean—oh well." I tried out a jaunty smile. "Was Cornelius in it?"

"You bet. The character Barnabas fits my stepson to a tee. Which means you can scratch Drustara off your list of suspects."

"Why so?"

"Because Cornelius was the one with the motive to kill—not Drustara. I'm afraid my stepson's actions, when held to the light of fiction, were reprehensible. But if a motive for murdering Cornelius is what you're after, then it's Thelma Unruh you should be talking to."

"I did, but—and I shouldn't be telling you this—she doesn't appear to have a motive."

"Vengeance seems like motive enough to me."

"*Vengeance?* You mean because he gave some other woman a ring?"

"Because he talked her into having an abortion."

I was stunned. The A word for Hernia, aside from *Amish,* is usually *adultery.* Although *abstinence* is heard more and more, now that folks no longer take it as a given. But *abortion*? To my knowledge, Thelma was the first woman I knew to have one.

"Cat's got your tongue, Magdalena, does it? At first Cornelius claimed they both were using protection, but that somehow it failed. That sounded fishy to me, so I pressed him. He then changed his story and said that only she was using it—was on the pill—and that she secretly stopped so that she could get pregnant. In her mind a baby trumped a ring. That's when Cornelius came to me and asked for a loan. Ten thousand dollars, to be exact. He'd managed to talk her into it by threatening to dump her if she didn't have an abortion."

"What a scumbag—oops! Sorry." I clapped a large, but exceptionally attractive, hand over my large, but well-formed, mouth.

"No need to apologize. I told you he was less than perfect."

"You only know the half of it."

She scooted closer. Unfortunately for me, Veronica is of the opinion that Americans bathe too frequently, thus destroying helpful bacteria. She also believes that clogging one's pores with deodorant is tantamount to killing millions of skin cells. While I'm pretty sure she has showered since the seventies, I think the nineties might have brought on a lasting drought.

"Tell me what you know, Magdalena."

I leaned away as far as possible without appearing rude. "I think you were had for ten thousand dollars. Cornelius and I are in the same investment club and the man was worth—well, not as much as I am, but suffice it to say, he was well-heeled."

Her unpainted mouth opened and closed several times without emitting a sound. When she found her voice, it was surprisingly husky.

"I should have known. I was played for a fool, wasn't I?"

"That depends. What was his story?"

"He said he'd lost all the money his daddy left him in some Nigerian Internet scheme, and that he'd learned his lesson, and was finally going back to college in order to get a real job someday. He seemed so contrite. Magdalena, there were even tears in his eyes."

"They're called crocodile tears, dear. Cornelius was far too bright to be suckered by a letter from Nigeria asking for monetary help in recovering lost assets. He's the one who warned me about them, and that was probably ten years ago. I'm truly sorry, Veronica, but your stepson did not need your money."

"But then why the sob story? *Why?*"

I shrugged before scrambling to my large, but uncommonly attractive, feet. Why, indeed. I don't understand why people do half the things they do. Why, for instance, do folks deface public property? Why do they litter? Why do they spit their gum out onto the pavement in front of the Bedford Wal-Mart? Why do they let themselves get so frustrated by other drivers that they react in anger? And this is just the small stuff. Why do they deliberately do hurtful things to other people . . .

"Magdalena, is your mind wandering yet again?"

"I think it's lost."

"I swear, Magdalena, if I didn't know better I'd say you were stoned on pot."

"Alas, that has never been an option—oops, did I say that? I mean, it isn't, is it?"

"Are you hinting around for a joint?"

"If I was, would you give me one?"

"Do I look stupid, Magdalena? You represent the law in Bedford County. Of course I wouldn't give you one— *not* that I have any to give. You should be ashamed of yourself. You have everything going for you in life: money, beauty, a handsome boyfriend, and that incredible voice of yours. Why would you want to risk any of that? What emotional hole are you trying to fill?"

"I don't have any holes to fill," I wailed.

"Magdalena, if you don't mind me saying so, wailing does not become you. It's very distracting."

And here I thought I'd already learned the lesson of humility. Let me tell you, there is nothing more humiliating than having an ex-hippie lecture you on comportment. Gathering my shreds of pride about me, as if they were a garment that had malfunctioned, I hoofed it back to my car with nary a peep. Pressing an elegant, albeit elongated, foot to the metal, I most certainly set a record for getting back to Hernia.

When all else fails, go to the one who isn't supposed to fail. Normally that would be the Good Lord, but at the moment I had his emissary in mind. After all, the Lord had more important things to do, like choosing which passengers on a doomed airplane are praying the hardest, and thus deserve to live, or which people, based on the intensity of their supplications, will be plucked alive from the devastation left behind by a hurricane. These are important matters to consider, whereas mine was entirely personal, and trivial to boot.

Reverend and Mrs. Fiddlegarber live in the parsonage owned by Beechy Grove Mennonite Church. It is the same house that was occupied by Reverend Schrock and his shrill wife, Lodema. Sadly, the good reverend has gone on to eternal rest, and as for Lodema, she is ensconced in a rest home for the severely disturbed that is located deep within the heart of the Pocono Mountains. After her husband's murder she regressed to the level of a six-year-old girl. In fact, I received a letter from her recently, printed in large block letters asking for a raise in her "ALAWANS." She was saving up to buy her first "BARBY DOL."

Never an optimist, I steeled myself for the worst as I rang the doorbell at 665 Poplar Street. Once again my pessimism was rewarded, and I found myself navel to face with our new preacher's diminutive wife, Petunia. A rose by any other name might still be a rose, to paraphrase the bard, but Petunia Fiddlegarber could only be a thorn.

"Greetings and felicitations," I said pleasantly.

"Is that Spanish?"

"Not the last time I checked. Is the reverend here?"

"Do you have an appointment?"

"Certainly. I was supposed to meet him here at two hairs past a freckle."

"Is that Pennsylvania Dutch?"

"If you insist." I cupped my hands to my mouth. "Oh, Reverend! 'Tis I, the one who signs your paychecks. Wherefore art thou?"

"Why, I never," Petunia sputtered.

"Then you haven't missed out on much. Believe me, it's overrated."

"What?"

"What did *you* mean?"

"You know, Miss Yoder, not everyone appreciates your flippancy. As a professional writer, I, for one, think that not only do you try too hard to be funny, but most of the time you fail. The result is an inability to communicate effectively. If you like, I could work with you—say, on a weekly basis. We could discuss my fee structure at our first session."

"But you write enema instructions, for crying out loud."

"They're not just instructions; I write informative prose of an inspirational nature. Perhaps you'd like to take one of the boxes home with you and study it. That could be your assignment for next time."

Thank heavens the reverend materialized before I had a chance to tell Petunia what she could do with her box. "Magdalena, how good of you to drop by!"

Petunia pursed her lips. "She doesn't have an appointment."

Reverend Fiddlegarber chuckled nervously. "I'm afraid my wife likes to joke."

"No, I don't."

"Please, Magdalena, come in."

"But Gerald—"

The reverend grabbed his wife's arm and literally pulled her from the doorway. I sailed into the house on a cloud of righteous indignation. Before heading to the back of the house, where I knew the reverend's study was located, I paused only long enough to glare at the thorn in my side.

Alas, I should have paused longer. But how was I to know I was heading straight for the lion's den?

18

I have been in the parsonage study innumerable times. In fact, I am the one who supervised its decoration. Since the Good Lord had been a carpenter, I thought knotty pine was a perfect choice for the walls. A preacher should have a bookcase to hold the Bible and a few commentaries, but not one so large as to give shelf space to works of so-called contemporary scholarship, much of which is aimed at diverting believers from the straight and narrow path. A desk is in order, serving as it does as a surface upon which to write sermons, but it need not accommodate a computer. (I have nothing against computers, mind you; it is the Internet to which I object, seeing as how it is little more than a superhighway system for the Devil. Al Gore should be ashamed of himself for having invented it.) Now, where was I? Oh yes, a desk requires a chair, a straight-back chair, one designed to encourage proper alignment of the spine. A church-issued calendar and a plain brown trash can complete the décor.

Imagine my shock, then, when I sailed into a room that was unrecognizable. The beautiful knotty pine had been painted white, wall-to-wall shelves had been installed along one side, and the pastor-appropriate desk had been replaced with a monstrosity that might embarrass even the most ostentatious televangelist. Sitting atop this altar to the ego was the most elaborate computer setup I had ever seen. The pièce de résistance, however, was a plush leather chair with built-in massage features. If that wasn't the Devil's doing, then I don't know what is. As for the calendar and trash can, the former featured cat breeds, whilst the latter was brushed steel and ultramodern in design.

"Look what you've done!" I cried.

"You like it? It's much cheerier, don't you think? And that other desk—whoo boy, I haven't seen one that small since the sixth grade. Where did it come from, an elementary school?"

I hate being found out. "It came from an eighth-grade classroom, not a sixth. And, I'll have you know, those were real knotty pine boards you painted over."

"Yes, and it took two coats, plus the primer. Oyster Shell is the name of the color. I didn't mind doing the work myself, but I've been meaning to ask, when will they start work on the rest of the house?"

"Excuse me?"

"Petunia wants you to start with the kitchen. She's used to a flattop stove. I think she wants to paint the cabinets the same shade of white as in here. And I told her not to worry, that the horrid linoleum would definitely go."

"Go where?"

"Ha, ha, good one. Unlike my wife, I appreciate your humor. She said there's so many layers of wax on that floor that when she tried to strip it, she found Jimmy Hoffa."

"Hey, wait a minute! That's *my* line."

"You're a hoot, Magdalena, you know that?"

A dumbfounded hoot, maybe. The nerve of the reverend and his wife to presume that in addition to a good salary and free housing, the church would spring for redecorating. What had been plenty good enough for the Schrocks wasn't good enough for them—and they were from *Maryland*, for crying out loud. The next thing you know they were going to demand a car allowance, as well as a provision allowance for when they went home to visit.

Dumb as I was, the reverend steamrolled on. "When will the car be ready?"

"*Excuse* me?"

"I trust it's a full-size model, like a Crown Vic or a Town Car. I've got a touch of gout and really need to be able to stretch my legs. Just not an SUV. Between you and me, unless you're a family of eight, owning one is just plain sinful. You haven't asked our color preferences yet, so I assume the final selection hasn't been made. I'm partial to silver automobiles, but Petunia prefers black. We've agreed that silver with black interior leather would be acceptable."

My heart began to pound. "What you do with your money is no concern of mine, dear."

"By 'your' money, you mean my salary, correct?"

"Yes—I mean, we haven't really discussed that, have we?"

"When you hired me at the retreat center in Maryland, you gave me your word that I would be compensated handsomely as pastor of Beechy Grove Mennonite Church."

"And indeed you will be. In addition to the use of this charming parsonage, which, frankly, you are well on the way to destroying, you will receive monthly payments of one thousand dollars, full-coverage health insurance, plus all the leftovers your heart desires from our many, and quite tasty, potluck suppers."

"You're just kidding, right?"

"Absolutely not—well, okay, Denticia Wapplemeister is not the world's best cook, and I'd stay away from Belinda Litwiller's concoctions—she likes using toothpaste for flavoring—but everyone else is capable of cooking up yummy things from time to time."

"I'm not talking about food; I'm referring to that pittance you call a salary. My wife makes more than that writing enema instructions."

"Pittance is such a relative term, don't you think? I daresay a thousand U.S. dollars a month would go over quite well in Bosnia. Agreed, the commute would eat into your paycheck, but think of all the frequent flyer miles you'd get. And anyway, you don't have to pay a mortgage here, and I'm sure someone as peaked as your otherwise lovely wife could give the insurance company a run for its money."

"Petunia is in perfect health, thank you. No, Miss Yoder, when I agreed to this post, I was under the impression that I would be well compensated. Clearly that is not the case. I'm afraid that either you meet my salary demands or I will be forced to seek a pastorate elsewhere."

"Demands?"

"Four thousand a month, the benefits you mentioned before, *and* match my contribution to retirement savings."

"Why, that's blackmail!"

"No, it's salary negotiations."

Ever the good sport, I chuckled pleasantly. "Okay, I'll cry uncle. Two thousand it is, but we'll only match your savings up to ten percent of your net salary."

"I wasn't kidding. It's four thousand or the highway. Sorry about that crude, colloquial expression."

"But you said we were negotiating."

"I was only trying to be polite. I'm serious, Miss Yoder, either you come through or Petunia and I will have to leave."

I sighed heavily, never being one to take defeat in stride. "Bon voyage, dear. But make sure you restore the paneling to its God-given natural state, or you'll have a lawsuit on your hands. Belonging to one of the more conservative branches of our church as we do, we at Beechy Grove Mennonite don't approve of frivolous lawsuits, but we have a Presbyterian attorney who doesn't object one whit."

"You wouldn't dare!"

"Exactly. It's our attorney who dares. Now, if you'll excuse me, I have a million things to do, including finding your replacement." One of the many other things on my agenda was to find someone who could suture together my broken heart. With Reverend Fiddlegarber now footloose, if not fancy-free, my marriage to the Babester would have to be put on hold. In order for us to get married while we could still stand—forget it; it was never going to happen. Where would I find another Mennonite minister willing to participate in a mixed marriage? Nowhere, that's where. I was doomed to grow old alone. No doubt I'd become cynical and bitter, perhaps even sarcastic. Despite my comely appearance, children in Hernia would call me a witch . . .

"Miss Yoder. Earth to Miss Yoder."

I shook my head hard enough to dislodge my brain, had I still been in possession of one. Gradually the pity-induced fog began to clear.

"Uh—what?"

"Perhaps we can compromise after all."

"We can?" I slapped my mouth with a shapely hand for having sounded too eager.

"Would you like to sit down? Have some tea? I had the rabbi bring some scones and clotted cream with him from Pittsburgh. Nice young fellow—although Petunia doesn't think much of him. By the way, she doesn't know about the comestibles the rabbi smuggled in for me, so I would appreciate you not saying anything."

"My lips will be sealed between bites. But first, lay it on me."

"I beg your pardon?"

" 'Tis I who should be pardoned. That's just something my worldly sister, Susannah, says. It means tell me everything."

"I see. Well, I've been doing some quick thinking—"

"Always a dangerous activity. Look where it got Adam."

"Indeed. At any rate, you are an obscenely—I mean,

extremely—wealthy woman, Miss Yoder. You are the richest Mennonite I know."

"*How* do you know this?" I wailed for old time's sake. "I sold my sinfully red BMW, my dresses are home-made, sewn from cloth purchased at the Material Girl in Bedford, my humble brown brogans are from Payless, and my sturdy Christian underwear comes straight out of the JCPenney catalog."

"People talk, tongues wag, surely you know how it is."

"The people at church? Which ones? Did Agnes Mishler say anything? Why, the nerve of that woman, and her pretending to be my friend."

"Miss Yoder, I can't get specific—confidentiality of the cloth and all that. My point is that you're loaded and have the means to make up the difference between our two positions. The church elders need never know."

I couldn't believe my ears, which, by the way, are in excellent condition. "And how is this a compromise?"

"Because I'll agree to stay in a position that is clearly undervalued, and you'll part with a small fraction of your vast fortune, one which is probably tax deductible anyway. We both lose a little, and we both gain a lot. What do you say?"

"Does this mean you'll still officiate at my wedding ceremony?" I asked, whereas I should have said, "Get thee behind me, Satan."

"Absolutely. Petunia will even agree to be a brides-maid. You have my word on that."

"Thanks, but no thanks. But an extra kitchen helper at the reception would be nice."

"So we have a deal?"

"Deal."

I passed on the scones and clotted cream, having suddenly lost my appetite. Dancing with the Devil is a surefire way to diet. Not that Reverend Fiddlegarber is the Devil, mind you; merely his agent. We all are from time to time, aren't we? Well, perhaps some of us more than others. After leaving the parsonage I headed straight over to put the screws to a woman who, some folks around here think, danced one too many times with Beelzebub, and has permanently crossed over to the dark side.

Drustara Kurtz is an ex-Amish woman. Tall, with auburn hair and milky skin lightly sprinkled with freckles, she is beautiful enough to be a movie star, or at the very least, to model sturdy Christian underwear in catalogs. At some point during her *rumschpringe,* her church-sanctioned period of rebellion, Drustara hooked up with a Methodist boy from over Somerset way and started attending his church's youth programs. Before her parents knew what was happening, she'd not only joined his church, but married him. Within a year they were divorced. From there it was a hop, skip, and a broad jump to the *Oprah* show, and all because she'd written a novel that critics called "achingly true." But face it, the book also lacked punctuation and was full of randomly capitalized words; those two aspects alone are guaranteed to turn four hundred pages of trash into a literary accomplishment.

Of course Drustara is no longer Amish. In fact, she has been placed under a ban by the bishop. Her family and friends must shun her or undergo censuring themselves. Even if her own mother was to meet her on the street, she would not be allowed to speak to Drustara. Until she repents, the red-haired beauty is dead to her people.

As small as it is, Hernia has three distinct neighborhoods: the prestigious historic district, the new development with the improbable name of Foxcroft, and Ragsdale. The last is not an official designation, but an uncharitable appellation that apparently uncharitable souls, myself included, use when we refer to several streets on the south side of town that have not been kept up well, and that, as a result, have become affordable to the less-than-middle class. All right, it's the poor side of town.

At the time she divorced, Drustara and her three-year-old daughter, Clementine, lived on Beacon Street, which, ironically, doesn't have even one streetlight. After Oprah plugged *The Dark Side of Heaven,* the vastly successful author built the second largest home in Foxcroft. No doubt about it, she would have built the largest, but that distinction will always be held by the Rashid mansion, which exceeded our covenants, but for which a one-time exception was made. The Rashids, by the way, are Hernia's first Muslim family.

I had never been inside the Kurtz house and looked forward to it. Not wanting to be a total boor, I opted to ring the bell instead of employing my knuckles of steel.

"Who is it?" I heard her call from somewhere deep within the house.

"It's Magdalena Yoder, no longer ugly, but twice as beautiful, but since that's a vain thing to say, I'll let you draw your own conclusions."

The heavy, ornate door inched open to reveal an anxious pair of green eyes. There was a body as well, and the telltale red hair, but only the eyes were unsettled.

19

"I paid my municipal taxes," Drustara said. "If you didn't get the check today, you'll get it tomorrow."

"That's nice, dear, but I'm only the mayor of Hernia; I'm not the county treasurer."

"I know who you are. But if you're not here to string me up by my thumbs, then why *are* you here?"

"Tsk, tsk, what a tongue. Is that what they taught you in that Methodist school?"

"I went to Penn State, and if by 'Methodist school' you mean the church I attend, the answer is no. I am who I've always been, just more so. Take it or leave it."

Having very little experience with assertive women who speak their minds, I prayed for direction. As is usually the case, none was forthcoming, although the weirdest thing occurred to me; perhaps Drustara Kurtz was a young version of Magdalena Yoder, and I should take it from there. Clearly this bizarre thought pattern was the result of crossed wires between Heaven and yours truly.

"I'll take it, but can we take it indoors?"

She stepped aside. "Suit yourself. But Clementine has been under the weather the past few days. A bad cold. I haven't caught it yet, which is not to say I'm not contagious. Oh, what the heck. Who am I kidding? I bet you're used to getting colds, what with you running hither, thither, and yon, sticking your nose into everyone's business."

Recoiling too fast can result in whiplash. "I will accept hither and yon, but thither is going just too far."

"So it's true what they say; you are one sandwich short of a picnic."

"Yes, but they never say which kind of sandwich. Don't you want to know which kind?"

"Okay, I'll bite."

"Cucumber and Nutter."

"You mean butter?"

"No whey! It's a dairy-free spread called Nutter."

"Nuts."

"Exactly. You should try it sometime."

"No, I mean you."

"Far too many people are normal, dear, so I'll take that as a compliment."

I looked around the living room for the first time. It was spectacularly beautiful, but not in the least bit ostentatious. If anything, the colors and furnishings were understated. My guess is that Drustara had used the services of an interior decorator. For most Hernians, decorating professionally means finding a page in the JCPenney catalog that one likes, and then ordering everything available on it.

"Wow," I said, almost at a loss for words. "This must have set you back a pretty penny. If I wasn't the polite, well-brought-up woman that I am, I might ask you just how many pennies this cost, although I would probably have you convert it to dollars. Math has never been my forte, and no, I do not mean forté. The former refers to a strong point, whilst the latter is a musical term. And yes, I am aware that so many people say forté nowadays, when they mean forte, that the dictionary lists it as the secondary pronunciation, but that doesn't make it right. Just because most people dress like slobs when they grocery shop doesn't make it right either, does it?"

She shook her head, sending masses of auburn waves into motion. "I take it back. You're not just nuts; you're stark raving mad."

"But in a good way, right?"

"Whatever. So, are you going to tell me why you're here?"

"I'm afraid it's not good news." I glanced dutifully around. "Where's your daughter?"

"Clementine is sleeping. We can talk here." She made no move to offer me a seat.

"Very well. It's about your former lover." Honest to goodness, the L word just slipped out.

"Which one?"

My jaw dropped. Not too long ago, when I didn't have a bosom to catch it with, I would have had to scoop it off the floor.

"Ha, gotcha, didn't I? You're like all the rest, you know? You think just because I ran off with a Methodist boy, I must be a tramp."

"Of course not, dear. I think that because you did the bedsprings bossa nova with Hernia's equally notorious playboy, Cornelius Weaver."

The green eyes took on a grayish cast. "Don't speak ill of the dead, Miss Yoder. That's scraping the bottom of the barrel—even for you."

"Forsooth, I speak the truth. I have just interviewed four other women who engaged in premarital, lateral relations with our town's most prosperous, and possibly most promiscuous, posthumous—"

"Miss Yoder, I'm sure you've heard this before, but you can be extremely annoying."

"In that case, just toss my book across the room. That's what I tell my readers."

She suddenly regarded me with interest. "You've published a book?"

"No. But if I *had,* that's what I'd say. Speaking of being published, my fiancé, the very handsome Dr. Gabriel Rosen, is working on a mystery novel, but just after the halfway mark, he ran out of ideas."

"I believe that's called the end of the book."

"Yes, but the publishing guidelines state he needs to have seventy thousand words."

"I see. Well in that case, tell him to buy the *Lord and Spencer Idea Gift Catalogue*. They sell single ideas for as low as nine ninety-nine, and you can get a complete plot package for three easy payments of sixty-nine ninety-nine. Believe me, it's well worth the money."

I nodded gratefully, and lacking a proper notebook, jotted down the information on the back of an old church bulletin. "Thank you so much," I gushed. "The Babester—I mean Gabe—thanks you as well."

"Mmm. Now tell me about Cornelius."

"Who?"

"My so-called ex-lover," she said softly.

"Ah yes. You see, a preliminary autopsy indicates that he died of a heart attack, possibly brought on by an overdose of amitriptyline."

"Elavil."

"You know this drug?"

"I suffer from depression, Miss Yoder. A lot of artists do."

"You paint as well?"

She sighed needlessly. "Writing is an art."

So is acting, I thought. Drustara Kurtz wasn't nearly as upset as I thought she should be. Not that there is a right way to be upset, but there is a wrong way—if one doesn't want to draw suspicion to oneself.

"Perhaps, Drustara, and my, what a lovely name that is—you have missed my point."

"That Cornelius was murdered?"

"Or perhaps not. You certainly don't seem taken aback."

"You mentioned four other women; that's your clue right there."

"I don't get it."

"If you're looking for a one-word answer, try *jealousy* on for size. Cornelius was living dangerously, making five women promises that he couldn't keep. Dangerous living often leads to death. Why should I be surprised?"

I shook my head in wonder. "Just a few short years ago you were horse-and-buggy Amish. How did you get to be this cynical so fast?"

"I was always cynical. That's one of the many reasons I left the community."

"You just said five women. I assume you're including yourself. But you do know that Cornelius was planning to marry Priscilla Livingood—don't you? In just three days."

"Of course I do. But it never would have happened; Cornelius would have found a way out of that as well. As to the fifth woman, she's your buddy the chief, am I right?"

This time I caught my jaw before it hit my bosom. "*How* did you know that? Nobody is supposed to know that."

"Miss Yoder, surely you are aware that men are the biggest gossips."

"Isn't that the truth! Drop a kernel of gossip at the Mennonite Ladies Sewing Circle, and it will take two weeks before it gets back to you, and by then it's so twisted, you almost think it's something new. Take the same nugget of info to the blacksmith's shop, and the very next day it gets back to you highly embellished, but other than that, none the worse for wear."

Her laugh was surprisingly melodious. Our similarities were almost frightening.

"You're a hoot, Miss Yoder."

"And a holler. So you're saying Cornelius told on himself."

She nodded. "I think he would have burst otherwise. Sleeping with the chief was so exciting for him, and on many levels. He just had to tell someone. But I think I'm the only one he shared this with."

Since no one else had brought up the chief, Drustara was probably right on that score. "There's something else I don't get: You're beautiful, wealthy, successful, outspoken, wealthy—did I mention wealthy? I can see why the others threw themselves at Hernia's most eligible bachelor, but why you?"

"He had enormous feet, Miss Yoder, and you know what they say about men with big feet."

"They require large shoes?"

"Exactly." Her delightful laughter enthralled me for another minute. "Seriously, Miss Yoder, as I'm sure you have discovered, my healthy bank account limits the playing field considerably. I knew Cornelius was a cad—may he rest in peace—but he wasn't after my money. He was intelligent, handsome, and wore big shoes. What else can I say?"

"So you weren't interested in marrying him?"

"Ach, *du lieber!*" she said, reverting to her native Amish dialect. "Why on earth would I do that? I have Clementine to consider. You don't honestly think Cornelius would have made a good father, do you?"

"Touché. So you were just—uh—friends with Cornelius."

"Is that judgment I see written all over your face?"

"Moi?"

"Yes, we were friends and more. But you don't have the slightest idea what it's been like for me to move out into the world. Sure, you're a Mennonite, and granted, even a conservative one, but that's a far cry from being Amish. When your sister married a Presbyterian, she wasn't excommunicated. It's darn hard for me to make friends, because even though I've managed to remove all traces of dialect from my speech—and what you just heard was an exception—my life experiences are not something to which most people can relate. That makes me seem odd, and, believe it or not, most people are afraid of odd. They are biologically programmed to be. At any rate, the only two people in this town who ever gave me the time of day were Cornelius and Zelda."

I gasped. "My half-sister Zelda Root? The one who is *two* sandwiches short of a picnic?"

"Why do you say that? Because she practices a different religion?"

"Not just different—it's wrong! She worships a man, for crying out loud. A live human being."

"And that makes less sense than worshipping a dead man?"

"Jesus was not just a man; he was God as well."

"Says who?"

"The Bible."

"Her holy book says different."

"She wrote it, for Pete's sake! You can't compare the two. That's absurd. Besides, a billion Christians bear witness to the fact that Jesus is the only way to know God."

"There are a lot more Buddhists than that, and they don't go to war over denominational differences. Let me ask you, Miss Yoder, where does it say in the Bible that God has a penis?"

"What?"

"Well, he's male, isn't he? What makes him male? The Bible refers to him as 'father.' You can't get any more male than that."

It was a good thing the heretic hadn't offered me a seat. I plugged my ears with my fingers and thumbs and, with the exception of one awkward moment when I opened the door, kept them plugged until I was safely in my car. Meanwhile my purse, which was hanging from my arm, slapped me in the face several times. I'm sure I deserved it; I should not have hung around for even a second of Drustara's blasphemy.

If the Good Lord wanted us to think for ourselves, he wouldn't have given us 1,074 pages of instructions, as per the well-known King James version of the Holy Bible, which has the place of honor on my nightstand. Independent thought is dangerous, in that it leads to the abandonment of traditional values. Traditional values are like fluoride; without them decay sets in. Drustara Kurtz is the perfect case in point.

On the other hand, if I couldn't hold my own in a religious discussion with an ex-Amish woman, how on earth was I going to make a marriage work when my other half had *never* believed the way I do? Just having a service conducted by a Mennonite minister in conjunction with a rabbi was not going to change anything. With my heart resting on the floorboards of my car, I drove across town to do what I had to do next.

20

Kheema Mattar
(Mince Meat and Peas)

Ingredients

¼ cup oil
1 pound ground beef
1 cup yogurt
1 tablespoon ginger-garlic
    paste
2 medium onions, finely
    sliced
1–2 green chilies, finely
    diced
¼ teaspoon turmeric

1 cinnamon stick
2 cloves
2 cardamoms
Salt to taste
3 tomatoes, finely diced
1 cup frozen peas, thawed
    and rinsed
¾ cup water
Pinch of coriander leaves,
    finely chopped

YIELD: 8 SERVINGS

Preparation

1. Heat oil in pan and add beef, yogurt, ginger-garlic paste, onions, and chilies. Mix.
2. Then add turmeric, cinnamon, cloves, cardamom, and salt.
3. Stir thoroughly and cook on medium-high heat till all the liquid is absorbed.
4. Cook this mixture till it reaches a light brown color, stirring periodically. Be careful not to allow it to burn;

sprinkle a little water in if need be.

5. Now add tomatoes, peas, and water and stir thoroughly. Mixture will be liquidy. Allow to cook for a few minutes.

6. Cover and cook on low heat till peas are tender. If mixture is still too liquidy, cook uncovered.

7. Garnish with coriander leaves and serve with naan.

Notes

• Fresh peas will need more cooking time than frozen peas.

• Discard whole spices before eating.

21

I let myself into the Babester's house. Creeping as silently as a cat in a fog, I searched the place until I found my beloved in his office, hunched over his computer. Quite unnoticed, I watched lovingly for a few minutes. Alternating periods of catatonia and intense clattering of keys clued me in to the fact that he was working on his manuscript. Apparently, without any help from me, or Drustara Kurtz, my would-be author had managed to purchase his own copy of the *Lord and Spencer Idea Gift Catalogue*.

"Ahem," I finally said, unable to bear my burden any longer.

"Holy shoofly pie!" Gabe shouted and nearly hit the ceiling with his head. The fact that he'd modified his swearword from cow excrement to a Pennsylvania Dutch dessert was something for which I could take credit.

"Hon, you nearly scared the pistachio out of me."

"Pistachio ice cream goes well with shoofly pie. May I read what you've written?"

"Magdalena, you know I don't like to share my work in progress."

"But you're never done, so it's always in progress. Now I'll never get to see it."

"What do you mean by that?"

"Gabe, where's your mother?"

"Outside, choosing a location for her garden."

"Garden?" Trying to imagine Ida tilling the soil was like trying to picture a rap singer performing at the court of Louis XIV. Like oil and water, the ideas didn't mix.

Gabe nodded in mock solemnity. "Someone told her there was a lot of money to be made by planting polyester bushes."

"It was a joke. I didn't think she'd actually consider it. Why didn't you stop her?"

He chuckled. "Because it got her off my back. I swear, Mags, she's worse than you; she's always trying to read over my shoulder."

"Well, you won't be having that problem any longer."

"Yup. As soon as she finds out that Miller's Feed Store doesn't sell polyester seed—"

"Not her—*me*."

"What?"

"Darling," I said, daring to use the word for the first time, "do you mind if we go downstairs to your buttery-soft Italian leather sofa to talk about this?"

"I think maybe I do very much. At the very least, I don't like where this conversation seems to be headed."

"But darling, you knew from the beginning, like I did, that we really didn't stand a chance."

"The heck we didn't! Who's gotten to you, Magdalena? Has that minister from Maryland been turning you against me?"

"No."

"Then who? What's this all about?"

"Gabe, we're not on the same page—we're not even in the same Bible. I mean we are, but you only subscribe to half of it."

"I don't subscribe to any of it—not literally. You've known that about me from almost the beginning."

"Yes, but I thought I could change you. That if I was

a proper witness to the Lord, you would eventually see the light and be saved."

"And I told you that as much as I hated you thinking I was wrong—doomed to Hell, or whatever your religion teaches—it was worth putting up with in order to spend the rest of my life with you. Just as long as you kept the sermons short and to the point."

"Are you saying now that you don't even believe in Hell?"

"Judaism is not about Heaven or Hell. It's about performing acts of loving kindness in this life. Darn it, Magdalena, now you've got me defending a faith to which I no longer subscribe. The kind acts, yes, but—shoot, I can't believe I'm even having this conversation."

I could feel my chin quiver. I hate it when my body betrays me. Pretty soon the tears would well up, and then my face would turn blotchy, and unless I did something drastic, a whimper might even escape my trembling lips.

"I love you, Gabriel Rosen." The force of my words surprised even me. "I have never loved anyone as much as I love you, and I never will! But it's over between us. It has to be; we are just too different. It never would have worked. But I thank God for the time we had together, and I pray that He will bless you, and keep you safe, and that someday—"

"I'll see the light and beg to be converted?"

"That's not fair! I'm pouring out my heart, and you—you—" Truth be told, I was grateful that he'd made me angry again. Anger can be a very destructive emotion, but I'd pick it over pain any day.

"Just go, Magdalena, and take your self-righteousness with you. Maybe someday you'll come to your senses and realize that when you start applying a literal interpretation to one collection of ancient tribal legends, you may as well do it to all of the others. So go, Magdalena, go with Zeus!"

I turned on a narrow heel to flee from the room, but

it was not going to be a graceful exit. In the doorway, standing as still as a garden gnome, and almost as pretty, was Gabe's mother, Ida.

"So," she hissed, springing to life, "you tink my son is not good enough for you?"

"Of course not! I mean, he *is* good enough, but—Mrs. Rosen, with all due respect, this really isn't your business."

"My son *is* my business."

I looked at Gabe, who looked like a deer caught in the headlights. It was then that I realized that, matters of faith set aside, our breakup would have been inevitable. Matthew 19:5 states that a man shall leave his mother and cleave unto his wife. But as long as Ida Rosen was in the picture, there wasn't going to be any cleavage.

"Tell me something, Ida," I said, trying mightily to control my voice. "Deep down inside—maybe even not so deep—you're happy that Gabriel and I are breaking up. Isn't that right?"

Ida rolled her eyes. "Oy, this one talks like a blintz."

"Ma, answer her question."

"*Nu,* vhat's to answer? Of course I'm not happy. How could I be happy? Gabeleh, is it too much to vant that you should marry a nice Jewish girl? New York vas full of them, but here? Nothing but shikses."

"Ma," Gabe moaned.

"No, it's okay," I said. "She has a right to her opinion. Everyone in Hernia is saying the same thing, but in reverse. But you, Gabriel, for your own good, you need to cut the apron strings. You're almost fifty years old, for crying out loud. Isn't it time you learned to cut your own meat as well?"

Gabe reddened. "I know how to cut meat, darn it, but if it gives Ma satisfaction, who am I to deny her?"

"A grown man."

"You're treading on thin ice, Magdalena. Who still lives in the house she was born in?"

"That's not a fair comparison; my parents are dead."

"Yet your mother still controls you. Isn't that right, Magdalena?"

I slipped off my engagement ring for the last time. It was a monstrous blue Ceylon sapphire surrounded by small, but exceptionally clear, diamonds. Susannah refers to it as "major bling." It was also a soap catcher that needed constant cleaning to look its best, and that, frankly, I was embarrassed to wear when it did look that way, because of all the attention it attracted.

"So this is really it, then," Gabe said. Talk about quivering chins.

"All over but the shouting," I said, forcing my mouth into what I hoped resembled a smile. "Only there won't be any. But I do have a favor to ask of Ida. And since I'm giving her back her son, it shouldn't be too much to ask."

"So ask already," she said. "You have my vord that I vill do it."

"You know Miller's Pond?"

"Of course. It's right in front of this house—before the road."

"That's right. It gets pretty scummy over the winter, and doesn't clear up until early summer. I want you to go outside, get a running start, and jump in the pond."

"*Vhat?*"

"Go soak yourself, Ida."

I pushed past her and ran outside.

There is no potion in this world, prescription or otherwise, that can heal a broken heart. They say only time can heal one, but it's an awful saying, because time stands still for broken hearts. When I got home, all I wanted to do, after taking a long soak in the tub, was to burrow under my sheets and stay there until the pain went away.

Having already experienced the simple life, I reward myself now—but not without some guilt—by making my bed with sheets that have a thousand threads per square inch. Made from the finest Egyptian cotton, they feel every bit as soft and buttery as Gabe's Italian leather couch. They do not, however, smell like butter. Well, not usually.

I'd just crawled into my den of white sheets and eiderdown comforters to hibernate when I got a whiff of this incongruous, but not unpleasant, scent. I peeked out cautiously. Perhaps there was a polar bear waiting to pounce on me.

"Freni!"

"Yah, as big as life and twice as ugly."

I fought back a laugh, but it overpowered me and escaped as a snort. I dug deeper into my den.

"Freni, please go away."

"Yah, I go, but first you eat."

"I'm not hungry!"

"You do not have to be hungry to eat these cross aunts." Her voice was muffled but still intelligible. Then again, maybe not. I poked my head out.

"Just which cross aunt did you have in mind, dear?"

"Ach, so now you make fun of me?"

"Freni, I'm not—oh, *those* cross aunts!" My dear kinswoman was holding a wooden tray in her stubby hands. On the tray was a plate of freshly baked, and buttered, croissants. Next to the plate of pastries was Mama's chipped stoneware pot, one that was reserved only for hot cocoa.

"So now maybe you eat, yah?"

"If you insist, but I'm still not hungry."

"I brought you some peach preserves for the cross aunts. The kind with the lumps."

"You mean 'chunks.' "

"Yah, that is what I said. Now, sit up, Magdalena."

I did as ordered. Freni set the tray on my bedside table and then almost tenderly tucked a starched white napkin into the neck of my pajama top. After pouring a cup of steaming cocoa, she handed me a dessert plate upon which she'd arranged two croissants, several pats of extra butter, and a gob of lumpy peach preserves.

"Now, eat," she ordered.

"Only if you join me."

"Ach!"

"I mean it. I'm not going to take a bite unless you do."

"But there is only one small plate."

"No problemo. I'll hold the tray in my lap; that will be my plate. You get the real plate—but we'll divide the rolls evenly. And we can share the cup, knowing as I do that you don't have cooties. But no backwash."

"Yah, but—"

"No if, ands, or buts allowed. Take off your brogans and scootch under the covers with me. If crumbs fall on the bed, so what? That's what washing machines are for."

I never could have imagined it in a million years. My seventy-six-year-old cousin kicked off her heavy shoes and hoisted her considerable keester up onto my bed. Snuggled next to each other, we drank the entire pitcher of cocoa and ate four and a half croissants each. By the time we were through, my bedclothes were covered with grease spots, jam stains, chocolate stains, and more crumbs than there are sand grains in the Sahara. The entire time we probably said no more than five words.

When we were quite done, with our fingers licked clean, we belched in turn (age before beauty) and then shortly afterward fell asleep.

22

"Hey, Mom, what's going on?"

I awoke to find my dear, sweet pseudo-stepdaughter poking me with the corner of her book bag.

"Alison! What time is it?"

She glanced at my bedside clock, which was still a blur to me. "Seven thirty, I think. Ya need ta get one of them digital clocks—hey, ya don't never sleep in the afternoon. Are ya sick?"

"I was," I said. "But I'm better now." A truer statement was never spoken.

"Yeah?" Her eyes strayed to the other side of the bed. "What's that lump under them covers? That ain't Gabe, is it?"

"What?" I jerked to a sitting position. There was indeed a lump under the covers. My dear kinswoman was still dead to the world, and had apparently pulled the covers over her head at some point.

"Y'are always yapping about how I shouldn't have sex before marriage, Mom. If you ask me, this ain't such a good example." She stepped sprightly around the end of the bed and whacked the sleeping lump with her satchel.

"Ach!" Freni squawked and popped up like Lazarus from the dead.

"Ooh, gross," Alison said. "I ain't got nothing against them gays, but my own mom with my cousin? That's sick."

Her words were music to my ears: *my own mom.*
And the fact that she considered Freni to be a cousin
of hers—well, it couldn't get any more touching than
that. The cousin in question, however, was not similarly
moved.

"Ach," Freni squawked again, and like a plump hen
pursued by a hungry fox, flapped her stubby arms and
virtually flew from the room.

"It's not what you think, dear."

"It's okay, Mom, I'm cool with that. I mean, I ain't,
but I want younz to be happy."

"Alison, for crying out loud, quit jumping to conclusions. I was having a hard time, and Freni brought me a
snack, and then we both fell asleep—not that I need to
explain anything."

The child can be as aggravating as gum on the soles of
my brogans, but then a second later she is more astute
than Aristotle. She digested my explanation, having apparently found it palatable.

"What kind of hard time?"

"Oh, nothing." I could feel my chin quiver just remembering my parting words to Gabe.

"Ya got that weird look on your face, Mom. The kind my
other mom had when I said I didn't love her no more."

"You did?"

"Yeah, but now I ain't so sure I meant it. I was real
mad at her, though, on account of she was acting all
goofy toward Pop, like she loved him more than me, and
he weren't even there when I was a kid."

I looked at the daughter I would never have, but still
did have, in a funny cosmic sort of way. True, I didn't
get a chance to carry her in my womb, but then again,
I didn't have to change a single diaper, or get up for a
middle-of-the-night feeding. But it was clear she loved
me enough to trust me with her feelings, so it was only
fair that I be straightforward with her.

"Alison, uh—well, Dr. Rosen and I are no longer
engaged."

Her expression reminded me of my favorite cow, Bessie, the first time we ever hooked her up to the automatic milking machine. "But y'are still getting married, right?"

"I'm afraid not."

"What happened, Mom? 'Cause whatever it is, I can go over there and fix it. I know I can."

"Not this time, dear. We've broken it off for good."

"Was it *her*? Was it Grandma Ida? Was it because she treats him like a baby?"

"You were aware of that?"

Alison plopped on the bed beside me. "I ain't blind, Mom. I ain't stupid neither."

"Nor a grammarian."

"Yeah. So it was Grandma Ida. Man, I knew it."

"It wasn't just that, dear. Dr. Rosen and I couldn't see eye to eye on some pretty important things."

"Ah, I get ya; it's that religious stuff, ain't it?"

"Yes, in a nutshell."

"No offense, Mom, but ain't that kinda stupid?"

"I beg your pardon?"

"Ya both worship the same God, right?"

"It's not that simple, dear."

"Well, it oughta be. If ya love each other, it seems to me that's all that should matter. Let God decide if He wants ta be pissed at ya because younz don't agree."

I sighed. The Bible says that a child shall lead them, but it doesn't say where to. Perhaps to the bathroom, where I could wash her mouth out with soap.

"Alison, it's not going to happen, so can we talk about something else?"

"Yeah, I guess." She was silent for all of three seconds. "Hey Mom, is it all right with ya if I get me a bikini wax?"

"A what?"

"Ya know, like a leg wax, only they don't stop anywhere near the knees. Shelby Saylor had herself one, said it hurt something awful. Even worse than pulling a tooth. She said I oughta be glad I don't need one, but I ain't so sure."

"Shelby Saylor is right," I cried as I clapped my hands over my ears. I wouldn't have thought in a million years that I would ever side with Shelby Saylor. The child is every mother's nightmare, except for her own mother, who doesn't seem to care one whit about her daughter's upbringing.

My hands have never stopped my ears from hearing. "I was kinda hoping ya would say that," Alison said nonchalantly.

"You *were*?"

"Yeah, it was kind of a dare. But I asked ya, didn't I?"

"You're darn tooting," I said, which is almost as bad as I can swear. Defying five hundred years of inbred reservation, I reached out to hug Alison, but she slipped away from my grasp.

"Don't ya be getting all mushy with me, Mom. I ain't about to take a nap with ya either."

I smiled, despite my broken heart.

Broken hearts, unlike broken limbs, do not require casts or crutches, so I had no excuse not to hit the sleuthing trail again. Besides, I'd heard that keeping active was a good way to keep from hurting. Then again, I'd also heard that time can heal a broken heart, and that turned out to be a load of *Haufa mischt*.

Whilst lollygagging about in bed (but only briefly) after Alison's touching visit, it occurred to me that I had been approaching the case from the wrong angle. I'd been investigating on behalf of Chief Olivia Hornsby-Anderson rather than on behalf of the town of Hernia. The five "suspects" I'd chosen to interview were all women who'd been romantically involved with the deceased, Cornelius Weaver.

Yet not only was the chief also involved with Cornelius, but they were doing the Sealy Posturepedic polka when he passed on to meet St. Peter. From what I've read, bad tickers, especially those that are unused to exercise, can be adversely affected by the rapid heartbeats brought on by sexual climax. How lucky we women are; we need only lie there, planning our menus, or reviewing the day's events, just as long as we remember to show some response at the critical moment. With a little planning, such as purchasing a good hairnet, we need hardly look worse for the wear.

At any rate, there were a number of factors not in Chief Hornsby-Anderson's favor. For starters, as a police officer, she should know CPR. Don't get me wrong; I'm not saying that CPR could necessarily have saved Cornelius's life, but it increased his chances. The fact that he died anyway had to be taken into consideration.

And then there was her questionable choice of me as prime investigator. Why not turn the matter over to the sheriff, or at the least, the inexperienced, albeit very handsome, Chris Ackerman? Could it be that the chief was hoping that I would make such a mess out of things that by the time she was forced to turn to professional help, it would be too late to make a coherent case against her? Well, if that was the case, she was in for a nasty surprise.

One of the very few benefits of possessing a cracked cardium is that the intense pain involved makes one less likely to give a rodent's rear about what other people think. Whereas just yesterday I might have been a wee bit nervous about putting the screws to the chief, now I really didn't care whom I screwed. So to speak.

Anyway, Chief Hornsby-Anderson (she has never invited me to call her Olivia) lives in Hernia's only apartment building. Why it is called the Narrows, no one seems to know. There are only eight units, four up and four down, and the chief lives up, with an inspiring view of the parking lot, and the back of Miller's Feed Store. Twice a week the chief can watch, from the privacy of her own balcony, the supply trucks unload. Amanda

Tutweiler, who used to live in 2D, rented folding chairs up there for sixty cents an hour. I'm told she had a waiting list a mile long, so I never bothered to put my name on it. Who says there's nothing to do in Hernia?

Even though it was not a delivery day, the chief took an inordinately long time to answer. She is an attractive woman, rather well preserved given her sunny California origins, but today she appeared blotchy and bedraggled. Immediately I recognized the signs of excessive lacrimal duct secretion. That is to say, she'd been crying.

"Oh, it's you," she said, sounding surprised, even though her door had a perfectly good peephole.

"No, it's my very much older, identical twin sister."

"What?"

"Nothing, dear. 'Twas merely a joke. Go ahead and attend to your needs, while I wait on the charming balcony."

She made no move to usher me into the apartment, and out again onto the balcony. "What needs?"

I gave her a sympathetic smile. "Wash your swollen face, run a comb through that jungle hanging from your head, and maybe even spritz those pits, for crying out loud, before they asphyxiate us both."

"Magdalena, I'm not going to invite you in, and frankly, neither my appearance, nor my odor, is your concern."

"I beg to differ, Your Chieftainship. I'm here to discuss the Cornelius Weaver case, and if I pass out and hit my head, I might get a concussion, possibly resulting in permanent brain damage, which means my sister, Susannah, would have power of attorney, and might decide to ship me off to Alaska and put me on an ice floe, and by the time the Supreme Court could hear my case, I'd have frozen to death, and I must tell you, Your Chieftainship, that I just plain don't like being cold."

"You're nuts, Magdalena. Practically even stark raving mad. Has anyone ever told you that?"

"No one has the nerve. It's the evil glint in my eye

that puts them off. Besides, I'm not crazy; I just act that way."

"And I'm supposed to invite you in?"

"You are a policewoman, after all. I'm sure you know how to defend yourself against raging lunatics. Still, if you like, we can chat here, even though the acoustics, thanks to the parking lot, allow my voice to be heard from a good quarter mile away."

"Very well." She gave me a warning growl. "If you so much as make a wrong move, you'll be sorry."

I couldn't tell whether she was serious or not. Some folks have such a dry sense of humor that their jokes go right over my head. Oh well, if she was genuinely afraid of me, that was her problem, not mine. Just as long as she didn't whip out her pistol and punch my one-way ticket to Heaven. That would certainly be ironic, given that I am a pussycat; even the pat of a kitten's paw against my face turns me to mush.

Keeping my long, elegant hands in sight, and a goofy grin plastered across my sculpted face, I slipped into her apartment and gave the sitting room the quick once-over. Chief Hornsby-Anderson would get along very well with Caroline Sha. The minimalist look is fine, as long as there is something to sit on. But this room was as bare as Mother Hubbard's cupboard. Could it be that the chief was planning to skip out of town, leaving me to hold the bag? That reference, by the way, is to snipe hunting, a sport at which I excel. Freni has some tasty snipe recipes— Now, where was I?

"You look like you're lost in thought, Magdalena."

"Yes, it's such unfamiliar territory."

"Touché. I'd offer you a place to sit, but since Hernia refused to pay for a mover, I sold my furniture before I left California. I've been meaning to shop for new stuff but haven't had the time. I did, however, buy a king-size bed in Bedford, no pun intended, the day I arrived in Pennsylvania."

"I'm sure that bed has already seen its share of use."

"Innuendo does not become you. Yes, my bed has seen a lot of use, but that's because it also functions as a desk and as my couch. I mean, really, what more do I need? The minute I get home every evening, usually around seven, I put on my pj's, hop in bed, and watch TV while I catch up on paperwork. Of course none of this is your business, so please, let's get on to police business. What have you been able to uncover in your investigation?"

"What a clever pun. Do you mind if I use it?"

"Excuse me?"

"Never mind, it was ill conceived. Yes, business. Well, there are six women whom I've put on my suspect list."

23

"No men?"

"Not yet. Anyway, all of these women were romantically involved with the deceased. They are, in the order in which I interviewed them, as follows. Priscilla Livingood, who has more store-bought parts than a John Deere tractor, is—I mean, was—his fiancée. I thought she would be snooty, but she's actually very nice. Works for a plastic surgeon."

"He does good work."

"Next up, we have Alice Troyer. She's a professional comedienne with a radish for a nose—I mean that kindly. Alice claims that she and Cornelius were engaged, had even picked out a whappalooza of a ring."

"A what?"

"An eye-buster, kinda like the ring I had." I glanced at the pale band of skin left by my ring. "Anyway, he dumped her the day before their engagement party. Alice says it came as a total shock."

"I bet."

"Carolina Sha, on the other hand, seems to have been aware that she was not the only one being wooed. Speaking of which, the woman is a little woo-woo, if you ask me. She lives in a paper house and doesn't use ice because she doesn't want to hurt the water, but she's happy to boil it for you. It's obvious that she's still bitter about not being chosen to be the next Mrs. Weaver, but

I honestly don't think she would kill a living thing—although she might feel differently about termites."

"It seems that Cornelius was a busy man."

"That's just the half of it. Did you know Thelma Unruh was a natural blonde? Very few women are, you know. And even fewer have a tower of Babel in their living room—well, a remnant, at any rate. It was obvious Thelma didn't like being cuckolded. Can that word apply to a woman?"

"No, and I think there has to be marriage involved."

"Whatever, as my Alison would say. Thelma insisted I speak to Veronica Weaver, the victim's mother. According to her, Cornelius needed to borrow ten thousand dollars, and he went to Mommy to get it. Mommy confirmed it, which didn't make a lick of sense, because I know, for a fact, that he was flush with bucks."

"You have a way with words, Magdalena."

"Verily. And Veronica also said he needed the money so that Thelma could get an abortion, something I need to follow up on. Not that I'm following up on my own abortion, mind you, but the veracity of Thelma's. Sometimes I think we'd be better off speaking German, despite its phlegm-clearing consonants and monstrously long multisyllabic compound words. At least it lets one know, by the case, which function each word performs in the sentence."

"You're wandering again."

"Wondering, as well. Why is it that, until recently, every non-English speaker coming to this country was expected to learn the host language? Can you imagine what a polyglot of tongues we'd be babbling if the Germans, Italians, French, Chinese, Japanese—if they'd all insisted on bilingual services? And what about the poor Albanians? Do you honestly think banks would bother to have Braille Albanian posted on their drive-through machines?"

"Now you're waxing political."

"Sorry. I shall endeavor to wane. Now, where was

I headed? Oh yes, the next bonnie lass on my list is Drustara Kurtz. She's a stunning redhead. I read an article recently that suggested the gene for red hair might have found its way into Homo sapiens via random matings with Neanderthals. Of course this isn't true, because the world was created in six days, and not six *long* days, either, or the Bible would have said so."

"Now you're on to religion."

"Better that than sex, since I don't know a whole lot about that. But anyone who says God doesn't have a sense of humor hasn't seen a naked man."

"Finally, something upon which we can agree. So that's the six suspects, huh?"

"Absolutely not. Veronica Weaver was his stepmother. She's not on the list."

The chief shook her head with tight little jerks. "No, no, Miss Yoder. You can't rule out anyone because of family connections. Stepmothers do kill their stepchildren. Haven't you read *Snow White*? What's more, birth mothers kill their children too, and vice versa. The Menendez brothers, for example. When it comes to murder, all bets are off. Anyone can be a suspect, and anything can be the motive."

I sighed to let her know that I hate being corrected. "Okay, so I have seven suspects in all."

"Yes, and who is seventh?"

"That would be you, dear."

"Me?"

"Most certainly. You were his lover as well. Perhaps he made the same promise of marriage to you, as he did the others. Then you discover he's planning to marry Priscilla Livingood. As they say, 'Hell hath no fury like a woman scorned.' "

"This is outrageous! I'm the chief of police. *I'm* the one who asked you to investigate."

"Actually, young Chris Ackerman did. Besides, like you said, anyone can be a suspect."

"This is egregious. I'm taking you off the case."

"I'm not sure you used that word correctly. You might want to look it up. Also, I'm not a licensed investigator, and I'm certainly not a real policewoman. 'Concerned citizen' is how I'd describe myself. So you can't take me off a case I was never on."

"I can have you arrested for obstruction of justice. Why I ever agreed to take a position in this Podunk town is beyond me."

"Now, *that* would be an egregious mistake. You see, as mayor of this Podunk town, I have it in my power to terminate your employment."

"On what grounds?"

"Suspicion of murder, what else?"

"But you can't—"

"Oh, but I can. That's the beauty of living in Podunk; we make our own rules."

"Yes, but the beauty of living in America is that I can exercise my God-given right to sue."

"It is indeed a wonderful country. I can countersue, and since you're the outsider, suspected of killing one of our own, what do you think your chances would be of winning?"

"I'll have the trial moved to Philadelphia—or Pittsburgh."

"Ah, the city of brotherly love, and the city of pierogies. Fill a pirogue with pierogies, Pittsburghers say, and you still wouldn't have nearly enough. Got to love them, though—the Pittsburghers, not the pierogies. Their fair metropolis is too far west to be an eastern city, and too far east to be Midwest. Ergo, they have developed their own culture, and practically their own dialect. Do you know what a gum band is?"

"Something with teeth and braces?"

"No, it means 'rubber band' in Pittsburghese. But back to the issue at hand, which seems to have gotten out of hand, but I think I have a handle on it. You see, my dear, I can count on one hand the number of successful lawsuits wherein the plaintiff was not a local.

On the other hand, just to be fair, we've only ever had one. The lawyer was brilliant, so I'll give him a hand. In fact, you have to hand it to him, because he was handicapped, as well as coming from Pittsburgh. And speaking of that burg, whose circuit court would you choose? Judge Morris Bluffman, or Judge Beatrice Ess? Bea Ess, we call her for short. But if filial affection is your preference, may I suggest you try and stay away from Judge Anne Thrope—*Miss* Anne Thrope, when I knew her. Anyway, she hates everybody." I spoke rapidly, which is a nonviolent, albeit passive-aggressive, way to assert authority.

"Okay, okay, you win," the chief shrieked in that high-pitched voice that is peculiar to Californians. "Go ahead and grill me, Miss Yoder. Grill me like a weenie."

"It would be my pleasure, dear, but first I have a few requests."

I grilled the chief while sitting on a lawn chair, on her balcony, facing the feed store. After all, no Hernian in her right mind would pass up a chance to see a truck unload or, at the very least, a stock boy burning empty boxes in a barrel. In one hand I held a mug of hot chocolate, piled high with miniature marshmallows; in the other, a ladyfinger—the cake variety, of course, not a real one.

"So," I said, pausing to lick my lips, "when was the last time you saw the deceased?"

"You know when; it was the moment he died."

"And you don't know CPR?"

"Who says I don't? Of course I do. I probably even cracked a few of his ribs. Check the coroner's report for that, will you?"

I nodded. "How long were you and Cornelius doing the Posturepedic hokey pokey, and believe me, that's not what it's all about."

"What?"

"There's more to life than sex."

"Macadamia, or filbert?"

"Excuse me?"

"Which nut are you?"

"This is a murder investigation, Your Chieftainship. This is no place for levity. Please answer my question."

"Corny—that's what he asked me to call him, so no comments from the peanut gallery—and I had been seeing each other from the day I moved here."

"That's been months!"

"Yes, the best months of my life."

"And it started the very day you arrived?" How did a strumpet attract the town's reigning playboy so quickly? Did she leave a trail of pheromones on her way into town?

"I ran down to Yoder's Corner Market to get some milk, and there he was, buying a tin of ravioli."

"And you—"

"I know what you're thinking, and no, I'm not a slut. We didn't sleep together for almost a week. We didn't need to. Corny said he found me refreshing, able to carry on a sophisticated conversation—unlike the other women he dated."

"For the record, we never dated."

"I wouldn't think so, given your age."

I treated her to a display of my teeth, which, depending on one's intent, is not the same as a smile. "During the months you were involved with Cornelius, were you aware of the other women in his life?"

"Boy, I'll say. His phone was always ringing. But in anticipation of your next question, they were not aware of me."

"They are now. There's not a sentient being in the county who doesn't know of the affair."

"Have they begun to collect the tar and feathers? Or is it to be a huge scarlet *A,* maybe with neon lights?"

"They were hoping to do both, but I convinced them that wooden stocks would suffice—provided they were too tight and stopped your circulation. We could take turns lashing you with an Amish buggy whip."

"Why is it that I'm not sure if you're joking?"

"Funny, but I feel the same way. Scary, isn't it?" I took a deep sip of cocoa. "Be a dear, will you, and refresh this. It's supposed to be *hot* chocolate, not warm."

She smiled. "My pleasure."

While she busied herself with hostess duties, I kept an eye on Kevin, a new stock boy at Miller's Feed Store. He'd come out back and was breaking down cardboard boxes to be fed into a fire barrel. Cool as it was, he'd taken off his shirt, and his muscles rippled in the firelight. Either his jeans were one size too small or he was well equipped, both in front and in back. How old was he? Eighteen? Maybe twenty? Just for one minute I'd like to get my hands on . . .

"Here you go, Miss Yoder. Hot, just like you wanted."

"Ach! I wasn't—I mean—I guess I drifted off. One is not responsible for images conjured whilst dreaming."

"Right. No need to play innocent around me, Miss Yoder. I'm the town slut, don't you recall?"

"Your words, dear, not mine. I was thinking 'strumpet.' It has more class, don't you think?"

"Please, drink your cocoa while it's still hot." She took a small sip from her own refreshed cup.

Ever an agreeable woman, I obliged her by taking a huge gulp. Now, I'm one of those few, but blessed, individuals who have asbestos throats. What is too hot for most folks is still only tepid to me. Pour boiling coffee into a cup, stir it twice, and it's just the right temperature. I even have to heat the milk I add, lest it render the beverage too cool for my tonsils.

That said, the refill the chief handed me was hot enough to singe the lungs of Lucifer. What's more, it had the vinegary taste of Tabasco. Olivia Hornsby-Anderson had played a dirty trick on me, but she wasn't going to get away with it.

My tongue screamed for relief, but I forced it to cooperate. "This is wonderful. Now be a dear and fetch me some more ladyfingers, will you?"

She nodded, her eyes wide with wonder at my ability to drink liquid brimstone. Even before I heard the glass door slide closed behind me, I was hard at work at the task at hand. Dumping my spiked cocoa over the balcony was too obvious and exacted no revenge. Yes, I know the Good Lord said, "Vengeance is mine," but with all due respect, He'd never been tricked into drinking hot sauce. No, what I needed was a solution that would spare my mouth further agony and fix her wagon at the same time. Aha! I knew just the thing.

24

Just switching mugs with my reluctant hostess wasn't going to work. Hers was white with bright orange script that read *World's Best Mom*. Mine was brown and had a pedestal base. What I needed to do was to pour her cocoa into a receptacle of some sort so that I could transfer my drink into her cup. Then I could pour her beverage into my mug and proceed to sip it smugly. But what could I use as a container?

Aha! And Mr. Langley thought I was too stupid to pass college physics. If only he could see me now. Maybe two things of equal volume and density *can't* occupy the same space at the same time, but they can be switched around with the aid of a sturdy brown brogan. And thank heavens I'd switched to brogans after my nap!

Quick as a magician I pulled off my right shoe, poured my doctored potion into it, poured the chief's cocoa into my mug, and then emptied my shoe into her mug. The transfer happened so fast, my brogan barely got wet—well, almost barely. But what's a wet foot between fiends?

I completed my diabolical deed just in time. "Are you enjoying your hot chocolate?" the chief asked. She had in her hand a plate piled high with my favorite snack.

"Scrumptious," I said.

"Really? Not too sweet?"

"It's perfect. I could drink gallons of this stuff." I chugged back half a mug's worth.

I saw her eyes dart from mug to mug as she assured herself that nothing had been switched. "Cheers," she said, and quaffed back half her mug in a single gulp.

"Good Scrabble word," I said.

She stared at me, her eyes as big and round as the saucers our mugs didn't have.

"*Quaff.* It's not a word one thinks of on a regular basis. Of course with that letter combo, it would be pretty obvious."

The chief exploded from her chair, knocking it over, and threw herself half over the rail. My instinct was to lunge for her and pull her back, lest I be the one to hear her splat on the concrete below. With my luck she'd drag me over with her, and we'd both go splat, and me not having made a final confession of sin. Then, instead of being greeted by Papa and Mama as I entered the Light, I might be saying howdy to Cousin Eldridge Hostetler, who did unspeakable things with his pony, and was mean to animals as well, and who always claimed there was no God. I know, once saved, always saved, but a deathbed confession doesn't hurt, does it?

Fortunately the chief expectorated before I could react, thus saving me from both puke and pulverization. When she was quite through gagging, she tore back inside, and I could hear the water running. She took her sweet time about returning, but I didn't mind, thanks to Kevin, the stock boy.

"How did you do that?" she demanded.

By then my shoe was steaming in the cool air, but she didn't look down. "Do what?" I asked sweetly.

"Switch the drinks?"

"Come again?"

"I have to hand it to you, Miss Yoder. You're not the yokel I thought you were."

"Another good Scrabble word—*excuse* me? You thought I was a yokel?"

"Oops, did I say that?" She clapped her hand to her mouth in what was supposed to be a coy gesture.

"So now you're mocking me?"

"Miss Yoder, you don't honestly think I would have taken this job, moved way out here to East Nothing, if I'd thought I'd have to contend with a powerhouse like yourself, do you?"

"*Moi,* a powerhouse?"

"You are a force to be reckoned with: highly intelligent, extraordinarily assertive, and extremely attractive to boot. Why are you wasting your time being mayor of Hernia when you could be governor of Pennsylvania, for crying out loud, to use one of your quaint phrases?"

"If the shoe fits," I said. "Of course I'll have to stuff it with newspapers while it dries, so it doesn't shrink."

"Aha, you've just answered my question. I forgot about the nut factor. Still, that shouldn't stop you from being governor of California, maybe even running for president of the United States. You're certainly arrogant enough."

I leaped to my feet, one sodden, one dry. "That does it. I'm not going to take insults sitting down. Do you have any more to hurl at me before I leave, pun quite intended?"

A strange look transformed her face. "Do you really have to go?"

"Criminals don't catch themselves. You ought to know."

"Miss Yoder—please, may I call you Magdalena?"

"May I call you Olivia?"

"Please do. Magdalena, I have a confession to make."

"Before you do, you have a right to remain silent. You have a right to call an attorney—"

"Not that kind of a confession, you twit. I just wanted to say that I—uh—well, this is hard to say."

"It needn't be. I already know that your handpicked underling, Chris Ackerman, is gay. And now you want to tell me that you are as well, and that you are attracted to me."

"No."

"But you said I was beautiful."

"Yes. I also think a lattice-top cherry pie is beautiful, but I don't want to date it."

I felt vaguely rejected. "Then, what did you want to tell me?"

"I wanted to tell you that, initial impressions aside, I have every confidence in you. If anyone can find Cornelius's killer, it's you."

"Thank you. If you don't mind, I'll get going now, before you have a chance to cancel your vote of confidence with a comment about me being a rube, albeit one with an aptitude for solving the Rubik's Cube."

"Nertz to Mertz," she said without missing a beat.

"What?"

"Nothing. It's from an old *I Love Lucy* show—but I forgot, you don't watch TV."

"And neither should you, dear. Who knows what you might see. I heard from Sam—you know, my cousin who owns Yoder's Corner Market—that there was a wardrobe malfunction on some show or another and that a bosom was inadvertently displayed. Of course that wouldn't have happened if the displayer had been wearing sturdy Christian underwear, but you get my point."

"Not everyone thinks it was inadvertent."

"There you go!" I headed for the sliding glass door.

"Are you all right, Magdalena?"

I turned slowly, all the while willing myself to be charitable. Given the speed at which Hernia's grapevine operates, I wouldn't be surprised to learn she'd already heard that I'd broken off my engagement to a Jewish Adonis, and was going to offer one of her shoulders for me to cry on. Well, just because we were now on a first-name basis, and might, someday, conceivably be friends, didn't mean I was going to spill my guts to her.

"Why do you ask, dear?"

"Because your right foot is making squishing sounds."

"Oh, that! I've always been a heavy sweater."

"Just the one foot?"

"Okay, I'm busted. But you have to admit it was clever, me pouring my drink into my shoe, and then into your mug. Do you think the cocoa picked up subtle undertones along the way? Foot flavors, as it were? Perhaps a little toe-jam bouquet?"

Olivia rushed to the rail again.

There are times, when my vocation impinges on my avocation, that all I really want to do is take a vacation. This was one of those times. Believe it or not, I do more than share clever quips as I traipse around Hernia in pursuit of justice.

The PennDutch is my bread and butter, and even though I can now afford to butter both sides of said bread, I feel that it is my duty to perform for my guests. Every evening I don a clean broadcloth dress (usually in a snazzy navy) and a starched white prayer cap, and polish my shoes. This night I had to dig out my backup brogans, which are a mite worn—"broken in," as we frugal types are wont to say. Anyway, given that it had been one of the very worst days of my life, I felt the urge to add an extra touch to my comely appearance. I decided to apply a lick of paint to the front door, so to speak.

That is why Freni, when she opened the pantry door, discovered me dabbing the contents of a cherry-flavored Kool-Aid packet on my moistened lips. You would have thought she'd found the family skeleton, by her reaction.

"Ach, *du lieber*!"

"Freni, you really should knock first."

"This is the pantry, for frying out loud."

"That's 'crying,' dear."

"Yah, but I am a cook."

I pursed my cherry red lips. "How do I look?"

"Like a harlot, yah?"

"Yes, but a pretty harlot, right?"

Freni shook her head and, mumbling to herself, bustled off to attend to a boiling pot. Whatever it was that brought her to the pantry was temporarily forgotten. I may be the daughter she never had, but I am, at times, as baffling to her as quantum physics. Rather than judge myself harshly on this count, I prefer to see myself as a much-needed spice in her life, perhaps curry. Never mind that I read somewhere that real curry is not a single spice, but a marriage of several spices that are freshly ground before being mixed together. The curry I buy for the PennDutch Inn comes premixed, in an attractive bottle, and the flavor is to die for.

In fact, Freni's very special chicken curry was on the menu for supper. Its fragrant aroma was what drew me out of the pantry and into the kitchen proper. I may even have lifted a lid and peered into a pot.

Suddenly, out of nowhere, a wooden spoon appeared and rapped the back of my hand. "It will make tough the chicken, Magdalena."

"Why so little?" I asked. There was enough curried chicken in the pot to serve only three Ohioans.

"The English," she said, referring to my guests, "are not liking curry. They say they want real Pennsylvania Dutch food, so they drive to Bedford. I tell them I do not write the menus, and that I eat this curry, and I am Amish, but they do not want to listen."

"They've *all* gone into town?"

"No, there is one who stays."

"Who?"

"Ach, I do not know her name. I am only the cook, not the social erecter."

"Director, dear."

"Yah, that is what I said. Magdalena, you know that I do not speak bad words about anyone—"

"Except your daughter-in-law, Barbara."

Freni frowned over the tops of her bottle-thick

glasses. "I think maybe you have hit the nail on his head. This woman is very much like Barbara."

"As tall as Goliath, but as sweet as your shoofly pie?"

"Ya, tall like Goliath."

"Freni, I was thinking that since there is only one guest tonight, and she's from Vermont—one of the thin states—and I'm not particularly hungry, why don't we make up a tray of your delicious entrée, and after supper I'll run it over to the chief?"

Freni shrugged her shoulders. Lacking a neck, her head bobbled like the head of one of those dogs you see in the rear windshield of some cars.

"Yah," she muttered, "but maybe they do not eat such fancy food in California."

"What? You've been cooking for the fruit-and-nuts crowd from Hollywood for years. If it's unpronounceable, or unidentifiable, they toss it back like a good Amish man tosses back headcheese."

"Always one with the riddles, Magdalena. Where are these Amish who throw headcheese? Iowa, I think."

"Yes, Iowa, from whence hails your daughter-in-law. I mean that the chief undoubtedly has a sophisticated palette, and a little curry is not going throw her a curveball."

"Ach, again the riddles!"

"Riddle-shmiddle. You're stalling. Out with the truth. Why is it you disapprove of me taking supper over to a lonely, grieving woman?"

She threw up her stubby arms in exasperation. "If I tell you the reason, will you climb off my back?"

25

Coconut Chicken Curry Flurry

Ingredients

¼ cup oil

3 medium onions, finely sliced

4 cloves

3 cardamoms

1 cinnamon stick

2 pounds chicken, cleaned and cut into pieces

1 teaspoon ginger-garlic paste

3 green chilies, split in half (optional)

Salt to taste

1 can (13.5 ounces) coconut milk, divided

½ cup warm water

¼ cup coriander leaves for garnish

Pinch of shredded coconut

YIELD: 4 SERVINGS

Preparation

1. Heat oil in pan. Add onions. Stir-fry till soft.
2. Add cloves, cardamom, and cinnamon and stir till mixture reaches a light golden brown.
3. Add chicken, ginger-garlic paste, chilies if desired, and salt. Mix thoroughly.
4. Then add ½ can coconut milk and stir. Let this cook slowly while adding warm water.
5. Cover pot and allow curry to cook on low heat till chicken is tender, approximately 20 to 30 minutes.

6. Add the rest of the coconut milk and mix till gravy is thick and smooth.
7. Garnish with coriander leaves and shredded coconut. Serve with rice or naan.

26

"I'll clamber down posthaste."

"It is this: The chief is supposed to be an example to the community, yah? Instead, she makes sweat in April with a man she does not marry."

"What?"

"For her the bed shakes when there is no storm."

"Oh, I get it. You're mad at her because she complains about our weather?"

Freni sighed heavily, brought to her wits' end by the dimwit I was. "The chief and Cornelius Weaver, they do the hickey poker. It is a sin, yah?"

"The what—ah, say no more! Your turn of phrase is far more descriptive than the actual name of that dance. But remember, Freni, not only does the Bible instruct us not to throw the first stone, it also commands us to show hospitality to strangers. And who could be more strange than a woman who puts hot sauce in cocoa?"

Despite the thickness of her lenses, and the grease and flour deposited thereon, I could see that my kinswoman was rolling her eyes. "Is that a historical question?"

"Something like that. Freni, I love you. Have I ever told you that?"

Fortunately when her eyes stopped in midroll, they faced forward. "Yah."

"Do you love me back?"

"Ach!"

"Between the two of us, we represent a thousand years of inbreeding. When it comes to expressing love, we are about as demonstrative as a wet dishrag. We can't even hug without those silly little pats on the back. It's either that or a death clench. If we were ever to hold each other in a still, silent embrace, what do you think would happen? Would we turn into pillars of salt, like Lot's wife?"

"Yah, salt," Freni said and added a pinch to the evening's dinner.

"Come on, Freni, let's try hugging like regular folks. Since you're vertically challenged, you put your arms around my waist, and I'll put my arms around your plump, but only slightly slumped, shoulders. We'll hold that position—no patting—while I count to sixty. What do you say?"

"I say you are *meshugganeh*."

"*What?*"

"It means there is grain in your silo, but it does not reach the top. I learn that from Ida."

"Why, the nerve of that woman! What else does she say about me?"

"That you are not—ach, I cannot say."

"That's okay. I know she thinks I'm not good enough for her son."

"Yah, that too, but—it is better I say no more."

"No fair! You can't stop now."

I've seen calmer looks on chickens with their heads on the chopping block. "So now we hug, yah?"

A bird in the hand is worth two in the bush, and my cousin's bush was an exceptionally tangled and overgrown mess. Her birds rarely found their way into my hands, so it behooved me to grab one whenever I could.

"Hug away!" I cried and threw my arms around the dear soul. But, and this was using the very reliable Mississippi One, Mississippi Two system, we'd hugged less than ten seconds before she pulled away.

"And now I will get back to work," she said.

"But you cheated! Even the real English—the ones from England—hug longer than that."

Freni muttered something that, although unintelligible, I interpreted as her final word on the subject of hugging. Although recently she has gotten better about handling her emotions, still, my temperamental cook has quit a total of ninety-eight times. I could insist that we persist in my attempt to overcome our genes, but it might well mean me having to finish preparing supper, and then cleaning up afterward.

"Righto," I said. "Cheerio, tut-tut, keep a stiff upper lip, and all that sort of rot."

"Yah, *meshugganeh*," she said, and turned to stir a pot of vegetables that was on the cusp of boiling over.

While she busied herself, I slipped out of the kitchen and into the dining room. Sure enough, the table was set for two.

It is a massive table, capable of seating twenty foreigners, or twelve Americans. Built from oak by my ancestor Jacob the Strong Yoder, it was the only piece of furniture to survive a tornado several years ago that flattened my house. Freni, perhaps in an effort to spare me a carbon copy of her daughter-in-law, had laid the place settings at either end of the table. Unless my guest and I used megaphones, we would be unable to carry on a meaningful conversation.

While it is true that I offer Spartan accommodations at a premium price, I also try very hard to make my guests feel important and welcome. After all, isn't validation what we all want most after food, shelter, safety, sex, good health, minimal taxation, recreation, competent sales clerks, easy-to-open boxes that are just that, glue that actually sticks, slow drivers who stay in the right lane, laundry products that never need improving, stiff

penalties for people who spit their gum out on side-
walks, and prescription bottles that can be read without
the aid of a magnifying glass? Personal validation is the
special touch that has made my humble inn such a huge
success, so, tired as I was, I was determined to validate
the herring out of the brave guest who'd remained behind. To that end, I moved my place setting.

27

The woman from Vermont reminded me that her name was Sidney "with an *i*," and that she was a writer.

"They're coming out of the woodwork," I said pleasantly.

"Writers?"

"That too. I was, however, referring to that line of ants moving along the baseboard. I can't figure out if they are termites or just regular house ants. Which ones have waists?"

Sidney, it saddens me to say, was not up to snuff in the manners department. Not only did she bring a notebook to the dinner table, but she had the temerity to write in it.

"House ants?" she asked, jotting something down.

"Well, they're not in the barn. Frankly, I don't mind them as long as they stay away from the food. The way I figure it, they have to spend the winter somewhere, so why not inside where it is nice and comfy? Same goes for field mice. Of course they have to stay out of the kitchen and public rooms, and my guests generally don't like them in their bedrooms, which pretty much limits Mickey and Minnie to the cellar."

She glanced around the dining room, her eyes as big as mousetraps. "You're joking, right?"

"Alas, I lack a sense of humor. The Good Lord, in His wisdom, bypassed me with the funny gene."

"You actually coexist with mice?"

"They're in the cellar," I reminded her crisply, albeit pleasantly. "It can get to below zero here in January, whereas the cellar is always in the fifties. What would you have me do, turn the poor things out into the cold so they could freeze their tails off? They don't have fur on them, you know. And, even though you haven't asked, I sweep up their cute little droppings with some regularity. It's no different than scooping out a cat box, is it? I just wish Minnie and Mickey weren't so shy. I miss playing with my pussy, which, by the way, I had to give up on account of my stepdaughter's allergies. And just so you know, she isn't allergic to mouse dander; I had her doctor check for that. After dinner, would you like to see the little darlings? Maybe even feed them some cheese? Although they much prefer smoked bacon. The whole cheese thing is a myth."

Sidney shuddered. "I'll pass on the mice, thank you. Any other critters allowed inside?"

"Don't be ridiculous, dear. This is Pennsylvania, not Maryland. I don't allow dogs, unless they're safely confined within a bra."

"I beg your pardon?"

"I'm referring to Shnookums, my sister's miniature something or other. Frankly, he looks more like a rodent than a dog. Folks have actually taken him for a rat. I certainly would not allow him to winter in my basement."

Sidney's pen was a blur as it raced across her notebook. I watched, fascinated, as she filled page after page. Finally she paused and looked up.

"Miss Yoder, tell me about your ALPO plan."

"Ah yes, the one you neglected to sign on for. Well, it's like this: For an extra fifty dollars a day, guests get the privilege of participating in the chores, much like they would if they lived with an Amish family. They get to muck out the barn, sweep the chicken house, gather eggs, clean toilets, make beds, etcetera. It's really great fun."

"I'll have to take your word for it. Now I'd like to ask you about the bed linens. Why are they so cheap and rough?"

"Cheep is what baby chicks do. My linens may be inexpensive, but they also add to the Amish feel of this place. Besides, tossing about on the hundred-and-sixty-thread-count bottom sheet—and my mattresses encourage tossing—is an excellent way to exfoliate."

"About the soap—"

"Isn't that a clever idea? Not everyone would think of taking a bunch of slivers left over from used bars and smooshing them together to form new bars."

She made a face. "But there are hairs stuck in them."

"Yes, but the color matches your own. That's why I had you state your hair color in your reservation. Personalized soap bars; what could be more welcoming than that?"

"It's disgusting, as is the food."

"What? Freni is capable of turning an old shoe into a culinary delight. She could call it Amish sole food. Get it?" I laughed pleasantly at my witticism.

"I fail to find that humorous. I took the liberty of speaking to your cook, and you wouldn't believe what I learned—well, you would, but no one else will."

"I'll have you know she cut off the part that the mouse chewed, and scrubbed the rest. But it won't happen again. Neither of us realized that mice are so fond of—"

"Stop, please! I don't want to know. What I was about to say is that she cooks with lard."

"Tut-tut, dear, you make that sound like an accusation."

"Miss Yoder, these days the only people who cook with lard are—uh, well, they're ethnic."

"But she's ethnic!"

"Which brings me to my next question. Why are you trying to pass yourself off as Amish, when I've seen you driving a car?"

I groaned inwardly, which, unfortunately, sometimes expresses itself vocally as well. "The brochure you were given upon check-in clarified that point. Since you either don't recall what it said or, worse yet, didn't bother to read it, I am *Mennonite,* and my cook is Amish. I am permitted to drive cars; she isn't. I have electricity in my home; she doesn't. I own a telephone; she doesn't—although she is allowed to use one. There are many other differences, but what unites us is a common history of religious persecution in Europe, our belief that only consenting adults should be baptized, and our nonviolent approach to life."

"Which explains the rats in your basement, right?"

"They are tiny little field mice, not rats, and my religion does not prevent me from killing them. It does, however, support the belief that human life is sacred, and that there is no justification for ending it. No death penalty, no assisted suicide, and above all, no war."

"Isn't that a little naive? What if there was a terrorist, wrapped in dynamite, about to walk into an Amish church and kill everyone in it, including little babies and sweet, defenseless old grandmothers. Wouldn't shooting that one man, before he could blow himself up, save many lives?"

"I suppose the fact that most Amish don't worship in churches, but in private homes, is not germane to the question?"

"Miss Yoder, you're stalling. Is it right to sacrifice many lives by not taking just one?"

"Only God can take what He gave in the first place," I said, quoting the official line. The truth is that, more and more, I am starting to see things from the other perspective. The Devil's perspective, I'm sure. I certainly did not need a guest, an outsider, to add fuel to the fire of my confusion.

"You honestly think God values the life of a hate-filled man—one whose stated purpose is to destroy Christianity—more than He does the life of an innocent child? Maybe twenty innocent children, depending on the size of your church?"

"Get thee behind me, Satan," I cried, and clapped my hands over both ears.

She jumped to her feet, jarring the table, which was set with gaily colored plastic tumblers I've collected from the Dairy Freeze in Bedford over the years. The water lapped dangerously close to the rims, threatening the charming feed-sack tablecloth I made one day last winter in a fever of creative activity. A neutral beige, the covering goes with most of my dinnerware, and the advertisement for Johnson's Udder Rub, with a high concentration of lanolin, adds a sense of fun to any meal.

"Miss Yoder, did you just call me Satan?"

"Absolutely not, dear. I was merely implying that the Devil was using your lips to lead me from the straight and narrow path."

"A straitjacket is more like it. I have half a mind to call the men in white coats to come take you away."

"Half a mind is worse than no mind at all. Believe me; I know of which I speak. Amelia Cornbody—who grew up on this very road, just beyond yonder dip and rise—had only half a mind, which got her elected to the Senate, where she bought into the whole corruption thing, hook, line, and sinker. Now she lives in a multimillion-dollar house, cavorts with sinful playboys, and owns her own yacht. I've heard she even flies to Egypt on taxpayers' money so she can play amateur archeologist. Meanwhile our school is overcrowded, the teachers grossly underpaid, and there are so many potholes in our roads that we've long since stopped naming them—except for the monster that opened up following last month's gully-washer. We named it Amelia Cornbody Canyon in hopes that she'd come back to look at it, so we could pin her down on a few issues. Instead, she sent a brass plaque and asked the town council to erect a monument beside her hole. Anyway, none of this would have happened if she'd been too smart to run for public office."

"Miss Yoder, are you a bleeding-heart liberal?"

"Moi?" I patted my bonnet-covered bun and tugged at my sturdy Christian bra. "Do I look like a liberal?"

"Well, I've heard all I'm going to hear. Miss Yoder, if you'd be so kind as to prepare my bill, I will meet you in the lobby in twenty minutes."

"You're checking out?"

"Just as fast as possible."

"But you haven't eaten Freni's delicious curry!"

"Dump it into Amelia Cornbody's hole, for all I care."

Those were the last words that Sidney from Vermont spoke to me. When I checked her room afterward, not only was there no sign of a tip, but one of the cute little burlap hand towels was missing. What's more, she had even taken her personalized soap.

With no one but Freni and me to eat the curry—Alison, who hates the stuff, had a bowl of cereal in her room— there was oodles left. I packaged it up in an old Tupperware container (curry will stain anything) and delivered it semipersonally. That is to say, I set it on the welcome mat, rang the bell, and fled like a roach when the lights are turned on.

It had been an exceedingly long day, and all I wanted to do was to topple into my own bed and pull my thousand-count sheet and eiderdown comforter over my head. Nighty-night, sleep tight, and don't let the bed bugs bite.

In fact, it had been such a stressful day that, when I did get home, I didn't even brush my teeth before crawling into my den. The only other times I've neglected my chompers were the night my parents died, and the first night of my honeymoon, following my pseudo-wedding to Aaron Miller. To not brush felt almost like a sin and was every bit as pleasurable as one. To sin with Aaron Miller was . . .

I thought I'd been asleep about ten minutes when I felt someone poking me. "Not tonight," I mumbled. "I didn't brush my teeth."

"Ya got that right."

I struggled to retreat back into the world of Aaron Miller, as hurtful as he was, in order to avoid the present world, one that included his biological offspring, Alison. It wasn't that I was choosing the adulterer over his daughter. I was choosing a simpler time. In that all-too-brief month in which I'd been deluded into experiencing heavy bliss, I'd felt utterly cared for. In today's world I had a murder to solve, not to mention a broken heart, one that there was no hope of mending. Alas, the present has a way of trumping the past.

"Alison?"

"I ain't gonna say that 'big as life' crap, but it is me. How come y'are sleeping in? Ya sick, Mom?"

"No, just tired."

"That's cool. But hey, ya need ta give me my lunch money. The bus is almost here."

"My purse is on the dresser, dear. Help yourself."

"Really?"

"Yes, really." I closed my eyes, so as not to wake beyond the point of no returning.

"Ya only got a twenty."

"Take it."

"Really?"

"Yes, dear. Now run along and catch that bus. Oh, and have a nice day."

"Yeah, I'd say the same back at ya, excepting ya ain't gonna have a very nice one, on account of that cute policeman is downstairs asking for ya. Hey, what's the deal with him, anyway? One of the boys at school said he was gay—the cop, not him—but I say, no way, José, 'cause whenever he looks at me, he has *lost* written all over his face."

I opened my peepers and peeped through a crack in my fortress. "*Lost?*"

"Yeah, ya know. Like the preacher's always yapping at church, about lost being one of them big sins. I didn't know what it was at first, so I asked Auntie Susannah, and she said it was like the hots."

"The whats?"

"Ya know, like sex. Anyway, this cop's got a bad case of that."

"Oh, you mean *lust*!"

"Whatever."

Fortunately for Alison, the bus driver, Miss Proschel, leaned on her horn. When she was gone I said my morning prayers, after which I took a spit bath and dressed for the day. Because my first stop was going to be the home of Hernia's horniest bachelor, I put on my sturdiest Christian underwear. One has to search high and low, and pay a king's ransom, for a brassiere with six hooks, and panties that come with a padlock, but trust me, there are times when they are well worth the cost and effort. Only a jewel thief with exceptionally nimble fingers could crack my code.

28

Doc Shafor lives on the other side of Hernia, in the shadow of Stucky Ridge, with a great view of Lovers' Leap. When I slowed to turn into his long drive, and saw him and his faithful hound, Old Blue, coming my way, I wasn't the least bit surprised. I lowered my window.

"Don't tell me," I said, "let me guess. Old Blue smelled me coming before I even left home, and after you prepared a delicious breakfast for me of ham and eggs and batter biscuits, the two of you have come to meet me."

The old geezer grinned. "Wrong. Old Blue smelled you coming yesterday, which gave me time to get up at five this morning and bake you a batch of *yeast* biscuits. Whipped up some honey butter for you as well."

"Will there be hot chocolate?"

"Do you think I'm an idiot? Of course there will."

"Then hop in, dears." Since both are a mite incontinent, you can see how much I adore the two of them.

We drove in amiable silence and, likewise, said little during the meal. Doc takes eating seriously, and given that he can cook circles around Freni, who is a great cook in her own right, I am serious when I eat his meals.

It wasn't until I'd drained my second cup of cocoa, and he his third of coffee, that we got down to business. "So, Magdalena, is my hunch right? Have you finally come to seduce me?"

I shook my head. "I keep telling you, Doc, I prefer older men."

"Older than eighty-two?"

"Much older than that. Try again when you reach a hundred."

"I'm going to hold you to that."

"I'll look forward to it."

"Well, then, if it isn't this fabulous gnarled body you're after, why the long trek out here? You break up with your New York studmuffin again?"

"It's for good this time, Doc."

"You always say that. A month from now you'll be sitting in that very chair telling me what a hottie he is."

"That's the second time this morning I've heard that word used in a vulgar way. How did you get to be so hip, Doc?"

"Which word is that?"

"Hot."

Doc leaned back in his chair and laughed. "Oh boy, if that's vulgar, then I better start training you a long time before Willard Scott wishes me happy birthday."

"Just so you know, I'm wearing my ultra-Christian underwear."

He laughed again.

"I'm serious."

"I know you are. That's what makes it so fun— Oops, I've offended you, haven't I?"

I fought back the tears. "I'm fine. No, I'm not. But it doesn't have anything to do with your teasing. Like I said, this time it really is over. With Gabe, I mean."

"Too much Ida? That, I understand. The time you sent us on that trip—"

"It's not Ida. I actually kind of like her. You and her—well, there's not many other people I can verbally spar with. Not equals, at any rate. No, it's the faith card."

Doc straightened. "He doesn't believe your way?"

"It's not *my* way; it's the only way."

"And you think he's going to burn in Hell forever and ever."

"What I think doesn't matter. But yes, it's what the Bible says."

"Sorry, but I can't help you with this one. I stopped believing in a punishing God the day my Belinda died."

"God punishes us only because we sin."

"Save your words, Magdalena. I don't need to hear about a gift of salvation through the death of Jesus, because if we don't choose the gift, then bam, we're doomed. What kind of free will is that?"

"Doc, have you become a Democrat?"

"You're kidding, right?"

I shrugged. I didn't know if I was kidding or not. I was as mixed up as a Jell-O fruit salad; that's all I really knew. That, and the fact that I hadn't really come to talk about Gabe.

"I'm switching subjects completely, Doc."

"Always a woman's prerogative, but thanks for the warning."

"As I'm sure you've heard, via Hernia's stupendous grapevine, I'm doing some investigating into the death of Cornelius Weaver, our town's second most notorious bachelor."

"I'll take that as a compliment. And yes, I've heard. He supposedly died of a heart attack, but there was a high dose of Elavil in his blood, right?"

I stared at him. "How did you know about the Elavil?"

"I have my sources. And yes, I know, they're not real, but then again, at my age I have some man-made parts as well."

"That Priscilla Livingood sure gets around."

"She's just living up to her name. But she's really a nice woman, Magdalena. I think you'd like her."

"I do."

"So, who are your other suspects?"

"Well, Alice Troyer, for one."

"Ah yes, one of this tiny burg's many claims to fame. A professional Mennonite comedienne. Won't wonders ever cease?"

"She's no longer a Mennonite—at least I think she's not. Anyway, we didn't talk about religion; we talked about the fact that Cornelius led her to believe she was the one he intended to marry. They even went ring shopping in Pittsburgh."

"Let me guess—the ring had to be sized before she could wear it."

"How did you know?"

"Oldest trick in the book. Hook them with promises, bed them, and then shove them out the door."

"Doc!"

He chuckled. "Not me, Magdalena. I don't promise them anything—except for a good time."

I blushed to the tips of my stocking-clad toes. "Spare me further details. Like I was about to say, Alice Troyer is livid. But still, she pointed the finger at Caroline Sha."

"Now *there's* a looker!"

"Excuse me?"

"The fact that she's bald only emphasizes her perfect features. Great body too."

"Yes, but you said '*there's* a looker,' as if I wasn't even in that category. So what am I, Doc, chopped liver?"

He slapped his knee. "So Ida *has* rubbed off on you. Magdalena, you poor insecure soul. I've been hitting on you since the day you turned eighteen. How many times have I said you were beautiful?"

"A million?"

"And one. And how many times have you disagreed?"

"A million and two?"

"Bingo."

"But I'm starting to believe it, Doc."

"Get out of town and back! What brought that on?"

"Doctor J. P. Skinner, I guess."

"The plastic surgeon?"

"Yes. He said I was—well, you know."

"I don't. What did he say?"

"But you do know."

"*Say* it, Magdalena."

"I can't. It'll sound silly."

"Say it loud, say it proud."

"No, I'm embarrassed."

Doc snorted. "You have got to purge yourself of that pride hang-up; it doesn't become you. Any other suspects on your list?"

I nodded. "Thelma Unruh—did you know she plans to turn that monstrosity of a house into a bed-and-breakfast? She actually thinks she can make it work because of that stupid wall."

"She probably can."

"What?"

"I've often thought of buying that house and doing the very same thing. Of course I wouldn't, not as long as you're operating the PennDutch."

"But they're just bricks, for crying out loud."

"Bricks that someone tried to use as a stairway to Heaven. Besides, it's a great house for a B and B. High ceilings, great crown molding, and a fireplace in every bedroom."

I gasped. "Oh my stars! You've slept with her too! What kind of a man-slut are you?"

Doc roared with laughter. "Did you say 'man-slut'?"

"I learned that from Susannah. It means—"

"I know what it means. Not that it's any of your business, but I haven't bedded either of the young ladies."

"But you just said—"

"You jumped to conclusions. You do that a lot, you know."

"That's how I get my exercise. But if you didn't do the twin bed twist—"

"Still using euphemisms for sex, I see. And dance terms, no less—but that was really scraping the bottom of the barrel. At any rate, sex is another word you need to say loud and proud. S-E-X. And for your information, an old goat like myself can go a-courtin', and have himself a grand old time, without it involving sex."

Don't ever throw down a gauntlet in front of me and not expect some kind of reaction. While I may have the heart of a Mennonite pacifist, my mouth is nondenominational. If Doc wanted me to say the S word, so be it.

"Sex!" I shouted. "Sex, sex, sex, sex, sex. Sexy sex. Sex in Essex, sex in Wessex, sex in excess, excess sex in Essex and Wessex."

Doc grinned. "You're downright weird. Now try the B word."

That was a little more difficult. My first two words were not *Mama* and *Papa,* but *modesty* and *pride.* The first was desirable, the second to be loathed. It is pride that leads us to believe that we are without sin. It is pride that leads to the destruction of one's soul. That said, difficult topics are often best expressed in song. I threw back my comely head, and to the tune of "America the Beautiful," tackled the B word.

> *Oh beautiful, my blue-gray eyes,*
> *My lustrous light-brown mane,*
> *For bounteous bosoms majesty,*
> *My chest is not a plain,*
> *Magdalena, Magdalena,*
> *I have a great body.*
> *I'll swing my hips*
> *And purse my lips,*
> *But stay away from me.*

Doc clapped. "Brava, brava! That was an inspiring rendition of 'Magdalena the Beautiful'—although I must admit I didn't care for the last line."

"Would you like me to sing another verse?"

"No, that will do just fine."

"Veronica Weaver said I had a lovely voice."

Doc smiled but said nothing for a long, painful period of time. While silence is golden, it can also be damning. Maybe Veronica was wrong and I really did sound like a donkey in heat. Or maybe I sounded like a choir of angels, and Doc thought I was getting greedy with my gifts.

"Speaking of Veronica," he finally said, "how is the old biddy?"

"Apparently out of pot," I said, and clamped a hand over my mouth.

"What did you say?"

"A parent who cares a lot." Okay, so it was a white lie, but who was it going to harm? The truth, however, could hurt my reputation a lot. In any case, I wasn't bearing false witness against my neighbor.

"I like you better when you stick to the truth," Doc said.

"Excuse me?"

"You heard me. Even pretending you didn't understand what I just said is a form of lying. Magdalena, we're old friends. We should be able to always tell each other the truth, because we trust the other not to judge."

I hung my head in shame. "Okay, I confess. I was curious about marijuana. I wanted to see what it was like to get stoned."

"Thank you. I respect that."

"You're not horrified?"

"Why should I be? Imagine that every one of us was required to wear a small electronic screen strapped to his or her forehead, with electrodes connecting it to the brain."

I waved my hand like a schoolgirl who's finally got her first right answer.

Doc sighed. "Yes, what is it?"

"Do the Amish have to wear those screens too? As you know, they don't use electricity."

"The screens are battery powered—they only take

three C batteries. Anyway, every thought you have, no matter how private or absurd, will flash up on your screen."

I waved again. "Do my thoughts appear on just my screen, or everybody's screen?"

"Just shut up, Magdalena, and I say that lovingly. The point I'm trying to make is that everyone, and I mean *everyone*, is going to have stuff flashing up on that screen that will shock the socks off their families and friends. I guarantee you, every single person on this planet has strange and bizarre stuff popping into their minds, even for just a millisecond. Whether or not they choose to dwell on it, that's another matter. That's why the church has ruled that the mere presence of a thought is not a sin in itself."

I swallowed hard. I think even Doc would be shocked by some of the weird things that flit through my mind. Once I imagined that I was able to transport myself back to caveman times—which, of course, never were, because they're biblically incompatible—and I had a huge box of matches and a flashlight. The cavemen were so impressed by my "magic" that they made me their queen, so I was able to tell them all about the Lord and convert them, even though there weren't any Christians then, because I wanted them to be saved just in case they, the cavemen, really did exist. That way they wouldn't be going to Hell. Then there was that time during Reverend Fiddlegarber's inaugural sermon, which was delivered outdoors on a windy day, when I pictured him flying, naked under his choir robe, over our heads as he ...

"Earth to Magdalena," Doc said.

I shook my head. "But the reverend has such big ears. And he insists on wearing a black robe with these enormous sleeves—none of our previous ministers ever wore a robe. Anyway, if he flapped both his arms and his ears just so during a strong gust, don't you think he could achieve liftoff?"

"Nah, I've already thought of that."

"You *have*?"

"Like I said, we all have strange thoughts. But the reverend would have to flap his arms as fast as a hummingbird flaps its wings, which is two hundred beats per second. Besides, he doesn't have hollow bones."

"Too bad, because lately I've been wishing he would just fly away."

"You're no longer satisfied with your pick?"

"Ding, dang, dong, Doc. When am I ever going to learn?"

"Hopefully, you'll never be through. So, Magdalena, back to your task at hand. You've mentioned Priscilla, Alice, Thelma, and Caroline as your suspects. Anyone else?"

"No. Aren't those enough?"

"How about Drustara Kurtz?"

"Oh yes, I forgot! Hey, how did you know? Priscilla again?"

"I was driving by Cornelius's house one day and saw them in a lingering parting kiss on the front porch."

"Did you linger to watch?"

"No, but I could see them in the rearview mirror. They weren't in any hurry to end it."

"The way I see it, Doc, is that there are four women who might have been very angry—angry enough to kill—at the man for not having proposed to them, and a fiancée who might have been very angry that her boyfriend wasn't faithful. So I've got motive, the means would be Elavil, and as for opportunity—they all had it. What I don't have is an eyewitness. What else is missing?"

29

"A confession."

"How do I get that? Beat it out of them? That was a joke, by the way."

"Yes, but a rather titillating image popped up on my view screen."

"If it involves me, erase it at once."

"Done. Okay, here's what I suggest: Throw a dinner party for these ladies."

"Doc, they hate each other. They're not going to show unless I neglect to mention who else is coming. As soon as they get to the inn and discover someone else is there they'll turn around and go home."

"No, they won't. All these women felt, at some point, that they were *it,* the special woman in Cornelius's life. They're all going to want a chance to drive that point home to their rivals."

"Go on."

"During dinner, concentrate on one guest—other than Priscilla—and, in your usual loud, but not too unpleasant, voice, comment on how she must have been Cornelius's true love. But make it sound confidential, as if you are speaking only to her. Trust me, there will be fireworks, and that's when the guilty party is most likely to let down her guard and say something incriminating."

"That's a wonderful idea, Doc, but how can I do that when I have an inn full of guests?"

"How many guests do you currently have?"

"Seven—well, nine, if you count the twin girls the woman from Mississippi is carrying. She's going to name one Sweet and the other Tea. Doesn't that stray beyond the borders of eccentric?"

"Would you be the pot or the kettle?"

"Doc!"

He winked. "Okay. Seven guests is no problem. Tell them you've arranged for them to have dinner with one of Hernia's living legends, an expert on local history. Arrange for them to be driven out here, and I'll fix them a dinner they'll be telling their grandchildren about. Who knows, I might even become one of the official side trips you offer your guests."

"Maybe. As long as you don't hit on them."

"Touché. But Magdalena, aren't you forgetting something?"

"I was *about* to say thanks. Honest, I was."

"It's not that; it's Chief Hornsby-Anderson."

"You mean Hot Lips?"

Doc's eyes danced. "Would you care to explain that?"

I filled Doc in on my shameful, albeit satisfying, sin of revenge. He laughed so hard that Old Blue started braying, which got me to braying, which in turn set off every dog on the south side of town.

"Shame on you, Magdalena," Doc finally said. "That was such a childish prank. Lucky for me I'm in my second childhood. Are you sure you won't reconsider dating yours truly? Think of all the fun we could have."

"Don't tempt me, dear. Anyway—getting back to business—Her Chieftainship is not on my list of suspects."

"Why not?"

"For starters, I have a gut feeling that she is innocent."

"I've always admired your gut."

"Thanks. My second point is this: Unlike the others, the chief was only using Cornelius. She neither wanted, nor expected, anything but pure, unadulterated adultery."

"Strictly speaking, since neither of them was married, it would be fornication."

I shuddered. "Doc, please don't say the F word. Now, where was I? Oh yes. My third point is that Chief need not have involved me at all in the investigation. She holds all the cards. She could have lied to the EMTs, and no one would know she was with Corny the moment he croaked—may he rest in peace. And she didn't have to tell me he had a high concentration of Elavil in his system. If she was guilty, this whole thing could have been swept under the rug, written off as simply a heart attack. Everyone in town knew about his overtaxed ticker."

"Your third point is well taken."

I stood. Doc, ever the gentleman, stood as well.

"Magdalena, you sure you can't stay for lunch? We could play rook—I know you don't use face cards—or anything you like."

"Sorry, Doc, gotta run. Say, you wouldn't mind if I took some of those biscuits with me, would you?"

"You going to Maryland?"

"No, just back into town to chat with Hernia's number one source of gossip, and listening to gossip always makes me hungry."

"Hmm, Agnes Mishler doesn't exactly live in town."

"Right, so guess again."

"The blacksmith shop?"

"Nope."

"Aha! My number one rival."

"He isn't your rival, Doc, because neither of you are in the running. Besides, he's my first cousin."

"You could marry him in South Carolina."

"Could, but wouldn't. Besides, he's married. Now, may I please have some of that thick-cut marmalade, and some real butter to go?"

I wouldn't marry Sam Yoder if he was the last man alive, and Big Bertha was broken, *and* my Maytag out of order. That's because Sam is more like an ill-behaved brother than a cousin. We're the same age and, because Hernia is such a small town, consequently we were in the same class from kindergarten through twelfth grade. Because we were seated alphabetically, Samuel Nevin Yoder occupied the desk directly behind mine. During those twelve years he cut my hair, dipped my braids in his inkwell, put gum in my bun, put a live toad in my paper bag lunch, sat on my paper bag lunch, put a dead toad in my desk, and made all manner of crude noises, some of which were accompanied by noxious odors. That said, and despite these years of torture, I felt a twinge of sadness when Sam married Dorothy. She wasn't even a Mennonite, for crying out loud.

Yoder's Corner Market stays in business only because most folks won't eat the animal feed available at Miller's Feed Store. Even Freni, from time to time, sends me into town to pick up a bottle of genuine imitation vanilla extract, or some other ingredient she didn't anticipate needing when she made her weekly trek into Bedford. This particular morning everyone in the community appeared to have been prepared, because Sam's usually packed parking lot was as empty as Aaron Miller's heart the day he stopped cleaving to me and clove to his first wife—in a manner of speaking.

The market has an irritating buzzer that sounds whenever the front door is opened. "Howdy," Sam said as he stuffed a magazine somewhere beneath the white apron he wears whenever he's on duty, which is most of the time. "If it isn't my favorite customer."

"Reading another girlie magazine?" I asked pleasantly.

Except for the white hairs that festooned the lobes, Sam's ears turned bright pink. "I don't know what you're talking about, Magdalena."

"Be careful, Sam. You already have the formidable Yoder nose. Keep lying like that, and you'll be able to turn the pages without using your hands."

His ears went from pink to red. "You won't tell Dorothy, will you?"

I crossed my toes within the privacy of my brogans. "Not if you cooperate with me."

"Cooperate how?"

"I want to know all the gossip there is to know in regards to Cornelius Weaver's death."

"Is that all? My gossip is free—always has been. You know that." He paused to rub his nose. "Wait a minute. Magdalena, are you thinking what I've been thinking?"

"I very much doubt it."

"Not that. What I mean is, do you think that the death of Cornelius Weaver was not entirely due to natural means?"

"It has crossed my mind. That's why I need to know everything you've heard about the late lothario and his between-the-sheets shenanigans. But please, clean it up a little."

"Well, as you undoubtedly know, he and our hot police chief were in flagrante delicto when he checked out. He slept with more women than a flea in a sorority house, but apparently Olivia Hornsby-Anderson knew some California tricks that drove him so wild, his poor heart couldn't stand it another second."

"Ha to the tricks part. I'm sure she's just another pretty face, but his time was up. What else you got?"

"Word has it that she's pregnant and plans to take a leave of absence and fly off somewhere secret to have the baby, then give it up for adoption, and then come back here like nothing's happened."

"Ha to that too. Who said that?"

"Gloria Reiger, I think."

"No wonder. Gloria has sixteen children, and the way her husband Caleb's been eyeing her, number seventeen will start to show before too long. Anyhoo, Gloria wants everyone to be pregnant. You know what they say about misery loving company."

Sam shook his head. "Those Amish, haven't they ever heard of birth control?"

"The more hands, the merrier—at least when it comes to doing farm chores. Anything else?"

"You're not going to believe it, so what's the point?"

"Try me."

"First you have to make a bet."

"I'm still a Mennonite, Sam—unlike some people I know. We don't make bets."

He didn't even blink. "This is a friendly bet. No money involved. If you believe there's even a ghost of chance that what I have to say *might* be true, you have to pay up."

"Sam, give it a rest. For the one zillionth time, I'm not going to kiss you. We're kissing cousins only in name. Besides, I had garlic sausage over at Doc's."

"I can tell."

"You can?"

"Don't worry, I find it rather invigorating. Now, about the bet, I stand here on my feet all day, and by closing time I can hardly walk. Dorothy refuses to give me a foot rub—she thinks feet are gross, along with several other body parts—and I could really, *really* use one. So if you lose the bet, off come my shoes and socks."

"And if I win?"

"First of all, this bet hinges entirely on you being honest. But since I know you would rather snip off your own tongue with pruning shears than let even one false word pass your perfectly shaped lips, I trust you. I just wanted you to know that."

"Oy veys meer," I moaned. Surely Sam was being

facetious. He had to know that I was capable of taking the art of lying to new heights, maybe even having it recognized as an Olympic sport. I'm not proud of this, mind you, but I will not deny that it does give me some sense of satisfaction to know that when I have fudged on the truth, I have done it convincingly, to the best of my ability. Besides, I have never lied in order to deliberately hurt someone, and, as stated earlier, I have never borne false testimony against a neighbor in court. But if, on the off chance, Sam wasn't being facetious, his words of trust, if I really believed them, would make me feel so guilty, I might be tempted to drown myself in a bowl of chicken soup, knaidlach bobbing against my forehead.

"I'd like an answer now, not tomorrow."

"Okay, okay, don't rush me already. Tell me what I'd win."

"A free shopping spree in this glorious establishment."

I sighed. "Same rules as last time I won a free spree?"

"Same rules: only one buggy load, and nothing from the specialty shelf."

"That means the jar of caviar will be here for another twenty years. It expired at the turn of the century."

"It's here for ambience, along with the pimentos and artichoke hearts. Now, what's your answer?"

"My answer is yes. Now, what's the gossip pertaining to Cornelius's unfortunate demise?"

Sam leaned over the counter so that my garlic breath was inches from his face. "I was dusting the specialty shelf, as a matter of fact, when two Amish women came in. I couldn't see them at first, but I recognized one as Drustara Kurtz's mother, Esther—you know how raspy she sounds. Anyway, she was trying to whisper but was obviously very upset about something, so they were loud whispers. I thought about coughing or shuffling my feet, but frankly I was just too curious."

"A man after my own heart—oops, don't read anything into that. Pick right up where you left off."

That didn't stop Sam from leering at me. "Esther was talking about all the pain the Nameless One had given her. She meant Drustara, of course."

"Of course. It must be incredibly hard to lose a child, even if it is just to the world."

"Are you going to keep interrupting me—no, don't answer. As I was about to say, the second voice belonged to Anna Schumacher, who, as we all know, sounds like a canary on steroids. Anna wanted to know if the wedding was still on, and if so, did Esther want to come to her house and help her bake pies for the Sunday meeting, on account of it might take her mind off things. Then Esther said that no, the wedding was off, thank you, God, and now she had an even bigger worry."

"Whose wedding?" I hollered.

Sam finally recoiled from the residue of Doc's sausages. "Give me a chance, will you? Do you want to hear it word for word, or not?"

"Not. Just give me a summary with all the pertinent facts."

"Impertinence is more like it."

"*What* did you say? Remember, it's up to me to decide if the information is worth giving you a foot rub."

"You see what you do, Magdalena? You get a man's blood going. There's never a dull moment with you. My Dorothy, on the other hand, puts me to sleep. Sometimes we put each other to sleep. Once we both fell asleep doing you-know-what."

"Not another word, or I'm going to have to poke out my mind's eye."

"So anyhow, the wedding was supposed to be between Drustara and Cornelius. Did you know that he was the reason she stopped being Amish?"

"That simply isn't true. It was on account of a Methodist boy she met during her *rumshpringe*. That one she married but is now divorced from."

"Guess again. That was how she covered it up."

"Covered up what?"

"The fact that she was pregnant with Cornelius's baby."

"You mean the darling Clementine?"

"You got it. From what I could tell, now, after almost four years, Drustara had finally pressured Cornelius into marrying her. Then she writes the tell-all book and appears on *Oprah*. Suddenly the wedding's off, and the next thing we know, Cornelius takes frying lessons."

"You mean *flying* lessons, right?"

"No. I meant what I said. That philandering scoundrel is taking frying lessons in preparation for Hell."

"Which are you, the pot or the kettle?"

"I only fantasize about cheating on my Dorothy; I've never actually done it. There's a difference."

"You should talk to Jimmy Carter, dear. But never mind that now. When was this conversation you overheard?"

"Just a day or two before Cornelius died."

"Hmm. Since Drustara was forced into exile almost four years ago, and her family banned from speaking to her, that would mean there is a go-between."

"A younger sibling maybe? One too young to be covered by the ban."

"Most likely. Sam, if I didn't know any better, I'd say you were a genius."

"Same back at you."

"What was the bigger worry her mother referred to?"

"I honestly don't know. Another customer walked in, and that was the end of the conversation. So, what do you think? Was that worth a foot rub?"

I sighed. Having known Sam my entire life, I knew there was no backing out of our deal. As for putting off the inevitable, that would be like delaying a root canal.

"Okay, I'll do it. But get me some rubber gloves and a clothespin. And, of course, lock the door."

Sam rubbed his hands together. "Sounds kinky already. I love it."

"The clothespin is for my nose, and the gloves are so I don't have to touch your feet. And two minutes is all you get."

I will pay for those two minutes for the rest of my life.

30

Garden Delight Curry

Ingredients

¼ cup oil
½ teaspoon mustard seeds
½ teaspoon fenugreek
 seeds
1 teaspoon cumin seeds
2 medium onions, finely
 chopped
2 medium tomatoes, finely
 diced
1 tablespoon tomato paste
½ teaspoon ginger-garlic
 paste
2 green chilies, split in half
¼ teaspoon turmeric
 powder
½–1 teaspoon cayenne
 pepper (or to taste)
1 teaspoon sugar

Salt to taste
Water as needed
2 large potatoes, cut into
 4 pieces each (bigger
 pieces prevent potatoes
 from being mashed)
2 carrots, peeled and cut
 into small cubes
1 zucchini, chopped into
 small pieces
1 medium green or red
 bell pepper, diced
1 head cauliflower, cut into
 small florets
1 cup peas
Coriander leaves, finely
 chopped, for garnish
 (optional)

YIELD: 6 SERVINGS

Preparation

1. Heat oil in a saucepan and add mustard, fenugreek, and cumin seeds. Cook till they begin to splutter, then carefully add onions. Mix well and sauté till onions are soft.

2. Add tomatoes, tomato paste, garlic-ginger paste, green chilies, turmeric powder, cayenne, sugar, and salt. Mix well. Cook this masala for 5 minutes. Use water as needed to keep masala from drying out.

3. Add all the rest of the vegetables except cauliflower and peas. Stir well and cook till vegetables are slightly tender.

4. Add cauliflower and peas; add very little water (¼ cup) to help steam vegetables. Stir well.

5. Cover and cook on low heat till potatoes and cauliflower are fork tender. The time could vary depending on your preference for doneness, 10–20 minutes. Add a little water if curry is too dry.

6. Garnish with coriander leaves and serve with naan and raita.

31

How was I to know that Sam did *not* lock the door? And how was I to know that Agnes Mishler would decide to bake anise seed cookies and find that her larder was low on exotic flavorings? I will, however, accept the blame for being stupid enough to kneel on the floor behind Sam's counter while I rubbed his cursed foot.

"Oh, my heavenly stars!" Agnes said between gasps.

"Nit not whant nyu nink," I cried, and then thought to rip the clothespin off my nose. "Honest!"

"It was awesome," Sam said, his face shining with pleasure.

I grabbed Sam's left foot and, struggling to my feet, managed to take it with me. Of course Sam, who'd been leaning back against the counter, had the somewhat unpleasant experience of feeling his noggin hit first the edge of the counter, and then the concrete. It was only the second time in my life that I heard a grown man cry.

"You see?" I wailed. "His foot is bare, and I'm wearing rubber gloves."

"Magdalena, you're my friend," Agnes said slowly, "so I'll try to keep an open mind. What *were* you doing down there?"

"I lost a bet—although strictly speaking it wasn't a bet, since I don't bet, but more of a friendly wager. Anyway, I lost, and as a consequence I had to rub his disgusting foot."

"Whatever you say, Magdalena. But really, would it be too much to ask of younz to lock the door?"

"It was locked," I bellowed. "Well, at least it was supposed to be locked." I glared at Sam, who was moaning on the floor.

Agnes leaned over the counter. "Yuck. You really were rubbing his feet, weren't you?"

"Desperate times call for desperate measures. I needed to get some info from him."

"Why didn't you just ask me?"

"Next time I will."

"What is it you want to know?"

"The latest scuttlebutt on Cornelius Weaver. Are there any new rumors, that kind of thing."

"The latest I've heard is that Norma Kleinfelder saw Alice Troyer's new comedy act in Bedford last night. It was at the Holiday Inn lounge, or someplace like that. They call it a comedy club, but I hear that it's mostly just filth. At any rate, Alice was telling jokes about Cornelius. How callous is that? Magdalena, she must have hated him something awful."

"Believe me, she wasn't the only one."

"Oh, but that's not the half of it. Guess who else was at the show?"

"I give up. Who?"

"Veronica Weaver, that's who. She was there with some guy—some redneck, Norma said—and she was fit to be tied. She ran up on the stage and started swinging at Alice. Called her a liar and every other name in the book. Veronica's date and the manager, or some guy like that, tried to keep the two women apart. They succeeded, but not before Alice got herself a black eye. Frankly, I've never been a fan of Veronica, what with her hippie ways and such, but between you and me, and Sam there, I say Alice got what was coming to her."

"Spoken like a true pacifist," Sam said from his position on the floor.

I gave him a gentle kick to the ribs. "Judge not, dear.

You know, what I don't get is, what was Veronica doing at a comedy club when her only child had yet to start pushing up daisies."

"What is she supposed to do," Sam growled, "roll around in sackcloth and ashes?"

"For a while, yes."

"I agree with Sam," Agnes said. "When Daddy died, I did nothing *but* watch TV. It took my mind off my sorrow."

"Cleaning house does the same thing," I said. Honestly, I wasn't trying to be mean, merely helpful. For the record, Agnes hasn't cleaned her house since her daddy died nine years ago in a coal-mining accident. Neither has she thrown anything out. The result is that every room, with the exception of the kitchen, is stacked to the ceiling with stuff, and she has to get around through a maze of unstable tunnels. How Freudian is that?

"Too bad we're not all as perfect as you," Sam said. He seemed content to remain sprawled on the floor.

"I'm not perfect."

"Yes, you are," Agnes said. "Sometimes I think we should rename our town; call it Magdalenaville, instead."

"Would I get a statue?"

"On one condition," Sam said. "That we import pigeons."

"If only domestic turkeys could fly," Agnes said. "Jonah Speicher has some big ones."

I suppose that was a joke—possibly even a filthy joke—but I didn't find it particularly funny. But the way Agnes and Sam laughed, you would have thought they'd been drinking. Every now and then one of them would repeat a hilarious word such as *turkey* or *statue,* and they would both dissolve into puddles of quivering jelly—all at my expense, of course. It wasn't easy for me to remain dignified and calm, like the mature adult that I am. What's more, it was downright weird to see them bond that fast, given that they'd known each other their entire lives and up until now had barely exchanged *hello*s.

Finally Sam staggered to his feet. "So, Agnes, what can I get for you?"

"Do you carry anise seed?"

"He doesn't," I said.

"Excuse me?" they said in unison.

"Trust me, dears. Anise seed would be found on Sam's specialty shelf, which really isn't all that special, but at any rate, I was just looking at it, and there isn't any anise seed."

"Magdalena knows all," Sam said, not without sarcasm.

For some unfathomable reason, this rude comment drew more paroxysms of embarrassing laughter. I might even have lost my cool, as Susannah says, had not our town's extraordinarily handsome, but heterosexually challenged, policeman entered the store. The laughter ceased immediately.

"What's going on?" Chris said. "I could hear you across the street in the station."

"Oh, nothing," Agnes had the nerve to say. "We just seem to be in a jolly mood today."

"The we," I said, "would not include yours truly, although I have been known to laugh in years past. Nineteen sixty-four was a particularly good year, if I recall correctly. Rather a fine, dry laugh, with fruity undertones."

Chris nodded. "Miss Yoder, I need to speak to you."

"Then you shall," I said, grateful for the interruption.

"Privately, if you don't mind. At the station."

I have been to Hernia's police station innumerable times, once even as an inmate, but I've never found it pleasant—until recently. The chief and her handpicked deputy are both native Californians and have brought with them from the West Coast a certain je ne sais quoi.

I know they brought it with them, because *quoi* is a scarce commodity east of the Allegheny River.

What used to be uninspired white walls are now sea foam green, and once-bare windows now sport balloon shades and fringed curtains with matching valances. The fabrics are soft shades of green with sophisticated accents of silver and gray. The lamps all have new shades, and instead of carpet remnants on the concrete floor, one is privileged to tread upon genuine olefin area rugs depicting abstract patterns. Even the cells have been spruced up, and the bunk beds are now covered in duvets that came with matching pillow shams (alas, one sham has been swiped). As one Hernia wag is reported to have said, "Our city jail has been redecorated by Queer Eye for the Crooked Guy." I believe this is a television reference, so I am still not sure what it means.

Although, to my knowledge, there was no one else in the building, young Chris Ackerman closed the door to his office. "Can I get you a cup of coffee or anything, Miss Yoder?"

"Well, some hot chocolate would be nice. I've got some leftover biscuits and thick-cut bitter marmalade—"

"Forgive me for interrupting, Miss Yoder, but I only said that to be polite."

I felt my heart do a belly flop in the acid pit that had suddenly replaced my stomach. "Look, I know I have a lead foot, but if I promise never, ever to speed again, and double my pledge on Support Our Local Police day, can you overlook it this one last time? I promise it's the last."

"Triple your pledge?"

"Okay," I said smugly, "but you drive a hard bargain."

"Yeah, I guess I do, because I don't know what it is that needs overlooking."

"But you said—"

"And you said you'd triple your donation, and that's

fine by me. Now, if you don't mind, I'd like to tell you why I asked you over."

With my thumb and forefinger I pretended to lock my troublemaking mug and throw away the key.

Chris didn't even chuckle. "I'm afraid I have some bad news."

"Did I do it? Am I being sued?"

"I don't think so."

"Then quit burning daylight and sock it to me."

"Miss Yoder, sometimes you don't sound even vaguely like a Mennonite."

"But I am one, so however I sound, that's how a Mennonite sounds." I threw back my head and did a marvelous rendition of a rooster crowing. "You see? That was a Mennonite sounding like a rooster. I can do a passable cow, a great sheep, but my best is a hen that has just laid her egg."

Tears filled the sergeant's eyes.

"Oh, don't get me wrong," I hastened to say. "The hen didn't feel any pain passing that egg. Childbirth pain is a punishment only we humans have to bear, thanks to Eve sinning in the Garden of Eden. It says so right in the Bible. Of course not all of us will have to experience that, because not every woman is fertile. My garden will forever be as barren as the Mohave Desert—"

"Gobi."

"I beg your pardon?"

"Forgive me, Miss Yoder, but I've heard this story before—actually, several times before. You always say Gobi Desert. And another thing, I hope you weren't implying that animals don't feel pain when they have their young, because they can feel pain. But I didn't ask you over here to discuss animal sounds or birthing pains. This is a very serious matter, and you must listen to me. Please. Without any interruptions. Is that clear?"

"Crystal clear, although being of the humble persuasion, I use glass, sometimes even blue glass, but if, perchance, I did use crystal, and it was blue, would that make me of the crystal blue persuasion?"

"Please! Not another word."

I folded my arms across my ample bosom. "I'm all ears."

Young Chris Ackerman did not need to sigh as deeply as he did to get his point across. And the crossed eyes were simply overkill.

"It's about the chief." He shook his head and sighed again. "Dang it, Miss Yoder, sometimes you really torque me off. Before I go further, I just want you to know that this is a very bad time for me, and for you to make me lose it by crossing my eyes when I should be crying, well—dang it all to pieces. Sorry, I just had to say that—heck, no I'm not sorry. You deserve more of a dressing-down than that. From now on, you're going to be quiet and listen. Do you understand?"

I nodded mutely.

"Good. So anyway, as I was about to say, Chief Hornsby-Anderson is dead. She was murdered."

I clamped both hands over my mouth, so tightly, in fact, that traces of bruises lingered for several days. Nonetheless, I was not successful in suppressing *all* sound.

"Hmphurdyknl?" I said.

Chris wisely ignored me. "I got a call early this morning from one of her condo neighbors. He was getting his morning paper when he noticed that the chief's front door was open. He investigated and found her lying on the floor of her bathroom. There was a gunshot wound to her head, but no weapon. Doctors at Bedford County Memorial Hospital pronounced her dead upon arrival. You may speak now."

I removed my hands from over my mouth. "This is horrible. I can barely believe it. She was such an—intelligent woman. A progressive thinker."

"She was like a mother to me." Chris burst into loud sobs, his shoulders shaking with each one.

"There, there," I said, employing my entire vocabulary of comforting words. "It will be all right."

"No, it won't!"

Occasionally even a walnut-size heart like mine is capable of overriding an emotionless upbringing. Here was a young man, young enough to be the son I never had, who needed more than words. And I had nothing to lose, possibly even something to gain, by going against my nature. It took a bit of a fight, but I'm happy to say that the good half of the walnut won. I gave Sergeant Ackerman the hug of my lifetime, and I didn't even make patting motions on his back.

"It will be all right," I repeated, "because I'm going to make it right."

32

With no one to ticket me, I broke a speed record getting home. I know, it's probably a sin to speed, but I'm not the only Christian to do so. Travel any highway and observe the driving habits of those folks who own cars with fish symbols on the back. Of course the fact that others break laws is no excuse for me to do likewise. I merely feel the need to point out that I am not alone.

At any rate, once back at the PennDutch, I filled a large thermos with Freni's hot chocolate—which is made from scratch, not some little packet—and loaded a wicker basket with cinnamon rolls and oatmeal cookies (one must eat healthy foods as well). Then I had the distinct pleasure of breaking the law once again on my return trip to the police station.

I doubt if Chris had moved since I left him. "You're back so soon?"

"I had a tailwind; Freni served beans last night. Now, stay here and hold down the fort."

"What do I do?"

"Nothing—except answer the phone if it rings, and eat what I brought you. I'll handle everything else."

"But you're not even a police officer."

"So deputize me."

"I can't. I don't know how it's done. Besides, I'm only a sergeant."

"Well, I am the mayor, and since I hired you, I do hereby deputize myself."

"Is that legal?"

"Legal-shmegal. All I'm going to do is get to the bottom of this. And when I do, I'll get back to you, or I'll call the sheriff."

"The sheriff?"

"You have called him, right?"

"Uh—no."

"Then, don't worry; I'll call him. He needs to know what's going on in his county. The chief was killed within Hernia town limits, but we don't know if her killer has stuck around or is elsewhere in the county. Once he—or she—steps one foot outside the town limits, he becomes the sheriff's business as well."

"Miss Yoder, I can't begin to thank you."

"No thanks needed, dear." I eyed with envy the gun strapped around his slim waist. Of course I could never bring myself to use a gun, but wearing one might still make me feel safer. Or not. I read recently in the paper about a ten-year-old boy in Philadelphia who was shot by gang members because he was playing with a toy gun in his front yard.

"You want to take my weapon, don't you?"

"Don't be silly."

"Believe me, Miss Yoder, I would give it to you if I didn't think it might get you into trouble. But I do have something you might consider."

"Tear gas?"

He shook his head as he pulled open his desk drawer. "Tear gas is tricky. You'd need training. But here." He handed me a can barely larger than a salt shaker. "It's pepper spray. A very potent variety. I took it from a tourist who was drunk and needed to be temporarily confined. She never asked for it back, and it's been more than ninety days. You're welcome to take it."

I took the tiny can and slipped it into my purse. It was surprisingly heavy. It also made me feel surpris-

ingly safe. My sister, Susannah, had been bugging me
for years to carry pepper spray, but her pleas had fallen
on a pair of shapely, but selectively deaf, ears. The Good
Lord, I'd told her repeatedly, will watch over me, and
when my time comes, it won't matter what I have in my
purse. Perhaps I'd been foolish on that score. God helps
those who help themselves, some say. And if I helped
keep myself safe with the aid of a little can, confiscated
though it was—whose business was it but mine, and the
Good Lord's?

"Thanks, Officer," I said.

"No problemo. Just remember to point the nozzle
away from you. Otherwise you could have a very bad
day."

I smiled. I had every intention of being careful, and
it wasn't me who was going to have a very bad day. As
a wise woman once said, "A hunch from a woman is
worth two facts from a man." I had a hunch that the
chief's killer and the person who murdered Cornelius
Weaver were one and the same. *That* person was going
to have the bad day.

The man who answered the door was an absolute
stranger to me. Bob Bigger was the given name of the
neighbor who had discovered the chief's lifeless body.
Bob appeared to be an affable man, rendered just a
mite subdued by his gruesome discovery. But the first
thing I noticed about him was his peculiar accent. My
guess was that Bob was born in one of the square states
well to the west of Pennsylvania.

"Mr. Bigger," I said, flashing him what was meant to
be a disarming smile, "my name is Magdalena Yoder,
and I'm mayor of this charming burg."

"Please feel free to use my bathroom. I know how it is
when you're on the go, with no place to go. Heh-heh."

"Excuse me?"

"That look on your face; I'd recognize it anywhere."

"I was trying to be disarming, ding-dang it."

"Oops. So then, what can I do for you?"

"Like I said, I'm the mayor, and also an unofficial deputized officer of the law. You may call me Your Honor, or Pseudo-Sergeant, or just plain Miss Yoder, or even Barrenness."

"Baroness?"

"Close enough. Do you mind if I come in?"

"Not if you don't mind looking at clutter."

All men should be the kind of clutterbug Mr. Bigger was. The only disarray I could see was a scattering of books across a large coffee table. One of the books was open, and I saw that it was printed in a foreign language. I have no doubt that foreigners could read it, but to me the strange markings were even less decipherable than chicken tracks. When viewing the latter, I can make out the tracks of my rooster, Chanticleer III, and my favorite hen, Pertelote.

"It's Sanskrit," Mr. Bigger said. "It's the classical language of Hindus, and the parent language of all Indo-European languages, including English. It wasn't until 1789 that Sir William Jones, an English official in India, observed that Sanskrit bore systematic similarities to Greek, Latin, and even Persian."

"You can read it?"

"Yes, but not perfectly. I'm teaching myself, you see."

"My fiancé—well, make that ex-fiancé—can read Hebrew."

"That is not an Indo-European language. Its closest relatives are Arabic and Aramaic. But I'm sure you did not stop by to discuss linguistics. If I were a wagering man—which I am not—I'd bet that you are here to question me in regards to the untimely demise of my neighbor, Chief Olivia Hornsby-Anderson."

"You'd have won your bet. That is indeed my business. Please, tell me everything as it happened this morning."

"I already told the young sergeant everything there is to know."

"Yes, but he is a bit *farklempt*—I mean, emotional—at the moment, so I'm afraid I'm going to need you to rehash it."

He rubbed a large, rough hand across his eyes. "Okay. Well, I was retrieving my paper when I noticed Olivia's door was open. I stuck my head in and called, 'Good morning,' but she didn't answer. It seems that more times than not, we pick up our papers at the same time, and occasionally we have coffee together. But she's never left her door open before, and besides, her paper was still lying there. I thought I'd bring it in and put it on the dining room table, but this morning I had a really strong sense of foreboding, so I kept calling for her. Then I started searching, and that's when I found her in the bathtub, with a bullet through her head."

Hearing the account firsthand from her discoverer had a powerful effect on me, particularly my knees. "Do you mind if I sit down?"

"Not at all."

We both sat.

"So then," I said, "you called Sergeant Ackerman?"

"Not right away. It was obvious Olivia was dead, but what I didn't know was the whereabouts of the killer. I hightailed it back to the kitchen, grabbed one of Olivia's butcher knives, and searched the closets. Under the beds too."

"That's police work, Mr. Bigger. You might have gotten yourself killed."

"Baroness Yoder, I served in the Iraq War, doing house-to-house searches. I know how to protect myself."

"I'm sure you do, but a knife is not a gun."

"True. But this killer doesn't like to make a mess, so I knew there wouldn't be any shooting at close range."

"What do you mean by 'doesn't like to make a mess'?"

"Olivia was fully dressed and in the bathtub. The killer made her get in it so that there wouldn't be a mess. Then the killer ran the shower to wash down all the blood."

"Hmm. It sounds like you know a lot about this sort of thing."

"Only from what I read. And from what I see on TV."

I noticed for the first time that one entire wall seemed to be taken up by a giant television screen. It was, however, too flat for that.

His eyes followed mine. "That's a plasma TV screen."

"Where's the motor—you know, the stuff that's inside?"

"It's in there." He picked up a remote control, like the one used by Susannah, and pushed a button. The picture that appeared was startling in its clarity.

"Is that thing expensive?"

"Yes."

"Mr. Bigger, I hope you don't mind me asking, but what do you do for a living?"

"I'm a writer."

"Get out of town!"

"I beg your pardon?"

"That's just an expression; I didn't mean it literally. It's just that this town is crawling with writers. Do I know your books?"

He pulled a slim volume from a shelf sagging from the weight of books. "This was my first book. Actually it's my doctoral thesis, which was a novella in French. I despise the cover, don't you?"

I took the book from him and turned it over. It was predominantly black, with the title, *Je suis un hareng rouge,* and the author's name printed in red.

He extracted a much thicker book from the crammed shelf. "Here's my most recent effort."

When he handed me the tome, I nearly dropped it; I've raised sheep that weighed less than that. I'll admit that it was with some trepidation that I perused the title. Heaven forfend I'd read the book and hated it. If

Mr. Bigger threw it at me, that would mark our town's second murder for the day.

Existential Questions Raised by Quantum Mechanics in the Post-Modern Age.

"So you're a philosopher as well as a writer?"

"Nope."

"A physicist?"

"Nope."

"But the title—"

"Believe it or not, it's a novel. My editor thought up that title. He thought it might be different enough to be catchy. All five people who bought the book must have thought the same thing."

"It looks very interesting," I said, invoking the common law of decency number three, the one that permits white lies that are told in order to protect someone's feelings. "I'll keep it in mind next time I'm at Barnes and Noble."

He smiled. "You asked what I do for a living, but I wasn't honest with you. I do write for a living—at least that is my intent—but it's hard to make a living that way. I admit that if it wasn't for my parents' trust fund, I'd be forced to find a more honest way to support myself."

"Drustara Kurtz can support herself."

"*The* Drustara Kurtz? The one who was on *Oprah*?"

"The very one. You know, she's very attractive, and very single. You two probably have a lot in common."

"Somehow I don't think so. She writes scintillating prose, and I write books that put college freshmen to sleep."

"We all need our sleep, dear, so don't put yourself down. Where are you from?"

That simple question took him aback. "What makes you think I'm not from here?"

"Your accent, for starters. For another, I was born and raised here, and know virtually everyone by name. Except for the tourists."

"Yes, well, I was one of those. I'm originally from

Iowa. Decided to drive across the country last summer, starting in New York, got as far as here, and never left."

"Oy!"

"Is something wrong?"

"Just that my information links have been falling down on their jobs."

"Come again?"

"I used to know every bit of gossip—from how large Amos Graber's wart had grown, to the number of lumps in the gravy Tina Blough served her mother-in-law. The answer, by the way, is twenty-one."

Mr. Bigger laughed. "Well, I keep a low profile. We writers tend to be solitary."

"Yes, but there is no excuse for me not hearing about someone as big—uh—as famous as you. I mean, you're not that big. Barbara Hostetler is taller than you, and could probably whip you with one massive hand tied behind her back, which of course she wouldn't, and not just because she's Amish, but because she's one of the sweetest people in the world. And come to think of it, she's from Iowa as well. Do you know her?"

"No. I used to know all the people in Iowa, but there's been a flux of newcomers from Latin America. Is she Hispanic?"

"*Hostetler* Hispanic? You're joking, aren't you?"

"Weren't you?"

"What?"

"When you asked if I knew her."

"Oh, that." I had not been joking, and I certainly had not been thinking. We Mennonites often know a number of coreligionists in other states, and when we meet folks from those states, we try to make connections to the people we know. We call this the Mennonite Name Game. Gabe says Jews do the same thing, except they call it Jewish Geography. But it was plain stupid to think that a nonethnic person such as Bob Bigger would know an Amish girl such as Barbara Hostetler simply because they both came from the same state, even a smallish one such as Iowa.

There are few things I hate worse than making a fool of myself. Both times it's made me crabby. And although being crabby is something at which I excel, I have found that I need to apologize less if I keep my mug tightly shut until the crabs have all dissipated. As for Bob, his crimson complexion made it quite clear that he was profoundly embarrassed for having embarrassed yours truly. Thus it was that we sat in awkward silence until I stood up to the plate.

"If Olivia's killer was as neat as you say, that pretty much eliminates one of the suspects on my list, but highlights another."

"Unless the killer was only pretending to be neat so as to throw the police off his, or her, tracks."

"Or the killer could be you, and you're playing games with me."

"That's always a possibility."

"You could be a neat person pretending to be a messy person who wants to create the impression of neatness as a decoy."

"Neatly said, but at this point I would like to state, for the record, that I have never knowingly killed anyone, Olivia included."

"Duly noted." I moved to the door.

"Oh no, you don't," he said.

33

I grabbed the doorknob and turned. "What did you say?"

"You're not getting away without giving me Drustara Kurtz's phone number. She *is* single, isn't she?"

Never let them see you sweat, someone once told me. I forget the context, but it was a futile thing to tell a middle-aged woman. I took a plain white hanky out of my recently formed cleavage and dabbed my brow.

"Your thermostat must be stuck on high," I said as I scribbled Drustara's number on the back of a church bulletin. I handed him the information. "But please, don't tell her I gave it to you. I'm not in the habit of matchmaking."

"Sure, thanks. Do you have a key?"

"I beg your pardon?"

"For Olivia's apartment. I saw the young sergeant lock it when he left, so if you don't have a key, you're welcome to use mine."

"You have a key?"

"Is that so unusual? We are—or were—neighbors. I'm home all day, and she usually wasn't. If she forgot to put the meat out to thaw, or thought she might have left the thermostat set too high"—he had the nerve to chuckle—"she'd call, and I'd take care of whatever it was."

"That must be a California thing. We in Hernia don't

generally lock our doors, and if we do, we simply leave the key under the mat, or above the door."

"Isn't that asking for trouble? A stranger could walk in at any time and walk off with everything."

"Ah, but that's just it; except for tourists, there aren't any strangers in Hernia—at least not until recently. We're like one big family, and you don't steal from family."

"You know, that's one of the things I like so much about this town." He sighed, and I could smell coffee on his breath. "That's also the thing I *don't* like about this town."

"Too clannish for you?"

He took the key from a hook by the door and dropped it into my hand. "Clannish is an understatement. Hernia makes any town in Iowa feel like London, or Paris, by comparison."

"Well, now you've got a phone number of an available woman you can pursue, and if that doesn't work out, I'll give you my sister's number. But you'll have to wait until she gets divorced. Her husband is a convicted murderer, which is neither here nor there, but explains why he's there, and not here."

"And you?"

"Oh, I'm here, but not always there, or so some would have me believe."

"I mean, are you available for dating? I see you're not wearing a ring. I also see a band of white skin on your ring finger."

I looked at my finger and feigned surprise. "Why I'll be dippty-doodled! How on earth did that get there? Excuse me, dear, while I dash off to solve yet another riddle."

Writers are a nosy sort. For them, everything is fodder for the grist mill that eventually churns out plots and characters. I'd sooner be stuck in an elevator with a hungry anaconda than with a writer of fiction. If a snake devoured me I would at least, eventually, return to the earth as fertilizer and soon become dust. The writer, on the other hand, would twist my life like a pretzel before committing it to the page, where it would sit for all eternity in the basement of the Library of Congress.

I knew without a doubt that Mr. Bigger was going to be watching through his keyhole, so I went downstairs, got in my car, and drove to the end of the block. After spending a good five minutes jotting down notes and squeezing out a blackhead, I hoofed it back to the apartment and crept up the stairs like a leopard on the prowl. Olivia's lock, thank heavens, opened soundlessly, as did her front door. I was in.

Despite my deeply held religious beliefs, I still found it spooky to be in a dead woman's apartment, especially a woman who had been murdered just hours ago. I know, put your faith in the Lord, and He'll take care of you. But will He take care of me like He took care of the twenty-some survivors of a recent plane crash that made national news, or like He took care of the two hundred *dead* passengers? And will He take care of me like He took care of the family of five who survived a tornado by seeking refuge in their basement, or like He took care of the family of eight who perished when their house disintegrated around them? And don't get me wrong, I'm not afraid of ghosts so much as I find them annoying. Both Mama and Grandma Yoder have interfered in my life post-corpus, so to speak.

Of course I started with the bathroom. Frankly, I was a bit disappointed with what I saw. I'd always thought Californians placed a high value on atmosphere, such as scented candles, flowery soaps, and the like, but the chief's throne room, the bathtub excepted, would have met with the approval of even the most dour of my acquaintances, myself included. The walls were beige, the towels soft, but brown; even the toilet paper said more about function than aesthetics.

With one hand covering my eyes, I drew the shower

curtain back slowly. I must have peeked through my fingers a dozen times until it dawned on my overloaded brain that there was nothing to see. The tub was a lot cleaner than the ones back at my inn. If the chief hadn't been cooling her heels in the county morgue, I would have made it a point to ask her which brands of cleaning products she used.

Mine is only an amateur eye, but it doesn't take long to search a mostly empty apartment. Nothing struck me as particularly out of the ordinary, except for the chief's eating habits. Californians, in my experience, tend to be grazers. That is to say, they devour an inordinate amount of uncooked greenery. I know this because my guests sometimes request various edible leaves and roots, the names for which either I've never heard before, or else I've heard used for things other than food. Once, in an effort to keep a conversation going with a Hollywood starlet, I asked her how the shopping was on Radicchio Drive. Without batting a false eyelash she told me about an upscale Japanese store where she'd just purchased a fabulous crouton for her guest bedroom. At any rate, the chief's larder contained nothing but boxes of cereal and frozen TV entrées and, of course, Freni's fabulous curry. In my opinion, aside from her affair with Cornelius Weaver, the chief lived a very lonely existence.

There was nothing else for me to do at the Narrows but take some photographs and try to lift some fingerprints. It was Olivia Hornsby-Anderson herself who taught me the art of fingerprint lifting, and the irony of it was not lost on me. When I was through with my police work, I said a silent prayer. We Mennonites do not pray for the souls of the dead, believing, as we do, that their fates have already been sealed. My prayer was for insight on how to proceed next, the wisdom to use my insight to its best advantage, and the strength to deal with whatever else my investigation turned up. I suppose I could have just asked God to solve the case for me, but experience has taught me that the Good Lord prefers that I travel the difficult route.

I learned to pray at my mama's knee, and she at her mama's. They were long-winded women, so their prayers never stuck to just one subject. Having asked the Good Lord's help with the murder cases, I prayed that He would heal the gash that Gabe had inflicted on my heart, I beseeched Him to make Alison more interested in her schoolwork, I thanked Him for my good health, as well as Freni's, and finally I asked Him to motivate Herman Lichty to see a good dermatologist about the ever-changing mole on his forehead.

Having got my spiritual ducks in a row, I locked the door to Olivia's apartment securely behind me. You can be sure I pocketed the key.

My guests were thrilled to be invited to Doc's house for dinner. My suspects were far less enthusiastic about dining at Chez Magdalena. It wasn't until I thought to bribe them with a door prize that *might* include a luxury vacation that they all agreed to come. Given the sensitive nature of the evening's true purpose, I gave Freni the night off. My pseudo-stepdaughter adores the woman, so I sent Alison home with her. As for the meal, there is nothing wrong with Chef Boyardee from a box. Besides, I intended to add some of my own toppings.

It was no surprise to me that Caroline Sha, the one who lived the farthest from my house, was the first to arrive. Counterculture people are, in my experience, either extremely polite or rudely indifferent to common courtesies. Caroline, a student of the East, would rather be early than show disrespect by arriving even a minute late. I watched through a lace curtain as she hurried up the walk and then slipped off her shoes before ringing the doorbell. While I very much appreciated her promptness, at the same time I couldn't help but find it slightly annoying.

I opened the door just a crack so that I would be heard. "No, thank ya," I called in my best Maryland accent, "we already done give once this year."

"Magdalena? Is that you?"

"Put away that gun, Homer, 'tain't nothing but a woman in a blue and white bedsheet."

"Magdalena, that *is* you, and for your information, most Marylanders speak better English than you. Shame on you for making fun of an entire state and perpetuating a stereotype."

I flung the door open. "How can it be perpetuating a stereotype when you're the only one to hear me, and you're not likely to pass it on?"

"That doesn't matter. Words have power and should never be spoken without intent. Those mean-spirited comments of yours are now woven into the fabric of the universe forever."

I pulled her in so that the chilly night air wouldn't be part of my heating bill. "Have you been watching *Oprah* again?"

"The woman is a saint, and I won't have you mocking her."

"Very well. I would ask you for your coat, but you're wearing only a sheet. Come to think of it, you ought to be wearing a comforter or a duvet over it, not a coat."

"It's a *sari,* and you know it."

"Sorry."

The doorbell rang again, and because I was standing right next to the chimes, I nearly jumped out of my brogans. "Ding, dang, dong," I said. "Oops, sorry again. I really need to work on my swearing."

"That's not swearing, Magdalena."

"Yes, it is. Those might not be swear words, but the intent was there."

"You're weird."

"*I'm* weird? I'm not the one who lives in a paper house—"

The doorbell rang again. More than a bit annoyed at

having my lecture interrupted by an impatient guest, I gave the door a good yank.

"Oh, my stars," I said when I saw what was standing there. "Oh, my ding-dang-dong stars."

34

Cows seldom ring my doorbell. Therefore, it is quite un-understandable that I should swear again, this time upon seeing a black-and-white cow, standing upright, on my front porch.

"Hello, Magdalena," it said.

"Excuse me, dear, while I pinch myself." I gave my arm a good tweak, but the bovine specter did not disappear. That meant either I was still asleep, or the next car to pull into my driveway would contain the men in white coats.

"Please tell me I'm not the first to arrive," the cow said.

"There's more of you? You mean like a herd?"

The cow snorted, sounding more like a horse than a Holstein. "That depends on how many you've invited. Who knows how many of us there are altogether."

I gave her the once-over. She had a small udder but sizable teats. When freshened, which is farm talk for having been caused to lactate, she could be a decent milker.

"What's your capacity, dear? How many quarts?"

"A gallon even, morning and night."

"I already have two Holsteins that average better than that. So listen, dear, can you move this dream along a little bit? Better yet, morph into a handsome man in his late forties. Just be sure he's single, but not com-

mitment phobic. Oh, and he has to floss and trim his
nose hair on a regular basis. I don't know why men
want us to be well groomed, but they can't be bothered themselves. Not that good grooming was ever an
issue for the Babester. He excelled at what he called
his 'metrosexual routine.' Hmm, in retrospect I wonder if that was part of the problem."

"What?" The cow pulled off her head. "Magdalena,
you're even weirder than they say."

I stared at the headless cow—except that she wasn't
really headless. Protruding above what I could now see
was a cow costume was the not-so-comely head of Alice
Troyer, the comedienne. Perhaps the fact that she was
dressed in a Halloween costume should not have come
as a surprise to me, but I've had a hard life and, in particular, a very difficult last few days.

"Alice! It's you, and you're not really a cow!"

"Magdalena, enough with the pretending. Who else
is here?"

I willed myself to appear as sane as the next person.
Given that the next person showed up to a dinner party
dressed as a cow, it didn't take a whole lot of work.

"Caroline Sha is here. And to answer your earlier
question, I've also invited Thelma Unruh, Drustara
Kurtz, and Priscilla Livingood."

A smile spread slowly beneath her radish nose.
"That's it?"

"Isn't that enough?"

"You know what I mean, Magdalena. I know you do.
You didn't fool me for a second. I'd bet my life that
everyone here tonight—with the exception of yourself—has thrown herself at Cornelius Weaver. May he
rest in pieces."

"How unkind of you!"

"Okay, so maybe you too were a victim of his
charm."

"That's much better. Now, come on in. I'm about to
freeze my tootsies off."

*   *   *

The rest of the Weaver harem arrived momentarily, and after a minimum of hissing and claw baring we proceeded straight to the dining room. I, of course, took my rightful seat at the head of the table, but not until I'd served each a tall glass of milk and two slices of home-made pizza from a box. As was expected of me, I said grace, extending the prayer until the milk was warm and the pizza cold.

"Is there something to drink besides milk?" Caroline asked the second I said "amen."

"Water."

"What's wrong with milk?" Priscilla said. "The female cow hormones help keep one's skin smooth."

"I thought that was called an acid peel," Alice said. After having received barely a snicker from the others, the standup cow-cum-comedienne had changed into proper clothing.

"Cow's milk," Caroline said, "is meant for baby cows—calves, that is. What right do we have to drink it at their expense?"

"That's not how it works," Drustara said, shaking her lovely auburn locks. "Modern dairy cows produce far more milk than their calves require."

"You're missing the point," Thelma Unruh said, adjusting her tinted glasses. "Caroline eschews animal products."

"So *that's* how *eschew* is pronounced," I said.

Priscilla patted milk residue from her lips, which were full to bursting with collagen. "But that's ridiculous— drinking soy milk instead, I mean. Doesn't that keep mama soybeans from making baby soybean plants?"

"Ha!" I shall not divulge the identity of the childish person who drew a numeral one sign in the air to signify a point scored.

Drustara's emerald green eyes narrowed into slits. "All this talk about not drinking milk is ridiculous. What you should be upset about is the way veal is produced."

"Pray tell," I said, although I already knew.

"The calves are isolated from their mothers and kept in pens so small they can't turn around, or stretch out when they lie down. The reason they spend their short lives standing in one position is so that their muscles atrophy, keeping the meat soft and tender. They are also kept in the dark, and never get to see sunshine. They never get to run and play, or be nuzzled by their mothers. Their liquid food is intentionally low in iron, which makes the calves anemic, producing the pale color of veal. These are baby animals, mind you, not cabbages. Anyone who eats veal, in my opinion, is either ignorant or heartless."

"But I love veal," Priscilla said.

"How do we know this isn't propaganda?" Thelma said.

"Because we raised dairy cows," Drustara said. "Papa sold the extra calves to Mr. Kleinhoffer, who produces veal. I rode along with him once and saw what happens with my own eyes."

"Ladies," I said pleasantly, "don't you think it's odd that Alice showed up in a cow suit, and that's all we've talked about so far?"

"It's not odd at all," Thelma said, putting her two cents in. "Visual stimulation is very powerful. If she'd come dressed as a carrot, we'd probably be—"

"If we didn't kill animals at all," Caroline said, "we wouldn't be having this conversation, and the calves would be out in meadows frolicking with their mothers, and not held in torture chambers."

"And you," Thelma spat the words, "wouldn't be interrupting me."

The room erupted into righteous rancor as my guests debated whether or not plants had feelings, the pros and cons of drinking cow's milk, and whether laws should be enacted preventing the raising of veal calves. While I don't mind spirited conversation, chaos was not going to advance my agenda.

I tapped on my water glass with a knife. Ruth Redenbacher, who attends my church, can play entire hymns just by tapping on partially filled glasses. She supplies her own glasses, which some say are of an exceptionally fine quality. My tumblers are cheap, as is my cutlery, so the ensuing sound was anything but musical.

"Order in the house, order in the house!"

That brought the volume down to a dull roar. I kept tapping until the irritating sound was all that could be heard.

"Really, dears, you're almost as bad as my fourth-grade Sunday school class. They, however, are forced to be there by their parents. You, on the other hand, are my guests, here by your own volition to enjoy my largesse."

"Then, bring it on," Alice said.

"Excuse me?"

"I've eaten cardboard tastier than this pizza. Please tell me this isn't all there is to eat."

"Are you in the habit of eating cardboard on a regular basis?"

Everyone laughed, except Alice Troyer, who scowled at me. "Magdalena, you'll never make it as a comedienne."

"You're quite right. Thank heavens, that was never my intention. But now storytelling I'm rather good at that, if I must say so myself. So ladies, feel free to eat your tasteless pizza, while I amuse you by telling you a story I heard recently, and thought you might all enjoy."

I ignored the moans.

"Once upon a time," I said, "there was a handsome prince named Conrad, who lived in a castle in the center of town. He was the richest man in the kingdom, and every maiden longed to be his wife. The prince, however, had no intention of settling down—"

"Yes, he did," Priscilla practically shouted.

I glared at her. "This is *my* story, and in my story he never intended to get married. So anyway, the maidens could be rather pushy, but the prince, being a man, didn't really mind. He set up a schedule and saw the women on a rotating basis, somewhat like in a harem, and might have gone on doing that forever. However, one of the fair maidens grew intensely jealous of the others, and whenever it was her turn to see the prince, she managed to slip a drug into his mead—there, I've always wanted to use that word in a sentence. At any rate, the drug wasn't potent enough to cause any harm by itself, but the prince, you see, had a heart condition. One day this drug triggered a heart attack and the handsome prince died."

"Was the prince misbehaving with the village constable?" It was Alice Troyer, of course, but no one laughed.

"That wasn't funny," Thelma said. "I loved the prince—I mean—well, you know what I mean."

"Indeed, I do," I said. "That's why you're all here. Now back to my story, dears. You see, unbeknownst to all the women in the prince's life, he was a very paranoid man. I have heard that great wealth sometimes does this."

Drustara tossed her fiery mane indignantly. "Who better to know this than you, Miss Yoder?"

"I wouldn't talk," Priscilla said. "I hear that you made a million dollars just from being on the *Oprah* show."

"You heard wrong; it was closer to two million."

Everyone gasped, except for yours truly.

"Then what," said Thelma Unruh, "are you still doing in this backwater town? If my bed-and-breakfast takes off, I'm out of here. I can't wait to leave this pitiful mind-set behind me."

"Magdalena stayed," said Caroline Sha.

"That's because she has family here," Alice said, much to my surprise. "And that's why Drustara is still here, even though her family doesn't speak to her."

"And don't you presume to speak for me," Drustara snapped.

I tapped my glass again, as much for the irritating noise it produced as to get their attention. "Ladies, please. I haven't finished my story. As I said, the prince was paranoid, and installed hidden video cameras in each room. After he died, the village constable found the cameras and was able to catch the woman who had slipped him the drugs."

"Bull," Thelma said.

"I beg your pardon?"

"You heard me. There weren't any hidden cameras in that house." She turned to the others. "She's just trying to scare us."

Alice snickered. "You meant palace, didn't you, Thelma?"

Thelma removed her tinted glasses, the better to glare. "I meant what I said. Come on, girls, don't be stupid. You know she's up to her games, and we all know we're the mice she's trying to catch." She turned to me. "And you're the big old Cheshire cat, Magdalena. That big grin of yours makes me sick. Just because we loved a man who was incapable of loving us back, that's no reason to mock us."

"But he did love me back," Priscilla said, sounding on the verge of tears. "We were getting married. In just three more days."

"There, there," I said comfortingly. Of the five of them, she was my favorite. Thanks to her, and Dr. Skinner, I had an entirely new self-image.

"Face it, Priscilla," Alice said. "Take away the silicone implants, collagen injections, artificial bone implants, cadaver skin grafts, not to mention the fat either sucked away or relocated, and Cornelius would never have looked at you twice. You were to be his trophy wife—all sixty percent of you." She leaned forward, pretending to examine Priscilla closely. "Joan? Joan Rivers? Are you in there?"

"Alice is full of malice," Thelma hissed.

Caroline stood, her fluttering robes creating a soft

breeze. "I'm not sticking around for this. There's enough bad karma here to hold me back for another two life-times."

I smiled kindly, ever the generous hostess. "Would you like some pizza to go?"

"No, I would not. Magdalena, you are what you eat, you know. Processed flour, animal milk cheese—it's a wonder you look as good as you do."

"It's all in the genes, dear, and I don't mean my Levi's. Of course I don't own any pants, because pants are men's clothes, and the Bible wants me to dress like a woman, which is really confusing if you ask me, on account of all the pictures of men in my King James Bible show them wearing long dresses, but I digress. Now, where was I? Oh yes, I've always heard that it's not what you put into your mouth that counts, but what comes out."

"And I don't disagree with you. I don't gossip, or call people names, and I try really hard not to let negative emotions, like jealousy, take over. So if you're still bent on catching Cornelius's killer by provoking someone into a confession, or even just a slip of the tongue, you won't be needing my presence."

"Nor mine," said Drustara. She stood as well. "I had a hard time finding a babysitter on such short notice, and may have imposed upon my neighbor too much. I thought this evening was going to be one of remem-brance, not a mystery dinner theater."

"Here, here," Alice said, as if she wasn't to blame for anything.

"Bull," Thelma said. "You're probably having a blast dredging up material for your comedy routine. Well, I have news for you, missy, there's nothing funny about this, just like there's nothing funny about your show."

Alice's radish-shaped nose was now radish-colored. "You little—"

Thank heavens the phone rang. While I ran to answer it in the kitchen, I waved at the women.

"Run along, dears. Shoo, shoo!" As the door swung shut behind me, I grabbed the phone. "Magdalena's love palace," I trilled into the receiver. "Brotherly love, of course, not the other. Although sisterly love would be more appropriate, given the circumstances. Then again it wouldn't apply at all, so I take it back. So, hello?"

"Magdalena, are you sitting?"

It was Deacon Leonard Kirschbaum from Beechy Grove Mennonite church. When the Good Lord created Leonard, He omitted any brain cells that have to do with humor. He did, however, receive an extra dollop of wisdom, which makes him invaluable as a church board member.

I pulled up a chair. "Yes."

"It's about Reverend Fiddlegarber."

"Oh no! Not him too!"

"I'm afraid so. Even though it didn't come as a complete surprise, it's still unbelievable. Magdalena, what are we going to do now?"

"First catch a deep breath. Then see if Reverend Lantz from First Mennonite Church can preach at the funeral, and then—"

"Reverend Fiddlegarber didn't die."

"Of course he did. You just said—"

"Magdalena, he took over your church."

35

"Jammin' " Gulab Jamun

For the syrup

2½ cups water
2¼ cups sugar
1 pinch saffron
¼ teaspoon freshly ground
  nutmeg

¼ teaspoon yellow food
  color
½ teaspoon rose essence or
  1 tablespoon rose water

For the Gulab Jamun

Ghee (clarified butter) for
  frying
Light oil for jamun platter
  and for shaping jamun
2 cups Carnation milk
  powder or any brand
  nonfat milk powder
1½ tablespoons self-rising
  flour

½ cup warm milk
1 teaspoon ghee
½ teaspoon crushed
  cardamom seeds
¼ teaspoon crushed
  saffron

YIELD: 8 SERVINGS

Preparation

1. Prepare the syrup: Combine water, sugar, saffron, nutmeg, rose water, and food color in a heavy-bottomed saucepan and bring to a boil, constantly

stirring till sugar is dissolved. Raise heat and allow syrup to boil for 5 minutes, then lower and let simmer 5 minutes. Remove from heat and set aside.

2. Prepare the jamun: In a wok or wide-mouth pan, add enough ghee to reach 2½ to 3 inches deep. Heat ghee over very low flame.

3. Set aside a platter brushed with a very thin film of light oil.

4. In one bowl combine the milk powder and flour.

5. In a separate bowl combine the warm milk and ghee; set aside.

6. Gently sprinkle enough milk-ghee mixture into the dry ingredients, mixing all the while, till a soft dough consistency is achieved.

7. With clean hands covered with light oil, separate dough into 24 equal portions. Take each portion and roll in your palm using both hands till a smooth ball shape, jamun, is achieved. Set jamun on oiled platter. Shape remaining dough in the same manner.

8. Make sure the heat for frying is on low (you may need to raise the temperature a bit).

9. Gently lower jamun into ghee (they will fall to the bottom).

10. Very gently move the jamun with a wooden spoon to ensure even browning on all sides. This will take some time.

11. The jamun will rise; continue to cook gently as the oil temperature rises. Proper cooking should take around 30 minutes total.

12. Remove and drain jamun with slotted spoon and gently lower into syrup. Allow jamun to soak in syrup for at least 1–2 hours before serving; stir with spoon to gently coat. Jamun may be refrigerated in a tightly sealed container for a few days. Be sure to warm or return to room temperature before serving. Some even like them cold.

13. Decorate with crushed cardamom seeds and a few sprinkles of saffron.

Notes

- The trick to making really nice jamun is to fry them over low heat. Be careful not to brown the jamun too quickly and be sure to cook them long enough. You may break the first fried jamun to ensure the inside is done, but after 30 minutes, it should be.
- If the jamun collapse in the syrup, fry them for a few minutes longer and try to soak again. Do not refry soaked jamun.
- Be sure each jamun is thoroughly soaked in the syrup before enjoying.
- Use only ghee or unsalted butter for frying the jamun; do not use oil.

36

Allow me to explain. Beechy Grove is not *my* church. Well, it is—but it's not *just* mine. True, I was dedicated there as an infant, then baptized when I supposedly reached the age of reason, and I was married there (albeit illegally), but lots of other people have celebrated their life stages there as well. Okay, so I am a deaconess, and a board member, and the church's largest contributor, and when I say jump, the pastor usually asks me how high, but can I help it if the Good Lord chose to bless me monetarily?

"Leonard, what do you mean he 'took over' my church?"

"Tonight was the board meeting, remember? We were supposed to vote on which direction this congregation is going to take for at least the next three years."

"No, dear, that's not until—oh, my heavens, oh, my stars! I wrote it on the calendar in the wrong square, so I drew arrows down to the square beneath it—never mind. Tell me what happened!"

"Well, there are seven people on the board, as you know, and the reverend. But tonight Fred Fisher wasn't there; he's on vacation in Baltimore—his wife always wanted to visit someplace exotic. And Mabel Plank wasn't there; she's helping out her sister in Intercourse—the one who broke her hip. Of course Jimmy Spegootz is still up in Canada, trying to wrap up his father's estate—I don't think he's going to inherit very much because the old man was a drinker. That's it for our faction."

Our *faction*. Shame, shame, triple shame on us, the members of Beechy Grove Mennonite Church, for having such things as factions. It wasn't always this way. Under Reverend Schrock our unified flock prospered. But with his passing—if one can refer to a murder in such peaceful terms—fissures immediately appeared, and even before I hired Reverend Fiddlegarber, our congregation had essentially aligned themselves behind two ideologies. One—the correct one, I must add—was the traditional. Believe me, there are plenty of folks like myself who believe that some of the more progressive Mennonite groups have thrown the baby out with the bathwater. The other faction was, as one might have guessed, more contemporary in their observance.

My beef with the latter is that they are free to join First Mennonite if ladies in pants, television, and waggling hips while dancing is what they want so badly. Why do they want to change the status quo when an alternative already exists for them? What are the rest of us supposed to do? Join the Amish? I don't *think* so! Big Bertha is one of my few delights in life. As an Amish woman I wouldn't even be allowed the electricity with which to operate her. Bye, bye, Bertha; that's what my option would be.

Unfortunately, relaxing the rules is not all the faction wants. They want a large screen at the front of church, upon which they can project the words of the hymns, and they want the freedom to jump up and down like Holy Rollers, and they want to start banging on doors seeking converts like Jehovah's Witnesses. *Charismatic evangelicals,* that's what they call themselves. C.E., for short.

"Magdalena, Magdalena—Magdalena! Are you still there?"

"Of course, dear. I'm in the state of Shock, and the

capital city is Dismay. So what happened at the meeting?"

"It was a slam dunk for the other side, that's what happened. All four of the others voted for going the C.E. route."

"All four? But that means Reverend Fiddlegarber—"

"That's exactly what it means. The reverend didn't waste any time fiddling around, did he?"

"But this can't be!"

"Of course it can, and it is. But it's only half of it."

"Shall I prostrate myself on the floor for the rest of the news?"

"That might be a good idea. You see, Reverend Fiddlegarber turned out to be more of a Fiddle*grabber*."

"You mean he sexually assaulted someone?"

"No, he hijacked the church."

"What does that mean?"

"Beechy Grove Mennonite Church is no more, that's what it means. He and his three puppets are now calling it the Voice of Armageddon Cathedral."

"But that's impossible. Four people can't hijack an entire church."

"Not to hear them tell it. They claim to have polled the membership and that one hundred sixty-three families are joining them in what they call 'a spiritual revolution.' "

"I don't believe it."

"You're not calling me a liar, are you, Magdalena?"

"Of course not, Leonard. But this is the first time I've heard about this. Don't you think that if they'd really polled the membership, someone would have told me? You know that a Hernian entrusted with a bit of gossip is like a Cornish hen trying to hatch an ostrich egg on the sly. Sooner or later, something's got to pop out and give the show away."

"Yes and no. I don't think they've polled everyone—certainly not me—but I have no doubt they've approached a good number of like-minded members. They seemed pretty confident."

"Then I'll sue. I have more money than a Christian has a right to have, and I'll spend every last penny of it recovering what's left of Beechy Grove Mennonite Church. Even if it's just the building—wait just one egg-hatching minute! The building! The deed is made out to Beechy Grove, not VAC."

"I beg your pardon?"

"Voice of Armageddon Cathedral. You just said it. Please, Leonard, stay with me."

"Actually, Magdalena, I'm one step ahead. Before calling you, I pulled out my copy of the deed. There's a clause that says, in effect, that the actual name of the congregation is subject to change, given the nature of Protestant churches, which, sad to say, is one of division."

"Division indeed. How many Protestants does it take to change a thousand light bulbs?"

"One for each denomination in America."

"So you've heard the joke. Leonard," I wailed—and wailing *is* appropriate at times like this—"what are we going to do?"

"I don't know. One option is to join First Mennonite; another is to stay and fight—I just don't know."

"How can we stay and fight when they've already wrested the church away from us?"

"We could fight from within. By that I mean fight spiritually."

"Of course." Leonard was free to mean anything he pleased, even if it didn't make a lick of sense. But I knew another way to fight, and dyed-in-the-wool pacifist that I am, I've never been known to back down from a good fight.

"Magdalena, I don't like the sound of that."

"Don't worry, Leonard. You crank up your praying machine—there's always room for prayer—while I drag out the big guns."

"The big guns? I don't like the sound of that either."

"When I'm through with Reverend Fecklessgrabber,

he'll rue the day he stepped foot into Beechy Grove Mennonite Church."

"May I remind you, Magdalena, that you're the one who brought him to Hernia."

"To say touché would be cliché. I take full responsibility for this, and I will rectify my mistake posthaste."

He sighed so hard into the phone, I could feel his breath stir the downy hairs on my forearm. "Good. I'm counting on you. Shall we take a moment to pray together?"

"*Now?* Over the phone?"

"Yes. Believers do it all the time."

Leonard is a world-class prayer. Once he gets started, you either have to wait it out by telling stories in your head, or take a nap. I had neither time nor patience that evening.

"I think I'll pass, dear."

"Pass on praying? Magdalena, what's gotten into you?"

"Leonard, I just remembered something vitally important."

"More important than praying?"

"God helps those who help themselves," I said. Then I hung up and raced for my purse.

Not every church can lay claim to owning a parsonage. Some congregations simply cannot afford the expense, whilst others find it too much bother. Then again, many ministers—or their wives—are too picky about their accommodations to settle for what the church is willing, or able, to provide.

We, the members of Beechy Grove Mennonite Church, have found that supplying agreeable quarters for our pastor allows us to pay him a much smaller salary than we would have had to shell out had housing not been provided. Our parsonage is a sprawling Victorian house in the heart of the historic district and is the envy of all who have seen it. In the past, virtually every candidate that I have interviewed for the job of minister has accepted the position by the time we are done touring the house. Many of them don't even see the church before saying yes. Why, then, I wondered as I pushed the doorbell, was Reverend Fiddlegarber so ungrateful?

There wasn't a single light on in the parsonage that I could tell, but the door was answered within seconds. "Reverend, it's me, Magdalena Yoder, as big as life and twice as pretty."

"What the heck do you want at this time of night?"

"To come in? Tsk, tsk, dear, you really should clean up your language."

"This is my house, and I can speak like I want in it."

"Actually, it isn't your house. That's precisely why I'm here."

"Go away, Magdalena, or I'm calling the police."

"Yes, please call Chris Ackerman. I was going to call him myself on the way over here, but I couldn't see the menu on my cell phone without my reading glasses. It wouldn't do to rummage through my purse while driving at a record speed, now would it."

"Shut up and disappear, or you'll be sorry."

"Your threats don't bother me, dear."

"They're not threats. I have a black belt in—"

"I have a black belt as well. It came with that store-bought dress I got in Pittsburgh back in December. 'Dry-clean only,' it says, but I'm telling you—"

The door was flung open so hard that it slammed into the stopper against the wall, causing it to vibrate.

"Come in," he barked.

"Why, certainly. But first be a dear and turn on the light."

He did as bade. "You are uninvited, just remember that."

"I wish I could say the same."

"Ah, so that's what this is about. Your chickens have come home to roost, have they?"

"Don't flatter yourself, Mr. Riddlegobbler. You're not

nice enough to be a chicken. I'd say a thieving blue jay is more like it."

"My title is *reverend,* and my name is Fiddlegarber."

"I don't think so. Reverend means worthy of being revered, and you are far from that. As for your last name, how can I be sure of it, when you're a fraud and a liar?"

"My credentials are real. My theology degree wasn't just one of those Internet deals where you send in twenty-five bucks, and they automatically send you a certificate. No sirree, ma'am. It cost me five hundred, and I had to take a correspondence course."

"Who finally ordained you? Reverend Jim Jones?"

"Get out of my house."

"It isn't yours."

"Don't be a sore loser, Magdalena. Besides, if you opened that tightly closed mind of yours, I might even find you a place in my operation. Exciting things are going to happen in Hernia, I'm telling you. The Voice of Armageddon Cathedral is going to be *the* single largest church in the United States when I'm through. Pat Robertson and Jerry Falwell are going to beg to be my water boys. Presidents are going to call and ask my advice. Heck, they're going to ask me for permission to implement their policies—make that *my* policies."

"And where will God be in this?"

"Excuse me?"

"You know, the Man Upstairs. Although he isn't really a man—"

"'Put your hand on the television screen,' I'm going to say, 'and feel the healing power of the Lord surging through you. Did you feel that, Sister? Brother, are you healed? No? Then maybe your faith isn't what it should be. To prove your faith, Brothers and Sisters, send in your checks, of a hundred dollars or more, so that I can buy that diamond mine in Botswana that the Lord has laid on my heart.'"

I'd heard far too much. "Out of *my* house, Satan!"

"You seem to have flipped your lid, Magdalena. What's the matter? Is that bun on the back of your head screwed on too tight?"

I whipped the winning envelope out of my purse. "Read it and weep, buster."

37

He stared at it, sensing for the first time that his wicked plan might not have been foolproof.

"Go ahead, Beelzebub. This is the deed for the parsonage. Unlike the church building, it is not co-owned by the congregation. You see, Lucifer, the old parsonage was in awful condition and had to be demolished. We sold the land to my cousin, Sam Yoder, who built his grocery store on the lot. At that time the church was deeply in debt, so the proceeds went to paying that down some. For a long time after that, we limped along without a parsonage, but we were having trouble getting a minister on what little we could offer him. Then this house came on the market, and it was perfect for the job, so I bought it. But you see, I didn't sign it over to the church because—come to think of it, I really don't know why. Every time I thought about doing that, something inside me said no. I guess that was the Good Lord looking out for us."

"Let me see!" He snatched the paper from my hand, and with each line he read from the document, his face grew redder.

"It's all there. And search the church records, if you like, but you'll find nothing that gives you the right to live in my house."

"Possession is nine-tenths of the law," he snarled.

"Unfortunately for you, I *am* the law."

"Squatter's rights," he hissed.

"Then squat on the curb." I consulted my watch, which is the same simple, unadorned Timex my parents gave me for college graduation. "The movers should be here in ten minutes."

"The movers?" he roared.

"Tsk, tsk, again. You are so full of emotion, dear, anyone writing your biography would be forced to use disruptive conversation tags."

"And you're stark raving mad."

"Clichés as well." I gifted him with a calm, Christian smile. "Will you be needing help with the small things? I'm afraid I don't possess a lot of upper-body strength, so furniture moving is out. But I can toss silverware into a paper bag, or pack up the pantry—just not both. And if you pick pantry, be appraised of the fact that I would be tossing those items as well, and I've been known to drop jars of spaghetti sauce, fumble-fingers that I am."

By now he was shaking with rage. "You will pay for this, Miss Yoder. As God is my witness, you will rue the day you double-crossed me."

"Is that a threat, dear?"

"Don't call me *dear*." He glanced wildly around, presumably looking for eavesdroppers. Finding none, he got back to the business at hand. "If by the word *threat* you mean that you will soon become persona non grata in these parts, then the answer is yes. I have been blessed with a magnetic personality, Miss Yoder. I will use my influence to increase my flock until we have swallowed all of the churches in Hernia. What will your world consist of then, Miss Yoder? Regrets? Just as woman cannot live on bread alone, neither can she live on regrets."

"Hmm. Well, I do regret not having called the movers five minutes earlier, perhaps saving myself from your— Ah! There they are now. Oh, I almost forgot; the movers are nephews, by marriage, to my cousin, Sam

Yoder. One's a Methodist, and the other three are Baptist. They are not opposed to using force if necessary."

"Come on, Magdalena, let's not be hasty. Surely we can work things out. Compromise—isn't that what it's all about?"

"I don't make deals with the Devil."

The truck began to back into the parsonage driveway. Reverend Fiddlegarber was practically on his knees.

"Everyone has a price, Magdalena. Just tell me yours. I'll see if I can meet it."

"Not *everyone* has a price, dear. I've even known animals with more principles than you. Take my favorite hen, Pertelote. Once she starts setting on her clutch, she won't budge from those eggs, even if you set a cup of mealworms an arm's length away. You see, a mother's love, for one thing, can't be bought."

A truck door slammed, causing the Spawn of Satan to jump like a coffee addict. "That's just instinct. I've counseled mothers who've abandoned their children. These women did so just because they'd fallen in love with guys who hate kids. Wave a million dollars in front of some of them, and I have no doubt—"

"Junior," I said to the driver of the truck, "no matter what he threatens, keep loading. When you're done, drive this man and his wife anywhere they want in a hundred-mile radius. I've already called the sheriff, so he won't be bothering you."

Junior, who is the size of a side of beef, grunted. "Whatta we do if he don't give us no address?"

"Then drive out to the dump and unload everything there. Your uncle wants the truck back tonight ASAP. You have any questions, reach me on my cell."

"You can't do that, Miss Yoder," the not-so-good reverend cried. "You can't leave me with these thugs!"

"Junior, did you hear that? He called you a thug."

The lad, who is the captain of his high school's football team, flexed the muscles in his Methodist biceps. "I ain't no thug."

"Of course not, dear." I turned to go.

Reverend Fiddlegarber, out of options, literally threw himself at my retreating feet. Fortunately, his fingertips only grazed my ankles. I hate kissing the sidewalk and avoid it whenever I can.

"*Please,* Miss Yoder," he begged piteously. "Please reconsider."

"Nope."

"Okay, you can have the church back; just don't kick us out of the house. I'm begging you."

"Shut up—dear." I started walking at a fast clip, the soon-to-be-disposed-of reverend crawling along behind me on his hands and knees.

"I'll make you rich. Richer than even you can imagine. You could own a jet and fly relief missions to Africa. Real ones. Think of all the good you could do."

"At the expense of you bilking widows out of their life savings?"

"What? You're walking too fast."

I stopped so he'd be able to hear what I said next. "This has been an ugly experience *Mister* Fiddlegarber— you do not deserve the title *reverend*. Nonetheless, just like the honey that was made inside the carcass of the lion that Samson killed, some good has already come from it. At least I now know the identity of Cornelius Weaver's killer."

Never underestimate the power of greed. Until my conversation with the fraudulent Fiddlegarber, I was willing to cut mothers a little slack in that department. Stepmothers as well. I may only be Alison's pseudo-stepmother, but I would never, ever even be tempted to kill her, not for a million, trillion dollars. Which isn't to say that, from time to time, I don't want her to simply disappear.

But now the scales had fallen from my eyes, and I could see that there were indeed folks out there who would do anything for money. And there was only one person I knew of who stood to profit from Cornelius Weaver's death: his stepmother, and only living kin, Veronica.

Of course I don't believe in the phenomenon of psychic ability, akin as it is to both witchcraft and new age philosophy. But if I did believe it existed, it would be because I have observed it over and over in my almost half century of existence. Therefore, I was not in the least bit surprised to discover the killer at her mobile home, waiting for me.

"Come in, Magdalena. I've been expecting you."

"So you have. Is that hot chocolate I smell?"

"Yes. And if I remember correctly, you are particularly fond of ladyfingers."

"But—"

"But not the real ones. It's a pretty stale joke, Magdalena."

"Just because you're a murderess is no cause to be rude."

"Ooh, touchy, are we? What's got your knickers in a knot this time?"

"You. I can't believe someone would kill their own son."

"Stepson. There is a difference."

"Not to me. I only have a foster daughter, but still— it's inconceivable."

"What choice did I have? I never thought Cornelius would marry. He was such a playboy, you know."

"To indiscriminately sow one's seed," I said, "is not something to be admired."

"Magdalena, you are such a prig."

"I'll take that as a compliment, because I am, in fact, quite proud of my priggishness."

"Isn't pride the worst sin your kind can commit?"

"My *kind*?"

"Never mind. Do you want to know my reason for killing Cornelius, or not?"

"Frankly, at this point I'm not sure. If you tell me, will I soon be signing up for harp lessons?"

"That depends. But I'd say probably. The other place, I hear, has been getting rather crowded lately."

"Oh dear. I hope you remembered to make yourself a reservation."

"Very funny. But I don't plan to go there for a long time. And that's why I needed the money, you see."

"What money?"

"Cornelius's, of course. As you well know, he was loaded. Worth millions, right?"

"Maybe." Is eleven million a lot these days?

"Until that plastic bimbo came along, I was the sole beneficiary of his will. I still don't know why he thought he had to marry Priscilla Livingood."

"Actually, if you strip away the face putty, and suck out all the silicone, you're still left with a very attractive woman who is nice to boot. But that doesn't matter now. What concerns me now is the fact that you are a cold-blooded killer."

Veronica's trailer is smaller than some closets I've seen. One minute the woman was standing in her living room, barely an arm's length from me, and the next thing I knew she was in the kitchen brandishing a wicked-looking butcher knife. She smiled when she saw that I knew she was armed.

"Magdalena, you have always been one for exaggeration. That heart of his was a time bomb that could have gone off at any minute, whether I got involved or not. All I did was give it a little push. And the drug was perfectly legal, you know."

"So is a knife, but that doesn't give me license to stab—or you, for that matter."

"I suppose you'd prefer a bullet, like the one I put through Chief Hornsby-Anderson's head?"

"Yes, if I had to choose."

"Sorry, but I can't oblige. I tossed that gun in the trash barrel behind Miller's Feed Store—and I do mean *tossed*. Made it in from the chief's balcony in one try."

"What do you want? Applause? Why kill her, when

she wasn't investigating the case? It was me you should have gone after."

"Don't worry, I would have gotten around to you, Magdalena, had you not come to me. Besides, I never liked that woman. She had the gall to sleep with my stepson one day and search my place for pot the next. You would think that being from California, she'd have been more enlightened on that score."

She lapsed into a prolonged silence.

"Listen dear," I finally said, "I'm sure you're concocting a nefarious plan in that little coconut-shaped head of yours. Just so you know, I don't want to be stabbed, burned, or drowned. And if it must be a bullet, make it right through the heart, because I'm partial to my noggin. That said, it would be futile for you to do anything, because Sheriff Johnson and Chris Ackerman are both waiting at the bottom of the hill. The sheriff has a lot of hair growing in his ears, but young Chris can hear a frog fart a mile away—oops, sorry about the four-letter F word. I tend to develop a potty mouth under extreme duress."

"Yes, frog is an ugly-sounding word for an ugly, slimy animal. But as to your claim that you have backup waiting just down the hill, I say *Haufa mischt*."

"Horse manure?"

"You're full of it, Magdalena. Always were, so I'm going to call your bluff."

"My bluff?" It's a good thing my braids are wrapped tightly to form a bun. Otherwise, had they stood on end, Veronica Weaver might have been able to tell just how scared I was.

"Magdalena, I want you to stand in the doorway of my mobile home and shout as loud as you can. Holler as much as you want. I bet your life no one is going to hear you."

"You're on, Sister." Of course it is a sin to bet one's life, but I didn't really think I was going to lose. Not *really*. You see, I suffer from a disease that is rarely found in female adults my age. Stupid Teenage Boy Syndrome, or STABS, is the belief that one is invincible. That, in a nutshell, is how society is able to ship teenagers off to fight our wars. You won't find the president, or the members of Congress, on the front lines.

"Okay," Veronica said, "but I can't have you bolting." She yanked open a kitchen drawer with one hand, still holding the butcher knife with the other, and removed a pair of handcuffs. "Here, put these on."

"You want to hobble me like a horse?"

"In a manner of speaking. But only your arms will be hobbled. Still, don't get any ideas. One can't run very fast without using one's arms for balance."

"This is absurd."

"Do you want to call for help or not?"

"I do, but first I want that hot chocolate I smell."

"Aren't you afraid it's going to be poisoned?"

"Well, you're obviously going to kill me, so what difference does it make? Besides, aren't death-row prisoners entitled to a last meal?"

"I suppose you'll be wanting the ladyfingers as well."

"Certainly. This is no time to be counting calories. Not when it appears that I'll be losing weight rapidly over the next several months. Hey, I just thought of something. After I die, you can dig me up every now and then, and record my rate of decomposition. Then you can write a self-help book titled *Death: The Ultimate Diet*. It's guaranteed to be a bestseller, given America's obsession with weight loss, and you'll become fabulously rich, thereby rendering your stepson's murder pointless, and probably hard to prove, and all because of me. So you see, it would behoove you to treat me nicely, since I am the reason for your future good fortune. Therefore, I implore you to put the carving knife down—it should only be used to sever the tails of visually challenged rodents—and make nicey-nice with your good friend Magdalena."

"Enough!" Veronica was clearly annoyed by my

blathering, but not so much so that she forgot and turned her back on me.

I, in the meantime, saw this is as my last opportunity to dissuade her from dismembering my very attractive composite of bodily members. I decided to start with reason.

"If you turn yourself in, dear, you can plea-bargain. Or you could claim temporary insanity. Keep your fingers clean in the lockup, and you'll go up for early parole. These days murderers serve less time than folks who were caught smoking marijuana back in the sixties."

"Haufa mischt."

"Trust me, it's true. And think of all the advantages. You'll probably be taught a trade, you can certainly take some classes, and you won't have to worry about what to wear. Food, shelter, TV and magazines, medical and dental plans—it's all there. There are billions of people in this world who would be thrilled for this kind of setup. To paraphrase the words of a certain president's mama, you'll be better off than you are now."

"If that's really the case, then let one of the billions about whom you speak serve my time for me."

"That means you'll do it?" Hope springs eternal even in the most shapely breast.

"Heck no. Now, drink this." She set the cocoa down on a laminate countertop, next to the handcuffs.

"Where are the ladyfingers?"

She scowled but fumbled for the package of goodies. "You can have two. No more."

The Babester, who doesn't speak Hebrew, nonetheless taught me the English translation of a Hebrew saying by a great rabbi, Hillel: "If I am not for myself, then who is? If not now, then when?"

There was no time for me to think, so now was all I had. I picked up the mug of steaming cocoa and without missing a beat flung it into Veronica's eyes. She screamed as the butcher knife clattered to the floor.

I lunged for the knife, but just how close I came to it, I still don't know. At some point I blacked out, and when I came to I was sitting on the floor of the tiny kitchen with my arms above my head. Looking up caused my head to spin, but I did it anyway. My hands, I finally realized, were cuffed to the refrigerator door.

"Witch," Veronica spat, coming from another room. (If you must know, she actually used the preferred AKC term for a female dog.) "You could have blinded me."

"Then I assume that I didn't succeed?"

Down as I already was, there was no point in her kicking me in the ribs. "Is this the thanks I get?" she barked.

"For what?"

"All those compliments I gave you."

"You mean I *don't* sing like a lark?"

"More like a lard bucket—if one could sing. You may be beautiful, Magdalena, but you have a horrendous voice. Everyone in Hernia would agree with me."

Easy come, easy go, as they say. And at least I had my looks. I decided to pose a reasonable question.

"So, now what are you going to do with me?"

Her answer was to kick me in the ribs again.

"Ouch!"

"You deserve that."

"*Moi?* What for?"

"You are so dang inconvenient, Magdalena. I honestly didn't think you'd catch on. I'm not in the least bit prepared. Thank heavens my dear, departed Latrum enjoyed handcuffs." She sighed, revealing the fact that she did not floss on a daily basis. "Now I have to run all the way into Bedford to get some rope, and maybe some dynamite."

"Dynamite! Whatever for?"

38

"I figure the easiest way for me to dispose of you would be to find an old abandoned mine shaft, and then blow it down around that hard head of yours. Sure beats digging a hole. Besides, I'm really too squeamish to follow through with the knife bit."

"Then, hand it to me. I'm quite adept at slicing and dicing. Splicing as well, but for that I'll need the rope."

"Shut up."

"Certainly, dear."

"Oh crap! I just remembered, my car's on the blink again."

"You mean on the blocks. Concrete blocks, to be exact."

"We're not all rich like you. Where are your keys?"

"My keys won't fit your car—oh, no you don't!"

She ducked around the counter and snatched up my purse, which I'd set on the floor by the door. Then she dumped everything out on the counter. Had not the only witness to this debacle been a whacko killer, I would have died from embarrassment, thereby saving her the trip for dynamite.

Out sailed three weeks of church bulletins; my cell phone; a half-filled tin of curiously strong breath mints; one rolled-up dirty pair of pantyhose; my dog-eared wallet; an especially bright blue jay feather; an empty gum packet; a half-empty bottle of hand sanitizer; a fistful of grocery receipts; loose change—mostly pennies—that rolled everywhere; a comb with enough hair stuck in it to coat a small mammal; a sample-size tube of hand lotion; and a teeny-weeny, itsy-bitsy bottle of Baileys Original Irish Cream liqueur.

"Why, Magdalena, you lush!"

The accused lush blushed. "That's not even mine—I mean it is, but it wasn't my idea. Doc Shafor brought that back from the plane when I flew him and Ida to Bora-Bora. He said to keep it with me for emergencies. For medicinal purposes. You know, like a snakebite or something."

"Snakes in Hernia?"

"Other than yourself? We've had a plague this year. I'm surprised you didn't notice."

"Shut up. Where are your car keys?"

I moved my lips soundlessly.

"Stop being a smart aleck." She grabbed a cast-iron skillet from the top of her miniature stove and shook it at me. "While I really don't care for knives, I have nothing against frying pans. I'd be happy to rearrange your hairdo for you."

"All right. Don't get your knickers in a knot. The keys are in my car."

"I should have thought of that. This is Hernia, after all. Well, amuse yourself while I'm gone by reviewing your pitiful life. That way, you won't have to rush through it the last minute before you die."

Before stealing my car, Veronica unplugged all her telephones and stuffed them into a tote bag. She stopped at the front door just to taunt me one last time.

"After you're done reviewing your life, feel free to browse through the fridge for something to eat. You know, for that last meal you were talking about."

"Got milk?"

"There's almost a half gallon of two percent."

"Got mayo?"

"Shut up."

"I keep trying, but I can't seem to get the hang of it. You might want to pick up some duct tape as well."

"Good idea."

"Toodle-oo, dear."

The door slammed behind her.

There was nothing in Veronica's fridge that loaned itself to digitless dining, except for a stick of butter left open on a bread plate. While I am fond of butter—no substitute will do for me—there is only so much one can eat without a companion food. But butter is primarily a saturated fat, which is only a slightly more appetizing way of saying congealed grease, and there are a number of things that can be done with grease.

Suddenly I had the nucleus of a plan. It was a long shot, but since it would probably be my parting shot, it was worth trying. Of course I prayed, as well as planned. And while I do believe in miracles, I think they have nothing to do with the intensity of one's prayers. I'm not sure why they happen when they do; I just know that I reject the notion of a God who plays with humans like a child playing with dolls. The folks who do not survive plane crashes, or hurricanes, or tornadoes, may be praying just as hard as the ones who do. I'm sure a few heathens survive now and then too.

At any rate, the next step in my plan was to turn the stove on—oops, that would be difficult even with my comely attributes. I meant, turn *on* the stove. Veronica's trailer, although small, contained a flat-surface stove. I leaned toward it, bent at the waist, and using my teeth for hands, I managed to turn the closest burner on low. I waited a few minutes, then, ducking my head into the fridge, grabbed the butter stick in my teeth and touched it lightly to the burner. It began to melt immediately.

It took me several attempts, but eventually I got enough melted butter to drip down into the right cuff for me to slide my hand out. Freeing the second hand was easier. At the front door I had to wipe my hands on my skirt in order to turn the knob, and I hereby confess to using my entire repertoire of swear words on that account. Ding, dang, dong, darn—I said them all.

Fortunately, the road back into town was all downhill. Unfortunately, it's still a long way to go on foot. One can only imagine, then, my joy upon hearing a car approach from behind. I waved frantically, and nearly plotzed from happiness when the vehicle came to stop in a cloud of dust.

"Thank God!" I cried.

"Yes, and you can thank me too."

"Thelma Unruh, it's you."

"The last time I checked. Magdalena, what are you doing way out here?"

"Never mind that. Open the door, dear, so I can hop in."

"Open it yourself."

"I can't. I'm covered in butter from my elbows down."

"Oh, all right." She obliged me and I slid in.

"Thanks."

"I suppose you want a lift too?"

"No, I thought I would just sit in your car for a minute and see what it feels like. You know, in case I ever want to buy a clunker like this."

"I don't like sarcasm, Magdalena. You know that."

"Sorry. Do you have your cell phone with you?"

"Yes."

"May I use it, please? It's an emergency."

"But like you said, you're all buttery."

"Quite. Then you use it for me."

"It's not charged."

"Land o' Goshen, Thelma! Why didn't you—never mind. Just drive as fast as you can to the police station."

"I have to stop by the house first."

"No, you don't. This is police business."

"What is?"

"This!" I waggled butter fingers in her face.

"That's real butter, isn't it?"

"Yes. Unsalted, but still very tasty."

"You know, there isn't a substitute on the market that approaches the real McCoy."

"Why, I was just thinking the same thing myself. And nobody makes butter better than the Amish— Wait! You're trying to distract me. Like I said, I'm on police business."

"Since when did baking become police business?"

"I wasn't baking. I had just caught Cornelius's killer when I got conked on the head—you don't really want to hear this, do you?"

"Of course I do. Look, I have to swing by the house to pick up my glasses. Then I'll take you anywhere you want. But in the meantime, I'm all ears."

"Thelma, dear, you're wearing your glasses."

"I am?" She touched her tinted specs. This was a woman who hoped to compete with me in the hostelry business?

"Don't worry, it happens to me all the time. Except I don't wear glasses, so it's my— Hey, you were supposed to go straight. The police station's that way."

"Okay, Magdalena, I confess. But you can't tell anyone, or I'll die of embarrassment. You see, I was visiting Amanda Church, who, by the way, isn't getting any better. And you know how filthy her house is, and that was before she got sick. So I had to hold it in, but I couldn't quite manage to hold it all, which is why now I've got to get home ASAP. You can use my phone at home—*after* you've washed the butter off your hands."

"Oh my. Two near deaths caused by embarrassment in one day—who would have thought? But not to worry. These lips are sealed. After all, been there, done that, as they say nowadays. But one can always learn from one's lesson, right? Or else they wouldn't be called lessons."

"And what did you learn, Magdalena?"

"To always carry a spare set of sturdy Christian underwear, especially if traveling to Maryland. No offense to Marylanders, but most of the underwear they sell there is fit only for heathens, and fit heathens at that, which, alas, not many are."

"What makes underwear Christian, Magdalena?"

"You know. I mean, it's obvious."

"Not to me. Describe them, so I know what to look for next time I go shopping."

"Well, they have to be white—colors are just too provocative. Especially red and black. And they must be one hundred percent cotton; synthetics are the Devil's playground. And last, but most importantly, they have to cover everything. If your body squeezes over the top, or bulges out at the bottom, you may as well be wearing a sign that says 'harlot.' Oh, and it's better if the underwear is hard to take off. Think of all the folks who might have been saved from following their carnal urges if only their Hanes Her Way had put up more of a fight."

"Why, I'll be dippty-doodled, to borrow one of your colorful phrases, Magdalena! I've been wearing sturdy Christian underwear all along, and not knowing it. Does that earn me extra points?"

"Points for what?"

"Minibar privileges in Heaven, that kind of thing."

"You're mocking me, aren't you?"

"You think?"

"Why, Thelma Unruh, shame on you! And here I thought we could be friends."

"You thought no such thing, and you know it. We've never liked each other, Magdalena, and we never will."

"You're just jealous because I'm a successful businesswoman, and you're only a wannabe."

"A wannabe what?"

"Give it up, Thelma. No one is going to want to stay in that drafty old relic of a house you own, with that spooky wall running through it."

"It's about to get even spookier."

"Why is that? You planning to hang Halloween decorations on it?"

"I'm about to build an addition with a corpse inside. Actually, I'm using some of the old brick so no one will be able to tell."

"Thelma, if you don't mind me saying so, that's weird even for you."

"Have you read 'The Cask of Amontillado'?"

"By Edward Allen Poe. You see, I'm not quite the rube you think I am."

"Oh, I've never thought of you as a rube, Magdalena. Just an arrogant buttinsky who needs to learn her place—*inside* my wall."

"What on earth are you talking about?"

"I'm going to kill you, Magdalena. But not right now. First I'm going stick you in the wall. Don't worry, I'm going to leave one brick out, so that I can hear you scream—hopefully for a long while."

That's when I noticed that Thelma was driving with only one hand, and the other held a gun, one that was pointed right at the side of my abdomen. I jerked away, which she found rather amusing.

"At this close range—Miss Have Everything—I'll blast your liver to smithereens. Your large intestine as well. Even if you survive, you'll soon be begging to die."

39

"Thelma—dear—what is this all about? What have I done to you?"

"Shut up. As if you don't know."

"Not you too! I can't stand being told to shut up."

"At least quit sniveling. It's so unbecoming for a beautiful, elegant woman like you, who has everything."

"There you go again with the everything. Would you care to explain?"

Thelma had slowed to well below the thirty-five-mile-per-hour city speed limit; apparently holding someone at gunpoint was not routine for her. If only I could manage to unbuckle my seat belt without being noticed, I could hurl myself to the pavement and try for a headfirst landing. My noggin, thanks to all the milk Mama made me drink, was as tough as a Kevlar helmet. Therefore, my best plan of action was to keep Thelma occupied until I could come up with a suitable distraction, one that demanded all of her attention. Perhaps if I passed gas . . .

"You're not listening, Magdalena! You ask me to explain, but you look like you're off on another planet."

"I was. But I'm all ears now. Tell me why you hate my guts so much."

"Why wouldn't I? You're rich, you're gorgeous, you're intelligent—need I say more?"

"Yes! Don't stop there."

"And you throw away hunky men like yesterday's newspaper."

"I only threw away two hunks—hey, how did you know about the second one?"

"Magdalena, everyone knows you dumped that handsome Jewish doctor, and for the stupidest reason imaginable."

"That he isn't *saved*? That's practically the most important thing in life—no, it *is* the most important thing. We are all born to be saved—that's our main purpose in life—otherwise God would have created us all saved in the first place. And don't confuse me by throwing free will into the mix. Who needs free will anyway, if the result of a wrong choice is eternal damnation?"

"I'm not going to argue with your bad theology, Magdalena. Nor am I going to recommend that you see a much-needed psychiatrist. I just want to know, how on earth do you plan to convert that hunky doctor by pushing him away? I hope you realize that if he burns in Hell, it's going to be your fault."

"Why I—I—I—"

"You seem to be stuck, Magdalena. Pat that buxom chest of yours, and knock some new words loose."

I rehearsed silently until I was able to spit out what was on my mind. "Who are *you,* a murderer, to be giving me spiritual advice?"

Her laugh had an avian shrillness about it. "God works in mysterious ways. Now, enough about you. I want to know how long it took for Veronica to sing like a canary."

"Oh, she ratted you out immediately." Of course it was a lie, but I was fighting for my life, not to mention Gabe's salvation.

"That really ticks me off! It was her idea to begin with. We were taking an organic gardening class together, and when she found out who I was, she kept suggesting things for us to do together. And all the while she's asking me how I *really* felt about Cornelius, and did I know that his heart was barely functioning, and that if he married Priscilla, then all his money would go to her."

"So? How *did* you really feel about Cornelius?"

"Well, I hated him, of course. He should've stayed with me; I would have loved him like no other woman could. I hated Priscilla too. That's what Veronica kept harping on—what a selfish, conniving witch Priscilla was. A total user. According to Veronica, that schemer with the fake body parts would have killed him anyway, sooner rather than later, by having too much sex. Someone other than her may as well benefit from Cornelius's millions."

"I don't understand. Why did Veronica have to involve you? She was only giving him Elavil. That hardly requires a team effort."

"Ha! That woman couldn't pour water out of a boot, if the instructions were written on the heel. As much dope as she smokes, she may as well have a head of cauliflower between her ears. Take what just happened, for example. There I am, all settled down in my comfy recliner, watching my favorite TV show—you really should watch TV, Magdalena—when Veronica calls me to say she has you shackled to her fridge, and can I come over to babysit you while she runs into Bedford to buy rope and dynamite. It's a good thing I spotted you walking along the highway; otherwise Veronica would have been busted, and I'd have to kiss my share of the money good-bye."

"Boo-hoo."

"I'll ignore that, Magdalena, but only because I'm so pissed at Veronica, I can hardly see straight. I swear, I've had to think of everything. I'm the one who thought of Elavil and wrangled a prescription. All she had to do was give it to him."

"Why, that liar!"

"I'll say. We made a blood pact not to rat each other out."

"Did you, dear?"

"Are you mocking me now?"

"Moi? Au contraire. Mais vous êtes une femme folle avec un visage que seulement une langoustine pourrait aimer."

"What are you babbling about now?"

"I was saying how lovely you look in that color. Puke green was always rather flattering on you."

Thelma Unruh gasped in indignation.

We were crossing Main Street at Hopkins, and the speedometer was only flirting with twenty. We were also just a block from the police station, and hopefully young Chris Ackerman. It was now or never.

I took a deep breath of my own. "Look out for that dog!"

The rest, as we say, is Hernia history. Thelma swerved and completely lost control of her car, but not before I'd thrown myself onto the pavement. That's the day the lights went out in Magdalena—but for only a few seconds. When I came to I saw the rear end of Thelma's car protruding from what remained of Hernia's police department. Cute Chris Ackerman was in the building at the time but managed to throw himself out of harm's way. Thelma, on the other hand, was knocked out cold for hours.

I must have looked a sight, covered as I was with bruises and bandages. Ida certainly noticed.

"Nu, vhat happen to you? You fall off your high horse?"

"Yes, and it was quite a fall. All the king's horses, and all the king's men—well, what can I say? It was fun having them put me together again."

"So now she's a shlut!"

It wasn't easy, but I overcame my urge to tell her to shlut up. "Is Gabriel here, please?" I asked pleasantly.

"Maybe. Maybe not. Vhat do you vant mit my son?"

"To marry him, and to give him all the foster children

his heart desires. I would offer to bear the fruit of his loins, but I'm afraid my orchard has never produced a crop, and alas, it probably never will."

"Den he is not here."

"Ma!"

The world's handsomest man gently pushed the world's most undesirable future mother-in-law aside. If possible, his face was made even more handsome by the concern in his eyes.

"Magdalena, I heard. How are you feeling?"

"Like I threw myself from a moving car and landed on asphalt—wait a minute, that's what did happen."

"Oy, a smart mouth."

"Ma!"

"Let her talk, Gabe. I know you probably hate my guts at the moment, but my plan is to win you back, and love you every day for the rest of my life. I even plan to tolerate the pipsqueak."

"*Gvalt!* I tink I am having a heart attack."

"This is the place to have it, dear. Your son is, after all, a heart specialist." I looked past her. "Look, Gabe, I know I treated you awful, and it must have felt like I was terribly condescending. I was wrong about so many things, especially about us not being able to make it."

"Like a camel wit a sheep, yah?" Ida waggled a stubby finger in my face. "Not an equal yoke, you say. Vell, Miss Yoder, the yoke is on you."

"Shut up, Ma—please."

"*Vhat* did you say?"

"Ma, this isn't your business. Either you shut up, or you leave."

I thought Ida would faint. In fact, I am ashamed to say that I was hoping she would, and that Gabe would refrain from catching her. Instead, she merely sputtered like a campfire under a slow drizzle, and when she was out of steam, she fled from the foyer in utter frustration. She didn't even leave any s'mores behind.

"Gabe, I'm sorry—"

"Don't," he said, and pressed his mouth so hard against mine, it would have been useless to even attempt to protest.

The wheels of justice hereabouts turn so slowly that many of them are dust covered, but Veronica Weaver was eventually convicted of first-degree murder and permanently confined to a Pennsylvania penitentiary. I heard just last week that she won their Martha Stewart Award for growing prize-winning organic vegetables in the exercise yard.

Thelma had a better lawyer and received forty years, instead of life. However, due to prison overcrowding, she is spending the next four decades in a Maryland prison. The good news is that, while she was unconscious, Thelma saw the Light. Unfortunately (but this is only hearsay) sturdy Christian underwear is unavailable for Maryland inmates. The poor dear was quoted in *Christian Convicts* magazine as saying, "Having to wear heathen undergarments is tantamount to a double sentence."

We were married on May twenty-seventh, high atop Stucky Ridge. It was a Jewish-style wedding, presided over by the rabbi from Pittsburgh, but the bride was definitely still very much a Christian. The way I figured it, if it was good enough for Mary and Joseph, it was good enough for me.

Jewish weddings, I learned, are truly family affairs. Traditionally the bride's family delivers her en masse, if you'll pardon the pun, to the groom, who waits beneath the chuppah. The chuppah is a cloth raised aloft as a canopy, and symbolizes the marriage bed. The one we used was a prayer shawl that had belonged to Gabe's father, and that his mother had saved specifically for her son's wedding—just not his wedding to me. Chris Ackerman held one of the corners, my cousin Sam another, and Gabe's nephews, Benjamin and Jerry, the other two.

Since this was only a Jewish-*style* wedding, certain liberties were taken. Standing in for my parents were Doc Shafor and Freni Hostetler. Susannah was my maid of honor, and a very proud and happy Alison was a bridesmaid. My half sister, Zelda, also served as a bridesmaid. Gabe's cousin Mordechai, a Long Island mortician, was his best man.

Although we had no flower girl, we did have a secret ring-bearer. In order to make it up to Susannah, for having called her pedigreed pooch names on several occasions, I agreed to let her carry him in his usual hiding place. The ring was securely fastened to his collar; not a dog collar, but that of a miniature tuxedo.

To my knowledge, the entire town was there—well, with the exception of half of Beechy Grove Mennonite Church, but that's a tale for another day. More than making up for their loss were Faya and Ibrahim Rashid, as well as the recently arrived Conner and Patty McBain and their seven children. They, by the way, are our very first Roman Catholics—although you can't tell that just by looking at them. Who knew? I'm sure that Ron, our lone Episcopalian, would have come, had he not been viciously murdered the year before. Even the Mishler brothers showed up, in a rare moment of decency. And of course Agnes was there; she played wedding music for us on a keyboard.

Curious townsfolk pressed close throughout the ceremony, and when, at the end, Gabe crushed the glass with one stomp, a loud cheer went up. By far the loudest voice belonged to Freni.

"Mazel tov!"

40

Mango Lassi

Ingredients

1¼ cups yogurt (plain)
⅓ cup cold water
½ cup mango puree

4 tablespoons sugar
½ teaspoon lemon juice
½ cup ice cubes

YIELD: 4 SERVINGS

Preparation

Blend everything, except ice cubes, till sugar has dissolved. Add ice cubes and blend till frothy. Garnish with mint leaves.

Notes

- Lassi is a yogurt drink indigenous to Punjab. It can be made salty or sweet or fruity.
- Variations of lassi can exist with the addition or elimination of ingredients. For example:

Salty Lassi: 2 cups plain yogurt, 1 cup cold milk or cold water, ½–1 teaspoon salt (to taste), 1 teaspoon cumin seeds, squeeze of half lemon, handful ice cubes. Blend.

Sweet Lassi: 2 cups plain yogurt, 1 cup cold milk or cold water, 2 tablespoons (or to taste) sugar, handful ice cubes. Blend.

Fruit Lassi: 2 cups plain yogurt, 1 cup cold milk or cold water, 1 cup ripe diced pineapple, 2 tablespoons sugar, handful ice cubes. Blend.

Substitute any fruit or ingredient in the amount you like. Let your imagination guide you.

Enjoy!!

Even Magdalena's honeymoon gets caught
up in mystery when an innocent dairy
contest has something much more
sinister churning behind the scenes.
Read on for a sneak preview of

AS THE WORLD CHURNS

Tamar Myers's next tasty and thrilling treat.
On sale February 2008

Not all men are created equal. I learned this fact while honeymooning with my second husband, the Babester, but I will leave the particulars to your imagination. Suffice it to say, whilst showering that evening I threw back my head and burst into joyous song. Of course I took care not to swallow too much water and drown like a turkey in a rainstorm.

"*Oh, sweet mystery of life,*" I trilled, "*at last I've found you!*"

"Hon, are you all right?"

"Right as rain! Never been better. Tut-tut, cheerio, and all that sort of rot."

Gabe stuck his head into the tiny bathroom. Fortunately the shower curtain was opaque.

"I thought maybe you'd hurt yourself."

"No siree, Bob. I am as fine as frog's hair."

"Boy, you sound happy."

"Never happier. In fact, I was just thinking—"

"Just a second, hon, the phone's ringing."

"Let it ring. Ta-ling-a-ling-ling."

"But it might be Ma."

As my sweet baboo ran off to answer that stupid machine, my rare good mood dissipated like steam from a mirror. We'd been married for less than six hours and this was the second time my mother-in-law had called. Our wedding was supposed to have cut the apron strings that tied son to mother, but what good did that do when the two of them were joined at the hip? It was going to take a team of orthopedic surgeons to separate this pair.

"Tell your mother to take a long walk off a short pier, dear." It's all in the delivery, you see? Had my tone been any lighter, I might well have bumped my head on the ceiling, thereby adding to the dent that was already there. On the ceiling, that is, not my head.

My dearly beloved must not have heard me. The walls of our Motel One (it charges by the hour) were sufficiently thin for me to hear his voice, but too thick to allow me to hear what was being said. Since he sounded agitated, I knew I'd been right—it was his mother. There are only two people in this world who can rattle my sweetykins: me and the woman who bore him.

I tried to dry off with the only towel provided, which was as thin as facial tissue and not much larger. Finally I scooped up the bath mat, picked off a few hairs, and used that instead. After donning sensible Christian pajamas—flannel, and a good deal thicker than the towel—I slipped into my heavy terry robe and prepared to face the music.

"Okay, dear, let her rip."

Gabe was off the phone by then and sitting on the bed, his back to the bathroom. His head was bowed, his face cupped in his hands. It was a typical post–Ida Rosen pose. Try saying that correctly three times in rapid succession. But beware: The prize for getting it right is a weeklong visit from the old badger herself.

I know, Jesus commanded us to love our enemies. But with all due respect, the Lord didn't have a mother-in-law. Also in my defense, I'd like to add that I don't hate Ida Rosen as much as she hates me. In fact, she *despises* me. Not only did I take her only son from her, but I refuse to lie down and let her run over me. Literally—with her car.

My handsome groom turned slowly. "Hon, I'm afraid I have some bad news."

"But you promised," I wailed. There are those who claim that only sirens are capable of wailing, but those folks have yet to meet me. "You said that we could have the first three days of our honeymoon all to ourselves. You said—"

"Babe, I'm sorry."

I eschew cussing, but sometimes a gal has to do what a gal has to do. "Ding, dang, dong, blast it all! If you think I'm going to share our room with—"

"The call wasn't from Ma; it was the warden from the state penitentiary."

"Excuse me?"

"Sit down first."

I waved a hand dismissively. "No, no, go on. Why would the warden be calling us? How did he even know we were here?"

"You left a contact number with Chief Ackerman, remember?"

"Yes, but it was just for emergencies." Our little town has only one police officer—a young and inexperienced one at that. Since I am the mayor, we are frequently in touch.

"This is an emergency. *Please*, sit down."

"No!"

He stood. "The warden said that Melvin is—uh—ah—"

"Spit it out, dang it!"

"Melvin is missing."

"Missing how? You mean like playing hide-and-seek?"

"They don't know. No one has seen him since lock-down last night."

"*What?* That's almost twenty-four hours ago."

"The warden said he didn't want to get us worried and then have Melvin show up in the bottom of a laundry bag like last time."

"He works in the laundry room, for crying out loud. He knows it doesn't get trucked out."

"Yes, but this is the same man who once tried to milk a bull. Am I right?"

I felt my chest imploding for want of oxygen. "Does this mean what I think it might?"

Gabe nodded somberly. "That son of a twitch has escaped."

The room swayed, then spun, and soon my poor brain couldn't keep up with all the motion. I have a vague recollection of Gabriel lunging for me. Then all went black.

"What happened?" I asked for the billionth time.

"You fainted, hon. When I told you that the warden called and said Melvin was missing, you just collapsed."

I gazed up into my pooky bear's big brown eyes. Or were they blue? He appeared to have two heads.

"I can't believe they let him escape. It's just so unreal."

"Here, babe, let me help you sit up."

"Mebbe she vants to stay on the floor." It was a woman's voice. A most unwelcome woman.

My blood ran cold. "No!"

"You see? She doesn't vant to sit."

I struggled, first to a sitting position, and then to my feet. Yes, I swayed a bit, but like the Empire State Building I am vertically enhanced. I read somewhere that it sways from side to side as much as several feet in high winds. I generally sway a bit less.

"Ida," I gasped through clenched teeth—not an easy feat, mind you. "What are you doing here?"

"Ma just got here, hon. She was kind enough to bring me my pajamas. I was sure I'd packed them—"

"Indeed you had, dear, but I *un*packed them."

"Oy! Married yust a few hours and already dis von's a slut."

"Ma! Please, stay out of this."

"Yes," I agreed sweetly, "stay out of this. *Far* out of this. I hear they're having a sale on condos in Fiji. If you hurry you can catch the slow boat to China out of New York tomorrow morning, and make connections from there."

"Gabeleh, you see how she talks to me?"

"Ma, you deserved it." He turned to me, flashing pearly whites that were the envy of dentists from Boston to San Diego. "You really unpacked my pajamas? You little minx, you."

I could feel myself blush. It started in my toes and worked itself up to the roots of my bun. At five ten I haven't been called "little" since the third grade, and I'd never been referred to as a minx. How sinfully, deliciously erotic. If it wasn't for Ida, I'd have thrown my stud muffin on the bed and shown him what puts the yo-yo in Yoder—if you know what I mean. Alas, I had to settle for giving him what I hoped was a suggestive wink.

"Hon," he said, "is there something wrong with your eye?"

Before answering, I glared at his mother for good measure. "No, my eye is fine. Gabe, we've got to get back to Hernia immediately. Susannah, Freni, Alison—they could all be in danger. I need to call Chief Ackerman, then the county sheriff—"

"I don't think he'd hurt them. It's you he's probably after."

Ida tugged on her son's arm. Apparently she'd yet to be filled in on the prison break.

"Who vants to hurt her?" She sounded hopeful.

"Melvin Stoltzfus. Our former chief of police."

"My sister's husband," I added.

"You see, Gabeleh, vhat happens when you marry a shikse? I told you it vas a terrible idea. Marry that cute little Schwartz girl, I always said. Wiz hips like dat, she could give me lots of grandchildren. But no, you gotta marry this—"

"Ma, butt out. Please."

"Vhat?"

"You heard me, Ma. And you're right; Magdalena is my wife. I won't have you talking about her like that."

Ida Rosen looked as if her only son had slapped her across the face. "So now you talk back to your mother?"

"I'm sorry, Ma, but you have to respect the woman I chose to marry."

"Respect, shmect. If dis von"—she pointed at me with her chin—"and me vere drowning, who vould you jump in to save?"

"I'd save you both. I'm a good swimmer, thanks to all those summers I spent at Camp Minimitzvah."

"Ya, but if you had to choose?"

"Then I guess I'd save Magdalena."

"For this I come to live in Hemorrhoid?" Ida Rosen stabbed repeatedly at her enormous bosom with a make-believe knife. "Oy, the pain. The pain."

"It's Hernia," I said, and grabbing her by her equally ample shoulders, steered her over to the bed. "And if you insist on dying now, dear"—I gave her a gentle push—"then do it here. You'll be much more comfy."

She allowed herself to topple back onto the mattress, which was surprisingly soft, and proceeded to moan about her multiple injuries, both to body and soul. Gabe, who wasn't at all fooled, turned his full attention to me.

"What do you want to do first, hon?"

"Besides get your mother on that slow boat bound for Fiji?"

He nodded.

"I'll call Susannah and break the news to her. I'm also going to tell her to get over to the PennDutch, pronto. Meanwhile you call Freni at the inn. Tell her to make sure Alison's inside, then lock the door. Then someone needs to call Doc Shafor— Oh shoot! What about Barbara and the triplets?"

My new husband pulled me to his chest and held me tightly, seemingly oblivious to his sputtering mother on the bed. I'm only human, ergo I should not be judged too harshly if I gently maneuvered him so that Ida could see my smile. But just to be clear, we weren't dancing.

"Don't you worry about a thing, Magdalena. They'll locate Melvin any minute, and I bet dollars to doughnuts that they find him *inside* that maximum security prison. And even if he did manage to make it outside, I won't let him hurt you."

I wiggled my way to freedom. "Me? I'm not worried about myself, dear; I'm worried about *you*."

AVAILABLE FEBRUARY 2008

TAMAR MYERS

AS THE WORLD CHURNS

A PENNSYLVANIA DUTCH MYSTERY

Magdelena Yoder may finally be married to
big-time Manhattan doctor Gabriel Rosen, but
she's still a small-town girl at heart, and thrilled
to be the emcee at the first annual Hernia
Holstein Competition. As a bonus, the
PennDutch and its barn are booked solid. But
then someone clobbers the contest's originator,
Doc Shafor, while he's admiring the cows, and
both Gabe and his daughter Alison go missing.
With the help of her best friend (and the
hindrance of her mother-in-law), Magdalena
vows to track down clues until the cows—
and her family—come home.

Available wherever books are sold or at
penguin.com

SIGNET

TAMAR MYERS

PENNSYLVANIA DUTCH
MYSTERIES—WITH RECIPES!

"As sweet as a piece of brown-sugar pie."
—*Booklist*

"Rollicking suspense."
—*Washington Post*

Available wherever books are sold or at
penguin.com